I0645066

Jessie has managed to defy the odds, overcoming a severe hearing loss and achieving a Black Belt. She seemed to have it all, a handsome and devoted boyfriend, success as a karate instructor…until now.

On the cusp of graduating from high school, a shocking injury changes her life. With her heart shattered and her faith destroyed, she finds herself headed in a new direction all alone. As she leaves for college, she needs to find the courage to conquer her self-doubt and rediscover hope before it's too late.

KUDOS FOR *HOPE*

"Jennifer Gibson's new book, *HOPE* is the kind of story that is good for all ages. Jessie, the main character, shows us how life with a hearing loss can make everything you do a real challenge. Jessie has a lot ahead of her as she enters college and is out on her own for the first time. All of these new obstacles make Jessie stronger and fight harder. Loved this book, well done, Jennifer!" ~ *Reviewer, M. Blanchard*

"I can picture Jessie and the other characters interacting as I am reading. You are terrific in writing relationships. Great writing and interesting to an "much older" reader as well. Wonderful accomplishment, Jenn! Congratulations!" ~ *Reviewer, S. Nelson*

"This book, like the other three in the series, is a heartbreaking, heartwarming tale of courage and determination in the face of obstacles that would defeat most of us. Another star in the crown of this talented author." ~ *Taylor Jones, The Review Team of Taylor Jones & Regan Murphy*

"Gibson excels in her character development, making Jessie both realistic and endearing. You just can't help but root for her and feel her pain. It's a book that I think every hearing person should read, as it can open your eyes to the obstacles facing those with disabilities." ~ *Regan Murphy, The Review Team of Taylor Jones & Regan Murphy*

"Jessie is such an inspirational character that I really hope this series takes off under lovers of YA books. It even has a wee bit of the paranormal if you count Parker... I really enjoy this series and want to congratulate the author for taking a girl with hearing loss to be at the center of a story worth telling. A 5 star read indeed." ~ *Reviewer, Denise Jones*

"Jessie is back for another young adult story about being true to yourself, overcoming obstacles and, as the title says, hope. Within the series I enjoyed this book the most. While it covers more of the same issues of living with as a teenager with a disability and not being discouraged, Jessie has grown a lot more since the first book and she becomes a truly inspiring character in Hope. Being partially deaf doesn't stop her from going for her goals, be that sport, romance or even from passing on her skills and wisdom. There are some wonderful moments in this book, as Jessie and her friends learn valid lessons from her situation. Moving." ~ *Reviewer, Molly Flanders*

"Very sweet story about strength of character and perseverance. I love the perspective of the young woman's personal battle. I wish more books like this were available to help people understand more clearly. It would make a great difference in society." ~ *Reviewer, S.D. Black*

ACKNOWLEDGMENTS

I did not expect to write a fourth book for this series, since it was originally designed as a trilogy. When I was hit with inspiration late one night, I realized that I was meant to continue the story of Jessie. It was a real treat to revisit her character and take her on a new adventure that revealed many more layers of her personality.

A generous thank you goes out to my parents, Dr. Cheryl Gibson and Dr. Glenn Gibson, for their incredible support and inordinate amount of patience while I wrote this novel. An enormous amount of gratitude goes out to both of you for your editing services, and helping me polish this book so that it shines like a star.

The inspiration for Parker and Serena came from my real life fur babies, Liam, Belladonna, and Molotov. Their unique and adorable personalities provided a rich storyline for Jessie's spirit guides. You will be missed Liam, aka Parker, may you rest in peace.

I would also like to express my thanks to the team at Black Opal Books for their continuous support and love for my books. I couldn't have published them without you.

My gratitude also goes out to my Aunt Susan and cousins Lisa and Michael for letting me hang out with you while I madly worked on my manuscript.

Many thanks goes out to my beta readers, especially Marilyn and Stephen, who graciously offered their support and feedback.

Midway through editing this novel, my mother, Dr. Cheryl Gibson, died suddenly and unexpectedly. She was a truly

remarkable woman, a compassionate soul who loved helping others, including animals. Mom gave me the courage
and inspiration to produce this series to help others with a
hearing loss – this book is dedicated to her and I hope that it
will continue to inspire others. In a way, I always thought of
Mom as a lighthouse, a beacon of hope in the darkness, always shining a light for us to follow.

" Hope will always guide you. "

Hope

JENNIFER GIBSON

A Black Opal Books Publication

GENRE: NEW ADULT/YA/SELF-ESTEEM AND SELF-RELIANCE

This is a work of fiction. Names, places, characters and incidents are either the product of the author's imagination or are used fictitiously, and any resemblance to any actual persons, living or dead, businesses, organizations, events or locales is entirely coincidental. All trademarks, service marks, registered trademarks, and registered service marks are the property of their respective owners and are used herein for identification purposes only. The publisher does not have any control over or assume any responsibility for author or third-party websites or their contents.

*In memory of Dr. Cheryl Gibson;
may her light always guide you.*

Preface

I drew in a long and deep breath, gathering what was left of my dwindling strength. At the blast of the whistle, we both darted at each other, delivering a flurry of punches and kicks. I could feel the sweat pouring down the side of my face and back of my neck. He was moving fast and hard. I threw a series of kicks then jumped away. He did the same. It was like fighting a mirror. My strikes weren't getting through. He did a roundhouse kick to the side of my head and I raised my arm to block it. The force of his kick was enough to slam my arm into the side of my face. I stumbled a little, caught off guard by his strength, then regained my composure.

He kept going, faster and harder with his hits. Next, he attempted to kick me in the mid-section then rapidly changed direction and aimed it at the side of my head. I raised my hand to block it, but it was too late. His foot collided with my helmet, and I felt the impact. I could swear I heard a loud clang, like a bell going off. The room suddenly spun around. I momentarily staggered. The figure of Ethan swayed in front of me. I dimly heard him calling out my name. The room began to fade from my vision. I fell heavily to my knees and everything went black.

Chapter 1

acceptance

He bolted toward me, driving a punch to my face. I ducked to the side and slapped it aside. Unfazed, he quickly delivered a side kick toward my ribs. I stepped back and pushed it away then followed up with a back fist strike to his head and a reverse punch to his solar plexus. When my fist came into contact with him, I shouted "hiya!"

"Halt!" bellowed Sensei Jonas from my left. He raised on open palm at me and exclaimed, "Point for Jessie."

"Oooh!" I said with an impish grin. "The score is now tied."

Ethan narrowed his eyes at me, pointed two fingers at them, then toward me, his sign for I'm watching you.

Sensei Jonas placed his hand between us. "Go into your fighting stance." He watched us take our positions. "Hajime!" he said, releasing his hand.

Ethan lunged at me with a flurry of kicks, first to my ribs then high up at my head. He nearly caught me off guard with his aggressiveness, and I had to move quickly out of his range. I dodged his moves, slapping away his strikes. We both dove at each other with a hard punch to the solar plexus, yelling upon impact. I cringed as his fist made contact with me.

"Halt!" Sensei Jonas yelled.

We scrambled back to our starting positions that were marked on the floor with red tape. I was panting hard and felt the sting of his hit with every breath I took. Sweat was rolling down Ethan's face, and his chest was heaving with exertion.

"Judges call!" Sensei Jonas looked at the corner judges, they all shook their heads.

"No score. Ready?" he asked as he cast a glance at both of us. When we nodded, he yelled, "Hajime!"

I darted at Ethan, eager to finish this fight. He delivered another strike at me. I jammed down my arm to protect that side of my body, and he ended up hitting my biceps instead. I proceeded to snap out a front kick at him. He immediately thrust his elbow downward on top of it. The sharp pain of his impact shot up my leg.

My focus wavered, and I limped away from him, giving myself room and a momentary break. He did the same thing, prowling around the ring like a tiger deliberating its next move. I gulped back the rising panic. I was determined not to lose this match. My eyes followed Ethan as he circled around me. He suddenly snapped out a kick, and I barely blocked it in the nick of time. He changed positions and quickly did a back fist to the top of my head. At the same time, I lunged toward him with a punch to his solar plexus.

"Halt!" exclaimed Sensei Jonas.

We went back to the red line and waited anxiously. My hands were shaking, and I was beginning to feel the exhaustion in my body.

"Judges call!" Sensei Jonas looked at all of the corner judges, two gestured at Ethan and the others toward me.

It was a tie again. Only he could break that tie if he added his vote. He closed his eyes for a moment, replaying the events in his mind. After what seemed like an eternity, he opened them and gestured at Ethan. He grabbed his hand, raised it upright in the air, and exclaimed, "Winner!"

I was vastly disappointed, but I had to remind myself

that he was more experienced than I was at sparring. We bowed to each other then to Sensei Jonas.

Ethan walked over to me and did a fist bump with his gloves against mine. "You did a great job, Jessie. You're becoming more confident and faster with your sparring. You are getting much better at anticipating my strikes."

"I am? Oh, thanks," I said.

He grabbed my hand and pulled me into a hug. I leaned into him, wrapping my arms around him. When we broke apart, he placed his hands on my shoulders, looked into my eyes, and asked, "You doing okay?

I nodded. "Feeling a bit tired. You made me work hard."

The corner of his lip rose up into a sly grin. "Good. Someone's gotta keep you on your toes."

"Ha! No kidding. Did you have to elbow my foot so hard?" I said, limping slightly.

He grimaced. "Sorry about that. Shall I carry you?"

"Ethan!" I squealed with surprise as he grabbed me.

He carried me over to the wall where my gym bag sat and put me down beside it.

"Here you go," he said wearing a playful grin. He pulled off his helmet and gloves, placing them in his bag.

I looked over my shoulder and spotted Sensei Jonas watching us, giving Ethan a bemused stare. Then he looked at me, raising his eyebrows.

I mouthed at him, "Sorry!"

I hope Ethan wasn't going to get into trouble for that little prank. Feeling somewhat embarrassed, I quickly took off my sparring equipment. My hearing aids squealed as I took off my helmet. I instantly felt frustrated when it did that. I settled them back on to my ears, and adjusted the volume. I stuffed the rest of the gear into my bag and hurried over to the front of the class to line up.

I looked down the line and had to admit that it was nice to finally be at the end with the other black belts. It felt right after training for so long to get where I was today. It was a good reminder that this was where I was meant to be, that I earned this spot.

Both Ethan and his father stood at the front of the class and bowed us out. When I bent down to snag my gym bag, Ethan came over to me and touched my shoulder.

"Hey, are you sure you're doing okay?" he asked, his eye brows creasing in concern.

I knew Ethan and that his concern was genuine. "I'm fine."

He reached up and brushed a stray lock of curly hair out of my eyes. Then he rested his hand on my shoulder, a warm and comforting presence. "I know you're still scared after your last head injury. There's no shame in that. You're just being cautious."

I sighed and looked at him. His short blond hair was tussled from the helmet. It suited him well, giving him a more relaxed and casual air about him. His face still had a sheen of sweat. I could see specks of gold in his hazelnut eyes. He had a strong jaw line and sensual lips. I reached up and held on to his arm. I could feel his strong muscles beneath my fingers and gave it a squeeze. "I know. It's always in the back of my mind, though."

He placed both palms on the sides of my face, resting them against my cheeks. I could feel the intense heat radiating from them. "Don't worry," he said. "I will try to pull my punches and kicks."

"Same here."

"That's a testament to your strength, knowing when to stop. It's the true mark of a black belt, having that ability to control our strikes and when to use it."

"I know, it's all about timing. So, when are you going to stop jamming my elbow?"

He raised his eyebrows at me, giving me a sly grin, "When are you going to stop kicking me there? Don't you know that it hurts to do that?"

"Oh! You cheeky monkey!" I said, giving him a playful slap on his arm.

"Ow! Hey! You're a black belt, where's your sense of control?" he said, skipping away from me.

I chased after him as he ran over to the door and bowed out.

◦◦◦

As soon I walked in the door at home, there was a rich aroma of gingerbread. It filled the house with the scent of cloves, cinnamon and nutmeg. Mom had been busy baking today for her clients. Her home business, Paige's Pastries, was really taking off this year, especially her cookies.

There was a large envelope waiting for me on the kitchen table. I picked it up, noticing the return address. It was from Sheridan College. My stomach suddenly felt very watery. I pulled out a chair and sat down. With nervous anticipation, I opened it, sliding out the contents. Holding my breath, I read it. "After much consideration, we are pleased to announce that you have been accepted for the Illustration program."

My eyes froze at that sentence. Relieved, I blew out my breath and brought trembling fingers to my lips. I couldn't believe it. When I filled out the college applications, I really didn't know what to expect. I knew that my marks were okay, even though they were not outstanding in any way. I decided to take a chance and submitted my portfolio of sketches and artwork. I was taking everything one step at a time, especially after everything that happened in the last couple of years. Sustaining a concussion and going completely deaf in one ear was traumatic enough for me. I was still trying to process these new changes in my life. I was working harder than ever to listen to people, particularly my teachers.

I stared at the letter in disbelief. A myriad of emotions ran through me. I was excited at being accepted, since this was such a prestigious program and allowed only a limited number of students. Then I suddenly became very scared at the thought of being on my own for the first time in my life. I felt a sharp pain of sadness for Parker and Serena and my parents.

Just then, Parker jumped up into my lap and exclaimed, "Purrup?"

I laughed and gave him a hug, holding his soft fur against my chest. His fur was a rich shade of brown with distinctive black stripes. I could feel his purrs rumbling beneath my fingers. He looked up at me with his bright green eyes, scrunching up his cheeks that made him look like he was giving me a big smile.

"Thanks, Parker. Funny, I was just thinking about you."

He said, "Purrup," a cross between a purr and meow.

I loved that about him, and his ability to comfort me with his sweet personality.

I began to worry about what I would do without him. My chest felt hollow as I thought about that. Parker reached up and touched my cheek with his paw. He leaned his head against me while I rubbed his fur.

Serena came into the kitchen, carrying a felt mouse, She plopped it down by my foot and gave me a squeaky meow, announcing that she had a treat for me.

"Aw! Thanks, Serena. That's so cute," I gushed at her.

Parker was the one who insisted that I bring her into the house during a particularly bad winter storm a couple of years ago. When I brought her in, she was a scrawny and tiny cat, less than a year old. It was obvious that someone had abandoned her. Today, she was a healthy and happy cat. She was virtually inseparable from Parker. The two of them were always together. Her fur was a beautiful shade of silver with hints of darker stripes in some places. She had a crooked tail which appeared to have been damaged at one point. It wagged sideways like a dog.

Tears began to well up in my eyes when it truly hit me how much I was going to miss everyone here. My throat suddenly felt very tight. Mom came out of the large walk-in closet carrying several plastic containers and placed them beside the tray of decorated cookies. Her red apron was covered in flour, her strawberry blonde hair fell in curly wisps around her face.

She gave me a warm smile when she saw me. "Hi, Jessie. Did you find the letter that arrived today?"

I nodded and held it out.

She gave me a curious look, walked over to me, and picked it up. As she read it, her face lit up. "This is great news, Jessie! I'm so proud of you!" She bent over and gave me a kiss on the cheek and a quick hug, being mindful of Parker.

"Thanks, Mom."

"So why aren't you doing a happy dance right now?"

"I just realized I won't be with Parker and Serena or you and Dad," I said, reaching down and patting Serena's fur.

Mom kneeled down beside me. "Oh, honey. I know it's not going to be easy. You will be coming home on the weekends and during the holidays. It's not that far away."

"Do you really think so?"

She nodded. "I've been through this, too. You will be very busy with school and homework."

"More than what I have now?" I asked.

"Oh, yes. It won't get any easier, but it's worth it," she replied.

"Great—now you're scaring me. What if I wasn't meant to do this?"

"Jessie, the fact that you were accepted to such a high-ranked and renowned college speaks volumes about your talent."

I stared at the letter for a long moment. My mind swirled with so many turbulent emotions. "It's such a big step for me."

Mom rubbed my arm. "It's okay to be scared. There will be lots of changes and most of them will lead to great opportunities."

"Okay," I said softly.

"Mmm! It smells good in here," Dad said as he strode in and plunked down his leather satchel.

He took off his jacket and sat down with a huff, raking his fingers through his hair. I noticed that his fingers were stained with ink. I'd surmised that he had a long day at school with his students.

"Guess what? Jessie got accepted into college today!" Mom exclaimed, waving the letter at him.

He promptly got up and read it. "Ha! I knew it," he said, beaming, raising his finger skyward.

"You're not surprised?" I asked.

He came over to me, giving me a squeeze on my shoulders. "Of course not. You work just as hard as everyone else. Why wouldn't it be any different for you?"

I shrugged my shoulders and stammered, "I—I guess because of everything that's happened lately."

He sat down, crossed his legs, and leaned back, looking very much like a professor, which is exactly what he was. "That makes it even more impressive, considering how much you've had to overcome."

I just had an unnerving thought that sent cold chills down my spine. "Um. That stalker is not going to follow me to college is he?" I asked nervously.

When I worked at the hospital as a volunteer last year, a strange man had followed me home and hid in the tree-house.

Both Dad and Mom exchanged worried glances. "They've already arrested him. You don't have to worry about that."

I raised my eyebrows. "Are you sure? I'm still looking over my shoulder and checking to make sure no one is following me."

"Why didn't you tell us that this was still bothering you?" Mom asked.

"I didn't want to worry you guys and I thought I was being too paranoid."

Dad leaned his arms on the table. "There's nothing

wrong with being cautious, particularly after that episode. To have someone lurking around on our property was extremely disturbing, even to me. It affected all of us. I'll tell you what. I'll give the constable a call."

"Thanks, Dad."

"So what should we do to celebrate this momentous occasion?" he said, eagerly clapping his hands together.

"We should ask Ethan and his family if they want to join us for dinner," I remarked.

"What a lovely idea, Jessie. Ooh, I'm already coming up with a list of recipes to try," Mom said, dashing over to the fridge, grabbing the magnetic notepad, and writing down her thoughts. She loved cooking and enjoyed spending time with Ethan's family.

Chapter 2

I woke up to the sensation of something walking along the length of my body. When I opened my eyes, I smiled broadly as he came closer to me. It was Parker. He sat on my chest, blinking his green eyes at me. He leaned in and gave me a furry kiss on my nose, his whiskers tickling my cheeks.

I giggled with delight, enjoying the way he greeted me. Then I felt a pang of sadness when I realized he wasn't going to be there in the mornings while I was in college.

"Aw, thanks, Parker," I said, patting his soft fur.

I could feel his rumbling purrs on my chest and beneath my fingers. I didn't sleep with my hearing aids on, for the same reason that most people don't wear glasses to bed. It was too uncomfortable. Because of that, I couldn't hear anything. Not even thunder or a vacuum cleaner. It was completely silent for me. All I could do was see, smell, and feel my surroundings.

I glanced at my alarm clock. I was up earlier than usual. Ironically, it was an ordinary alarm clock and the sound was turned off. I wouldn't have been able to hear it, anyways. I did have a small portable alarm that was placed under my pillow and vibrated when it was time for me to get up. It was the same one that I had used at summer camp.

I looked down and saw Serena curled up into a tight furry ball by my knees. Parker reached out and touched my nose with his warm, soft paw.

"Good morning, Parker."

I saw him open his mouth and squeeze his eyes shut, a sign that he was meowing at me. I found that amusing, since it meant that I was able to lip-read my cat. I had a feeling he was hungry and wanted breakfast.

Just then, my pillow began to shake. It was a strange sensation, as if there was a swarm of angry bees under my head. I grimly reached under the pillow, pulled out a white puck-sized clock, and turned it off. I had always found it annoying, since it was so effective at shaking me wide awake.

I gave a kiss to Parker's furry forehead, got out of bed, and went to my closet. I grabbed a pair of jeans, undergarments, and a soft pink hoodie. Parker padded beside me into the bathroom, happily wagging his short tail which made him appear more like a bobcat. I didn't mind that he was missing a full tail. It suited his personality quite well and made him more unique, like me. That was probably why I liked Parker and Serena so much. Whereas other people would've rejected them because of their flaws, to me, it made them even more special, since I knew what it was like to be different.

Parker jumped onto the closed lid of the toilet seat and onto the counter beside the sink. He watched me curiously as I stripped off my pajamas and pulled on my clothes for school. I quickly added some makeup, covering up some new blemishes, and tied my curly blonde hair into a ponytail, the curly spirals cascading over my head. Parker swiped at my lipstick, knocking it off the counter. He watched it fall to the floor, tilting his head to the side and wiggling his rump.

Once I was finished, I went over to the desk beside my bed and opened a small plastic box. I picked up the pink hearing aids covered in fake rhinestones that I had glued on. I inserted them into my ears, pushing in the soft earmolds. It took several seconds for them to activate. I waited impatiently for the sounds. Sometimes it was a shock to suddenly hear loud noises around me from somewhere else in the house. It would catch me off guard, and I had to figure where it was coming from. Today, it was blissfully quiet. All I heard was the soft hum of the furnace.

I went out the door and headed downstairs. Serena and Parker followed alongside me as I walked into the kitchen. Rummaging through the cupboards, I grabbed two small dishes and a can of cat food. While I opened the can, I glanced down at them. They were turning around in excited small circles, meowing loudly at me. I scooped a small spoonful of cat food on to each of their plates and placed them on the floor in front of them. They happily gobbled it up. I topped up the bowl of dry food and added fresh water to their dish. When that was done, I made my own breakfast of yogurt, with Mom's freshly made granola and fresh raspberries, and poured a glass of mango smoothie. I quickly ate my breakfast and went back upstairs to grab my backpack and pink sneakers.

As I made my way over to the door, I saw Dad gathering up a stack of papers on his desk and putting them in his leather satchel.

"Morning, Dad," I said, peeking my head through the door to his office.

"Morning, Jessie. Have a good day at school," he said, giving me a warm smile.

I waved at him and went out the door. Since I had been working as a volunteer at the hospital, Mom and I had made arrangements for me to use her car so that I could go back and forth to school. Her rule was that I had to keep it full of gas. It wasn't a fancy vehicle, just a small compact car. I tossed my backpack into the passenger seat, buckled in, and turned on the ignition. I drove down the long country lane that was lined with maple trees. They were turning green with fresh new leaves. The air was crisp and cool this morning, a sign of early spring. Old cornstalks stood forlornly to my right. The field on the left side was waiting to be planted with sunflower seeds, my favorite flower. I drove past the red mailbox at the end of the lane. It read "McIntyre'" and had several dents in it from someone playing mailbox baseball. It was a common occurrence around here, where no one could witness the damage until after it was too late.

I turned onto the main road and headed to the city. The rolling hills and farmland gradually changed into an urban sprawl with cookie-cutter townhouse and apartment buildings. Traffic became more congested the closer I got to the central core. I went past fast food restaurants, the industrial section and a local mall.

I slowed down as I approached my school. It was a simple two-story brick building with tall columns on either side of the doors and a sign that read "Beaverdale Middle School/High School." The school was surrounded by tall pine trees and lush grass. The parking lot was already getting full as I pulled into a free spot. I found it immensely satisfying and a relief not to have to take the bus anymore. I couldn't take another year of bullying. I grabbed my backpack, locked the car, and went in. I marched on the slick glossy floor to my locker. When I switched my backpack for books, I headed over to the counselor's office and picked up the FM system that was being charged. The transmitter was a small, lightweight rectangular box with a cord attached to it so the teachers could wear it around their neck. I had two tiny receivers, little boots that clipped onto the ends of my hearing aids.

I walked over to my classroom, past a sea of students. It was nearly packed wall to wall, and we bumped shoulders with each other as we tried to get to our classes. My first class was with Mr. Brown, who taught art, my favorite subject. I approached his desk, which was covered with numerous art history books and a stack of artwork, and handed him the FM system. He looped it over his head and asked if it was turned on. Dimly, I realized it wasn't. I reached out and flicked the switch to ON. The sound in my hearing aids suddenly increased in volume and his voice instantly became stronger and richer.

"Oh! Before I forget—I just got a letter from Sheridan College. They accepted me!" I told him.

He blinked at me then reached out and shook my hand. "Congratulations, Jessie."

"Thanks," I replied shyly.

"You do understand that it's a very heavy work load? It's a lot more than we do here," he said, his tone serious.

"Um, yes, I think so."

He leaned his hands on the desk and gave me a solemn stare. "It's entirely different at Sheridan, less than half of the students graduate from that program. It won't be easy."

I gulped loudly then nodded.

"Are you absolutely sure that you can handle their classes?"

I stammered, caught off guard by how serious he was being and I wondered if he was speaking from his own experiences or more concerned about my ability to keep up. "T— that's my intention. I love art."

"Now I'm not trying to scare you, I just want you to be fully prepared," he added.

I suddenly felt even more nervous and began to wonder what I had gotten myself into. Did I make the right choice?

"Okay, I understand," I replied then walked over to the long wooden table.

There were no desks in this class, just several long tables pushed together that formed the shape of the letter U, leaving the middle open for Mr. Brown to watch us work.

I sat down, pulled out my sketchpad and pencil case, getting ready for class. A few minutes later, the bell clanged loudly. Mr. Brown stood up, checked off the attendance list, then placed the clipboard on his desk. His brown hair was clipped short on the sides, leaving the rest long. He swept part of his hair to the side and pushed his black glasses higher on his nose. Then he began rolling up the sleeves of his blue and white striped shirt. He wore khaki slacks and shiny brown business shoes.

"Okay, folks, today we are going to talk about how we define art. Is it about perfection? Does it need to be realistic?" he asked as he strolled over to us. "I want everyone to open their Art History books to the section featuring Canadian Photorealistic artists." He paused, waiting for us to find it, then continued. "Their paintings are so detailed that they often resemble photographs with perfect compositions. These types of artwork can take many months to complete. Artists such as Alex Colville, Robert Bateman, and Ken Danby are just a few examples."

I flipped through the glossy pages displaying their paintings while he spoke, noting the extensive details and layers of paint.

"However, it could be perceived that type of perfection is considered to be too much like a photograph. While it's remarkable to achieve that level of realism, some people consider it to be too boring or monotonous. There's a general consensus that having a flaw or a less than perfect image, deliberate or not, is actually more interesting to view. There are many cultures where artists deliberately add a flaw to their artwork. It's not about being perfect, it's about being purposely imperfect."

I stifled a giggle as I tried to say the words "purposely imperfect" several times in a row in my head.

"For example, the Navajo weavers believe in adding a different color or an altered line so that the spirit can escape. This is known as a spirit path."

Cool, I thought.

"Today, I want all of you to write an essay about the differences between perfection and imperfection in art. I'm looking for a creative response.; I want to know what appeals to you and why. Before you do that, I'm going to leave you with this phrase 'There is beauty in everything, you just have to know where to look.'"

That sent a chill down my back. It struck a chord with me. It made sense that I didn't mind imperfection, I saw more value in that. Parker and Serena and myself were flawed and I thought that was what made it more special. I'd learned to look past imperfections and see the real personality behind it.

After that class, I grabbed my gym bag from my locker and went over to the arena that was situated across the parking lot at school. I quickly got changed into my lacrosse equipment and joined my gym mates. This month, our co-ed phys-ed class was doing lacrosse, which I found similar to hockey. I was wearing my own hockey gloves, shoulder pads, and helmet. I enjoyed the speed of this sport, and it felt good to be in the arena again, even though there was no ice at the moment. My gym teacher, Mr. Collins, stood in the middle of the floor with his hands on his hips as he waited for us. A whistle hung around his neck. He wore black track pants with white stripes down the side and a white short-sleeved polo shirt with the school's logo embroidered over his heart. His stark white hair stood straight up in short spikes that reminded me of a hedgehog. He was a muscular guy, his arms and biceps with quite large and seemed to be straining against the sleeves of his shirt. I knew that he was also involved with the weight lifting team and wrestling team, which would account for his strong physical body.

There were twenty of us on the floor. He divided us into two groups. Our team was given yellow bibs to wear, while the other team wore red. I was the mid fielder, which meant I could go anywhere I wanted. I stood off to the side, while two players stood in the circle at the center line. As soon as Mr. Collins blew the whistle, they immediately hustled for the ball. Jacob, who was on my team, scooped it up and started running down the floor quickly. I sprinted after him, ready to pitch in. He clashed with another player, who caused him to fumble the ball. One of my other teammates, Neal, was right behind him, and he swiftly picked up the loose ball. He made a beeline over to the goalie, deftly ignoring the slashes across his stick from the defense. I ran to the far side of the crease, ready to pick up any rebounds. Neal darted at the goalie, did a quick fake to the side, and tried to shoot the ball into the upper right corner. It bounced off the goalie's shoulder, and everyone made a mad scramble to snatch up the ball.

Julie, her long blonde ponytail sticking out from under the helmet, managed to snag it and tried to snake her way through the thick line of defensemen. Suddenly, she pivoted around and ran behind the net, throwing the ball at me. I leapt up in the air, caught it, and ran around to the front, cradling the stick in my hands. The guys slashed hard at my stick, trying to get me to drop it. I could feel the sting of their hits on my forearm where it missed the padding. Fortunately, I was used to pain and ignored it. I kept going, running past the defense until I could find an open spot. Then I saw it. I quickly shot the ball just over the goalie's shoulder. It zipped through and into the net. I felt relieved and exhilarated at the same time.

Getting this goal was a very personal and huge victory for me. I felt that I had to work much harder around my classmates, especially the ones who were on the varsity hockey and football teams. They were hard-core athletes. Even though this was supposed to be a fun co-ed gym class, the guys were not always open minded or remotely keen on having girls play with them.

Jacob and Julie came over and gave me a fist bump with their gloves. We started again at the blast of the whistle, snatching up the ball and making a mad dash across the floor. Jacob dropped the ball and the other player scooped it up, running into our end toward our goalie. I ran as fast as I could over to the guy in the red bib. It was Scott, one of the players that I did not get along with. He was always rude and arrogant to me, making chauvinistic remarks. I caught up to him, smacking his stick and trying to get him to fumble the ball. He deftly spun away from me and quickly passed it off to another player. I ran behind the net, ready to intercept the offensive players. Sure enough, the ball was passed back to Scott who stormed toward me. I veered in his direction, trying to ward off his shot. He quickly fired it out. It hit me in right in the collarbone, which stung. He picked up the loose ball and ran off with it, circling around the goalie. He did a sharp flick with his stick and the ball zipped into the net.

We marched back to the center and began again. During the hustle, the ball rolled toward me. I dashed over to it, scooped it up, and ran down the floor. Two of the red shirts immediately formed a tight line in front of me, I pivoted around them and kept going. Then I spotted Jacob and tossed the ball over to him. He took off and passed it to another player, who scored quickly. I gave Jacob a fist bump when we got back to the center. We continued to play for another thirty minutes until Mr. Collins blew the whistle twice to signal that the game was over.

I started to head over to the locker room when I heard someone yelling in the background. Then I felt a hard tap on my shoulder. I turned around to find Nick reaching out to poke me with his lacrosse stick. I couldn't hear him very well with my helmet on. I slowed my pace and turned around to face him.

"Yeah?"

He took off his helmet and ran his fingers through his hair. "Why didn't you toss the ball to me?" he asked.

His face was red and sweaty. I wasn't sure how much of that was from his anger.

I was perplexed by his attitude. "What do you mean?"

He jabbed a finger into my shoulder, "I kept yelling at you. I was wide open several times. If you had passed it to me, we could've gotten more goals!"

I had no idea what he talking about. "I don't recall hearing you. Which side were you on?"

"I was on your team!" he said, giving me exasperated sigh.

"No. I meant, on my left or right?"

"What difference does that make?" he asked, shrugging his shoulders.

"I'm deaf in my right ear. I can't hear anything on that side."

"Seriously? Then you shouldn't be playing lacrosse!" he said, leaning in closer to me, jabbing his finger into my chest angrily.

"I'm sorry, I didn't mean to ignore you," I replied meekly.

"You don't belong here, go find a different club to join," he said as he shoved past me and stormed over to the boys locker room.

Tears stung my eyes as I stood on the floor, shocked by his harsh words. I hadn't realized the consequences of my deafness in that ear. I also had a profound hearing loss in my other ear which made it even harder for me to pick up what I was missing. I was still learning how to deal with these new changes, and today proved to me how much it affected the way I perceived sounds and the impact it had on others.

Chapter 3

MOMENTUM

I was walking around at Ethan's estate, deep in thought about what Mr. Brown said to me about college and Nick's reaction about my deafness. It still stung and my chest felt awfully tight from the tension and worry. It made me wonder what else I was missing.

The gym and arena were tricky places for me to train since it was always so loud and chaotic. The high ceilings, squeaky shoes, and slick floors made the sounds bounce around. Even though I tried my best to anticipate what I needed to do next, I often made a lot of mistakes. I'd learned how to deal with my hearing loss since I was five years old when I lost it from meningitis. I had dealt with my share of being bullied and the isolation that came with it. I had to accept it and move on. It taught me to keep moving forward, even though that was not easy to do since I took it so personally.

It shook me to the core when I realized how much harder I was making it for the rest of the team. I was blissfully un-aware of them shouting at me. I had no recollection of them trying to get my attention. I began to wonder if he was right, that I shouldn't be playing sports. It nagged at me like a painful toothache.

I sat down on the wooden bench beside the pond and watched the water as the wind created ripples, turning it into a colorful abstract painting. Pink petals floated down from the trees, softly floating down onto the water like boats. There was a strong scent of lilacs in the air. Their white and purple blossoms gently swaying in the breeze. It was a beautiful spring day with the sun out in full force. It was warm enough for me to wear a long-sleeved pink shirt, jeans, and pink sneakers.

Ethan's family lived on a large property with a river on one side and a large pond on the other. Several floral gardens and fragrant trees with fresh blossoms surrounded me. It was a majestic and luxurious place to visit. To Ethan, it was his home. For me, it was a safe place to retreat from school. His orange cat, Saffron, came strolling over from a nearby bush, her fluffy tail happily swishing back and forth. She jumped up into my lap and started purring. I could feel her vibrations through her paws. I gave her a quick smile, even though I wasn't feeling very happy at the moment. I stroked her soft fur while I continued to ponder the situation I was in. It struck me as odd as to how adamant Mr. Brown was about me understanding how difficult the program would be at college. The more I thought about it, the stranger it seemed. Did he think that I wasn't capable of going there? There was something he wasn't telling me, which I found disturbing. It nagged at me. I couldn't decide whether I should be upset or angry about that.

Saffron's purrs rumbled against my chest, and I held her close, snuggling into her fur. I saw Ethan descending the stairs situated between the old stone house and garden filled with pink tulips and white peonies. He strode across the circular driveway and headed over to me. He wore dark blue jeans an indigo blue T-shirt, with an orange long sleeved shirt over top.

"Hey! So that's where you've been hiding. I see that Saffron found you first," he said.

I gave him a brief smile. He sat down beside me, and I

could smell his cologne, a mix of fresh snow and Balsam that reminded me of Christmas. His blond hair glowed in the sunlight, turning it blonder than usual. He had a lean face with a square jaw and slight dimples that appeared whenever he smiled broadly. In this light, I could see that his hazelnut eyes appeared more green with golden flakes in them. He placed his hand on the back of my neck, a warm sensation that felt nice against my skin.

"What's going on with you? You're acting distant today," he asked me.

"Sorry, I was just thinking about what happened lately and things people have been saying to me."

He gave me a puzzled look, his brow creasing in concern. "What do you mean? Talk to me," he said as his hand slid down my arm. He laced his fingers with mine. It was a familiar and comforting feeling.

I told him what Nick said at lacrosse and Mr. Brown's strange reaction about college.

"That doesn't make a lick of sense. I think that what matters the most is what you believe in. Only you know what's best for yourself."

I nodded, feeling grateful for his support. He reached up, brushed a strand of hair away from the side of my face, leaned in, and gave me a kiss on my cheek as soft as a feather.

"I know," I said. "I'm trying not to let them get to me but once in a while, I get caught off guard. I can't help but wonder if there's any truth in what they say."

"You know, there will always will someone who will try their damnedest to rip apart your self-confidence. They'll be quick to judge you and assume that you're an easy target," he said, reaching out to give Saffron a pat on the head.

Her purrs grew louder, I could feel them rumbling against my lap.

"It certainly feels true. You know that's smart advice," I replied.

He gave me a sheepish smile. "It's from Grandma Rose. She said the same thing to me."

I laughed. "Yeah, it does sound like her."

Ethan adored Grandma Rose, and he often went to her for advice. She wore hearing aids, similar to mine. She was a confident and spunky lady and I liked that about her. Even though she lost her hearing later in life, she didn't let it slow her down. She was the kind of person who spoke her mind. I knew that we would get along well when she saw my hearing aids. In a way, she taught Ethan how to see the person behind the disability. He learned from her that it's a different way of life and how to see it from a unique perspective. It taught him how to be more receptive and open with someone like me. He was one of the few people that I'd met who understood what it was like to have a hearing loss.

"It's nice to see you smile," he said. "It makes you even more beautiful."

I blushed, feeling the warmth spread through my face. I suddenly felt very shy. He leaned in, letting his lips touch mine—a hot and moist sensation against my mouth. I began to relax, letting the worry fade away, and eagerly returned the kiss, placing my fingers on the back of his neck and letting them slide up into his silky hair. I was blissfully happy, dizzy with joy. I felt him smile beneath my lips.

Saffron stood up and butted her furry head against our chins. We broke apart, laughing.

"Aw, I'm sorry Saffron. Did you feel left out?" I gave her a hug and quick kiss on her forehead.

"You know, supper's probably ready by now," he said.

Saffron jumped down and padded away, her fluffy tail waving in the air like an orange feather. Ethan grabbed my hand and pulled me up into an embrace. After a nice, long moment, we headed across the driveway and up the stairs into the kitchen.

Not surprisingly, I found Mom standing next to Ethan's mother, Katie, chatting as they stirred the pots on the stove. Katie loved trying out Mom's new recipes, and I think the two of them enjoyed exchanging stories about us.

Grandma Rose was setting up the kitchen table, laying down the napkins and utensils. She gave us a big smile when we came in. Coming over to me, she gave me a generous hug.

"Congratulations on being accepted into college, Jessie!" she said enthusiastically.

"Oh, thanks," I replied shyly.

She grabbed my hand and gave it a gentle pat. "Well, I think you're a wonderfully courageous young lady, especially with everything you've been through."

"I agree, Jessie," Ethan's mother chimed in. "You are a truly remarkable person."

Mom beamed as she watched us. I was trying hard not to blush from all of the attention.

Grandma Rose peered at my hearing aids. "I must say that I'm loving the new sparkly gems on your hearing aids. They suit you!"

"Thanks, I was trying to make them look more chic, I guess."

"What a fabulous idea! I wonder if I should do that too?" she said as she organized the table.

"Sure, why not?"

Ethan rolled his eyes. "You two are like peas in a pod you know?"

"Of course, we are," I replied, giving him a smug grin.

He walked over to the counter, picked up a couple of bowls of soup, and carried them over to the table.

"Did you need any help?" I asked.

"I don't think so, dear, go ahead and have a seat," said Grandma Rose.

After a few minutes of everyone bustling around the kitchen and placing the food on the table, we all sat down. Ethan's father, Sensei Jonas, grabbed a bottle of wine and began pouring a glass for all of us. The wine was from his own vineyard, and he was happy to share it with us.

He raised his glass. "For Jessie and Ethan being accepted

into college and university. Congratulations on your success, and may you have a bright future."

There was a chorus of "Hear, hear!" and "Cheers!" around the table, and everyone pinged their glasses with their respective neighbors. There was a loud clatter of utensils as we all started sipping the soup, our spoons clinking against the bowls.

"Oh my, this is lovely, Paige," remarked Katie.

"Thank you. It's creamy coconut chicken curry."

Katie smiled. "That's quite a mouthful!"

They both laughed at that. It was one of my favorite soups that Mom made, and it was clearly a big hit here. She loved to experiment with food, trying to find interesting combinations of flavors. While we sipped the soup and chatted, it dawned on me that, since Ethan and I were going to separate schools, we wouldn't be seeing much of each other. It was tricky enough now since he went to a private school, although I got to see him throughout the week at karate and on the weekends. It meant that the distance between us would be even greater.

"So, Ethan, I hear that you're taking Psychology at university. How did you get interested in that subject?" Dad asked.

"It think it's because I liked solving puzzles, particularly anything to do with the mind. After working at Camp Balsam, it made me realize that I could make a difference with kids who have disabilities. Even though they all had their fair share of learning disabilities, mental and physical impairments, I still loved working with them. To me, they stood out as truly unique individuals."

I nodded in agreement. "He's right. We didn't see their disabilities, we saw the real kid in them. They were really smart."

"I want to continue helping kids like that, I want to help them reach their full potential," Ethan said earnestly. "They need someone to guide them and help them stay strong."

"Good for you, Ethan! We could use more psychologists like you," Dad said.

"By the way, have you guys decided what to do about the prom?" Katie asked.

It was at that moment that I realized I hadn't even thought about it.

"Um—no. Why?" I replied hesitantly.

"I believe that your school has the prom next month, is that right, Jessie?" Mom asked me.

"I think so," I said, wondering what she was up to.

"Ethan's school has their graduation prom next fall and, unfortunately, both of you will be already at college and university," Katie added.

My eyes flicked back and forth at both mothers. Ethan and I looked at each other and he said, "We haven't discussed it yet."

"Then it's settled, you guys should go to Jessie's prom! It would be a wonderful opportunity for both of you to have a good time together," Mom said.

I coughed, the soup caught in my throat. Ethan slapped my back. I was momentarily speechless. Literally. Then I realized this would be the perfect opportunity to prove to my classmates that I did have a boyfriend. Some of them had claimed that I made him up since they never saw him.

I looked at Ethan who appeared equally as speechless. "What do you think?" I asked him. "Are you interested?"

There was a long pause, and I could sense everyone staring at us. I gulped loudly.

Ethan blinked a couple of times. "Yeah. That would work. In fact, it's perfect!"

Whew! I thought.

"Hey, Dad. Can we get a limo to go to the prom?" Ethan asked Jonas.

"Oh, sure, no problem, son."

We all started conversing back and forth about our plans, our voices overlapping loudly. I had to strain to hear them speaking and it forced me to focus more on reading their lips. I managed to catch a snatch of the conversation between the guys. They were talking about tuxedos.

"What are we going to do about a prom dress, Mom? I don't have anything nice to wear."

Her face fell. "Oh, dear, you're right about that. I guess we're going to have do some shopping."

I was not a big fan of dresses and dreaded the thought of wearing one.

"I have several bridesmaids dresses that we can alter to fit you, Jessie," remarked Katie.

"Why, that's a great idea!" Mom said.

"In fact, while you're here, you should try some of them on," Katie suggested.

Grandma Rose nodded. "It would be like a fashion show, Jessie!"

I groaned, not exactly thrilled with that prospect. "Sure, why not?" I said, trying to be polite.

After supper, the guys began cleaning up the kitchen while we headed upstairs to look at the dresses. Katie's room was supremely spacious with a large sofa under the window, a walk-in closet, and bathroom off to the side. The room had a tall ceiling, which made it seem much bigger. The bed itself was also king sized and there were small tables on either side, stacked with books. There were numerous photographs of simple nature shots, all of them featuring a tranquil theme by the sea. This bedroom was elaborately decorated, very much like the ones I had seen in magazines. It felt like it was professionally designed.

Mom and I sat down on the sofa as Katie strolled into the enormous walk-in closet and began pulling out dresses. She handed them to Grandma Rose, who laid them on the bed for me to see. Some had glittering gems on them, others were low cut, some were decorated with ruffles. They were in a variety of soft shades of lilac purple, pink, peach and soft baby blue.

"Wow, that's a lot of bridesmaid dresses," I remarked.

"It is, isn't it? I didn't realize that until now. We do love family reunions and weddings," Katie said, smiling as she gazed at the dresses then back at us.

Grandma Rose sighed. "Those were such wonderful weddings, weren't they, dear?"

Katie nodded. "Yes, it was certainly nice to see everyone again. We really need to do it more often."

"I don't think I have been to a wedding, have I, Mom?" I asked her.

"You did when you were younger but you probably don't remember that," she replied.

"Okay, Jessie, why don't you try some of these dresses, and we'll see which ones fit you," Katie said to me.

I took a deep breath, grabbed a couple of them, and carried them to the large bathroom. This room was equally as luxurious and spacious as the rest of the house. It featured a large tub that resembled a hot tub, toilet, plus a vanity table with a mirror and chair, as well as a long marble counter with two sinks in it. I carefully draped the dresses on the back of the chair and stripped out of my clothes. I pulled on a sleek purple dress that felt silky smooth to the touch. I turned around, walked out of the bathroom, stepped on the hem, and started to fall. There was a collective gasp and everyone lurched forward. I quickly grasped the frame of the doorway and managed to regain my balance just in time. I grabbed the dress, lifted it off the floor, and moved closer to them.

"Hmm, that's an interesting color on you, Jessie," Mom said.

"Try sitting down to see how it feels," Katie suggested.

I slowly walked over to the sofa and sat down then realized that I was slowly slipping off. The silky material made it nearly impossible for me to sit still in it. I leaned on the armrest for support. "What kind of material is this?"

"I believe that one is made out of silk. That's why is so smooth. Isn't it lovely?" Katie said.

"How do I sit in it?" I asked.

Grandma Rose laughed. "Carefully, dear."

I went back to the bathroom, tried on another dress, and paraded out like a model on a catwalk. This one was a shade of mint green. I looked like a tree frog wearing it. "What do you think?" I asked them.

"I'm not sure that's your color, Jessie," said Mom.

"Okay. I'll try the other one on." I went back into the bathroom and switched dresses.

I walked out and spun around. This one was indigo blue. I noticed when I strode forward that there was slit along the side that came nearly up to my thigh. It made me feel a bit too uncomfortable. It felt too grown up for me. I went back into the bathroom and wriggled into a tight peach dress. I looked in the mirror and noticed that my skin tone was almost the same shade as the dress. I looked naked and decided against it. I tugged on a pink champagne dress featuring a simple low cut neckline. It sparkled in the light, the tiny gems glittering whenever I moved. I walked out and did a little spin.

"What do you think?" I asked nervously.

Grandma Rose gasped with delight.

"That shade of pink suits you very well, Jessie," Mom said.

I glanced down and tugged on the straps, pulling them up higher. "Do you think it's too low cut for me?"

"It's fine, Jessie," Mom said, "stop fussing with it."

"I think that's the one," Katie remarked.

"Do you really think so?"

Everyone nodded their heads.

"What are you going to wear for shoes?" Katie asked.

They looked down at my bare feet. I wriggled my toes. "I hadn't even thought about that. I just have regular gym shoes, nothing fancy."

"Do you have any high heels?" Katie inquired.

"No, I don't."

She put a finger on her lips for a moment. "What size do you wear?"

"Size seven."

"Oh, dear, I'm a size eight," Katie replied, then she turned to Grandma Rose, "You wear a six right?"

Grandma Rose nodded.

I knew that Mom wore a size eight, which meant her shoes would be too big for me.

"Do you want try on a couple to see if they fit?" Katie asked.

"Sure, but I can't walk in high heels," I replied.

"It takes practice. Lots of practice," Katie said, giving me a smile.

She went in the closet then brought out several pairs of shoes. She knelt on the floor and placed a shiny pair of black high heels beside my feet. The heels were as skinny as pencils. I gingerly stepped into them, and she helped adjust the straps. I could already feel the pressure of the heels going into my foot. It was not very comfortable feeling, and I felt unsteady standing in them. I took a couple of steps forward, my feet wobbling like Jell-O. My arms started to windmill as I tried to maintain my balance.

"Whoa. I feel like I'm walking on stilts."

I took a few more steps then stumbled. Katie caught my arm before I fell forward.

"Maybe you would feel more comfortable in sandals?" Mom said.

I nodded, feeling grateful that she made that suggestion. I couldn't even bear the thought of having to walk in shoes like these, especially on the stairs.

"We can look for a pair of shoes this week," Mom added.

I felt a bit disappointed that I couldn't wear high heels. It made me feel out of place, like a country bumpkin. I accepted the dress and said thank you to Katie.

"I'm so glad that you could wear it, Jessie. It's nice to see it being used again," she said, giving me a hug.

We went downstairs to find the guys. They were all sitting in the living room, conversing. Ethan stood up and strode over to me. He grabbed my hand and tugged me outside onto the side porch, out of view from everyone else. Pulling me into his chest, he gave me a warm hug. I leaned into his body, feeling the heat of him radiate out to me. He eased away, bent down, and gave me a long, sensual kiss that left a tingling sensation on my lips. After we broke apart, I joined my parents and waved goodbye to everyone as we stepped into the car and drove away.

Chapter 4

onward

At breakfast, Mom and Dad asked me about getting in touch with the college about helping me get set up.

"You'll need to find out if there's any funding or bursaries for students with disabilities," Dad said,

"You should talk to your counselor about making sure that Sheridan has an FM system and whether the teachers are prepared for you," Mom added.

I nodded as I munched on my toast. "Okay, I'll see what I can find out."

During a break in between classes, I stopped by the counselor's office and informed them that I had been accepted into college. They pumped my hand enthusiastically and gave me their congratulations. Then they ushered me into my counselor's office.

It was a simple room with white walls decorated with various posters that featured motivational themes. Along one wall were numerous display stands filled with pamphlets and booklets from universities and colleges. I sat down in the stiff plastic chair across from the metal desk. It was piled up high with various books and a stack of paper-work off to one side. A cup of tea sat on the corner which I suspected had gone cold by now.

Mrs. Kessler was an older lady, reminding me of a kind-ly grandmother. Her white hair was clipped short in a pixie cut which suited her well. She wore a white knitted shawl across her shoulders over a blue short-sleeved blouse. A pair of glasses hung around her neck on a chain.

I nervously played with my pencil case. "Um, I have a question about the teachers at Sheridan. Would you know if any of them have used an FM system before?"

She glanced at me for a long moment as she pondered that. "I'm not entirely sure about that. Some may have expe-rience in the past with other students. We'll be speaking with them prior to your arrival to ensure that they have eve-rything set up. You're in a unique position since most of your classes are more hands on, as opposed to lectures. You will need to decide if a notetaker would help in this situa-tion. However, I do know that they have an accessible learn-ing office there, and we can make arrangements for them to help us find suitable accommodations for you."

I nodded. "Okay, do they have assistive devices such as an FM system available for me to use?"

"You will need to purchase the equipment and be re-sponsible for keeping it charged and bringing it to class. Remember, they will treat you like an adult, and it will be your responsibility to handle everything on your own."

I gulped, suddenly feeling very nervous. "Are they ex-pensive?"

She nodded. "I'm afraid so. However, you may qualify for a bursary that would help cover the cost, and it would be yours to keep."

"How do I apply for it?" I inquired.

"I can get the forms for you. Your doctor may be re-quired to fill out part of it as proof that you have a hearing loss. Don't worry, this is standard procedure and you shouldn't have any problems with it."

"Okay, how do I get funding to help pay for school supplies and tuition fee?" The more questions I asked, the more worried I became. I began to wonder if this was feasible. What if I couldn't afford it? How was I going to pay for the rent?

"There are government support programs that can cover some of those costs."

"Really? How much would they cover?"

"In the majority of cases that I've seen, it's more than half," she replied.

"Would I qualify for it?" I asked her.

"Most likely, but I can't guarantee it. You would need to apply for it and wait to see if it's approved. I would do this right away to ensure that you get some assistance and funding by the time you start college in the fall," she said.

"How do I apply for it?" My palms were getting increasingly sweaty as I asked more questions. I was beginning to panic, wondering if any of this would work.

"I have the paperwork here, and I can help you go through it," she said then stood up and opened a filing cabinet that was situated behind the desk. She pulled opened the middle drawer and rifled through the folders, pulling out various sheets of paper. Once she collected all of the forms, she handed them over to me, along with a list of various websites on it.

She pointed at the sheet with her pen. "You can also apply for additional support programs online. I would check out those websites to see if you qualify for any of them."

"Okay I'll do that," I said then glanced at the clock on the wall. I realized I needed to leave. "Thank you so much for your help."

She gave me a kind smile, her eyes crinkling at the corners. "You're welcome, dear."

I gathered up the forms and headed over to my next class, trying hard not to feel overwhelmed with all of the paperwork.

❦

Later that night, I worked with Ethan at the dojo, teaching the kids' class. I had a small group of little girls around the age of eight, with bouncy pony tails and impish grins. They were a cute bunch and eager to learn new moves. I loved working with children at this age. Their bright yellow and orange belts stood out against their white uniforms, reminding me of giant colorful bow ties.

"Okay, are you guys ready to follow me?" I asked them.

They happily bopped their heads up and down.

"Good. Bow to me, then go into a horse stance."

They promptly delivered a snappy bow then moved their left leg out to squat down with their hands tightly curled into fists that sat on their hips.

One of them wasn't really doing much of a squat, her legs were nearly straight which made her stand tall, compared to the rest of the group.

I nodded to her. "You'll need to go a bit lower. Bend your knees and pretend that you're sitting on a really fat pony."

She began to giggle, which made them all join in. I did a facepalm and sighed. They were all bending over, looking at each other, and snickering.

"Okay, let's try again. Follow me," I said, going into a horse stance, watching them as they copied me.

I turned to my left into a forward stance, bending my front leg and locking out my back one. I did a sweeping low block with my left arm then moved forward to do a punch. I looked over my shoulder to watch their progress. They all wore serious looks on their faces, completely engrossed in the movements. They copied my actions dutifully as I continued on with a variety of kicks, punches, and blocks, going back and forth across the floor. We practiced the same kata several times until they seemed to get the hang of it, remembering the moves correctly. They resembled tiny little warriors, with their determination and loud kiais, punching with all of their might.

I gave them a high five once they were finished with their katas. "That was awesome, guys! You got all of the moves right and did a good job with your stances. I know it's not easy, especially when you get tired."

They beamed at me. "Thanks, Sensei Jessie," one girl with long brown hair in a french braid replied. "I think you're a good teacher even though my mom says that handicapped people shouldn't work with kids."

I felt crestfallen and very surprised by her comment. "Why not?" I asked her.

She shrugged her shoulders. "I don't know. She says that she doesn't like you."

I was momentarily speechless. "Oh, I'm sorry to hear that."

"I like you just the way you are," she said, playing with the ends of her belt. "I think your hearing aids are pretty."

"Aw, thanks."

She came over and gave me a hug.

"Uh oh. I seem to have an octopus stuck on me," I said.

She giggled, then the rest the of the girls came over and did the same thing. They held on to my waist and my legs and I couldn't move.

"Hey! What about me?" Ethan said when he saw them. He pouted, sticking out his lower lip.

"Oh no. Sensei Ethan has a pouty face."

The girls looked at him, squealed with laughter, then ran over to him, wrapping their arms around him.

"Great. Now I can't move," he said.

Their giggles grew louder as he attempted to walk, dragging his leg across the floor. It was rather comical.

After a few minutes of being silly, Ethan held up his hands. "All right guys, it's time to get your sparring gear on. Shoo!"

They ran over to the wall where their bags were stored, sat down, and began putting on their equipment.

Ethan stood beside me as we waited. He bumped his elbow with mine. "Hey, you okay?"

I tilted my chin at one of the girls, "She said that her mom didn't like me because I am 'handicapped.'" I mimed air quotes when I said the last word.

He turned and faced me. "That doesn't surprise me. Dad had to convince her parents to let you teach this class and work with her."

A cold shock ran through me when he said that. It felt like someone dumped a bucket of ice over me. I stared at him in surprise. "What? Why didn't you tell me?"

"Because Dad knows that you're a great instructor and he told them that. He wanted them to see for themselves how good you are with the kids. It's his club. No one else has the right to tell him what to do."

The rising anger that I felt was beginning to deflate like a balloon. I was filled with a sense of disappointment and confusion. "Why can't people see past my disability? I don't get it."

"Fear or maybe misinformation? Prejudice? I don't know. I wish they would take the time to get to know you before they judge you so quickly," he replied earnestly.

"It still hurts when someone tells me they hate me."

"I know and I wish I could take that pain away from you," he said, wrapping his arm around my shoulders.

"You know—it's funny how people like that try to define who I am. I mean, yes, it does have an impact, in terms of how I function and interact with them, but it's not who I am on a personal level. I just wish they could look past my hearing aids and see the real me," I said. There was a sense of weariness in me, a tiredness in my body from this seemingly never-ending burden.

He nodded as he listened, resting his hand on the back of my neck and giving it a gentle squeeze.

"It's ironic how I thought that everything would change when I finally got my black belt," I continued. "I mean, I did feel different, like a new person when I received it.

Stronger and more empowered. But now, I realize that it's the rest of the world and the way they perceive me that hasn't changed. This feels like another test that I have to go through again. Only, this time, it's not for me, it's for them."

"Don't worry about it, okay? Both Dad and I see the truth about you, we know what you're capable of and how strong you are. You don't need to change anything about yourself."

"Thanks, Ethan. I guess that I thought this kind of crap would be over by now. That I didn't have to keep proving myself to people like them."

After a moment, he cleared his throat. "By the way, have you thought about joining me in fencing? Want to try it out?"

"Me? Why? What are you up to now?"

He grinned. "I thought you might like it."

"Stabbing people? Sure, sounds kinda therapeutic," I said, remembering the last time I watched him fence. "Isn't that a private club, though?"

He nodded. "The one at school is, I also fence at another one in the city."

"Why two clubs?' I asked.

"They offer different weapons and instructors. I get more training this way."

"Oh, cool. Yeah, I'll join you."

The kids came running back to us with their equipment and ready to go. We got them set up in the ring and began the sparring match. This kept us occupied for the rest of the class.

Chapter 5

TOUCHÉ

Ethan picked me up and drove me to the fencing club that was located twenty minutes away. The weather was miserable with the rain coming down in sheets, leaving giant pools of water. I watched the reflections in the puddles during the drive, noticing the colors rippling on the surface. The droplets on the window turned into a myriad collage of colorful dots with upside down images of the streets lights, buildings and signs.

"How long have you been going to this club?" I asked him while he turned onto another street.

"About four years I think," he replied, casting a quick glance at me.

"Did you go to tournaments with them?"

"Oh sure, many times," he replied.

"How did you manage to do both karate and fencing? Isn't that exhausting?"

He shrugged his shoulders. "Not really. I just learned how to balance my homework and chose which classes and tournaments to go to. Now that I have experience in both sports, I know which ones are more fun."

"I'm impressed. I wonder if I'll ever get a chance to fence in a tournament?"

"Sure, why not? I went to my first tournament after I got my yellow armband," he replied.

"Armband? You mean like we do with the color belts in karate?"

"Yeah, it's very similar, except we wear the patches on the sleeve of our jacket," he said.

"Oh, that's cool. Has long does it take to get a yellow armband?"

"Anywhere from six to eight months. It depends on how quickly the fencers learn the required skills."

"So it takes longer to reach the next level?"

He nodded. "Yep. It requires a lot more finesse and technical skills although everyone learns at a different pace."

Curious, I asked, "What color armband are you?"

"Blue," he replied.

"Is that an advanced level?"

"Yes, red and black are next and those are for high level athletes."

"What do you mean? Like the Olympics?" I asked him.

"Yes and long term fencers who have been fencing for many years."

"Wow," I said quietly.

He slowed down and turned the car into the parking lot beside a large brick building. We got out of the car. I picked up my gym bag while Ethan grabbed his large fencing bag. It looked a lot like a golf bag. He slung it over his shoulder, and we quickly dashed across the parking lot, avoiding the puddles.

Once we stepped through the glass doors, we shook off the rain and headed over to the atrium, our boots squelching loudly on the slick floor. Then we turned down a long hallway and marched past a row of lockers.

"How old is this building?" I asked.

"Pretty old. It was used as the main gym for a private school that was originally next door," he replied, hefting his bag higher on to his shoulder. I suspected that it was heavy.

"Weird, I didn't see any other buildings beside it."

"Ah, it burned down a long time ago."

"Oh. I didn't know that. How did that happen?"

"My parents said that it was hit by lightning," he replied.

I shuddered. I was not a big fan of storms, especially after being caught in a tornado a few years ago at school. I still had flashbacks of the dark green sky and swirling thick clouds filled with bursts of lightning. The wind had shattered the windows in my classroom, and we had to scamper down to the dimly lit and cramped basement. I didn't relish the thought of going through that again.

"The city said the gym was still in great shape and decided to keep the building. My coaches have been using it as a fencing club. The university also uses it for their varsity team."

"Universities have fencing teams? I didn't know that."

He nodded. "Isn't that cool?"

We turned left then right into a spacious gym with a high ceiling and wooden floors. Dozens of wires were strung overhead, looping down along the walls. There were sleek black boxes attached to the walls on both sides beneath each row of wires. Black tape on the floor outlined a long rectangular box going from one end of the wall to the next. It was nearly fourteen meters long and two meters wide. I counted them and noticed that there were at least eight of them, plus two long metal platforms the same size. They were located at the back of the gym.

I gestured at them with my thumb. "What are those?"

"Those are the metal pistes for the competitive fencers."

"Oh, why are they different?"

"They're the same ones that are used in tournaments. It gives them a chance to get used to them since they feel different than fencing on a wooden floor."

I glanced down at the floor. "So the areas taped on the floor are the same thing?"

He nodded and gave me a quick smile. "Yep. Pretty much everyone uses them. It can get pretty crowded in here, especially when it's close to a tournament. We've had over twenty four fencers in here at one point. It was nuts."

"What are they called again?" I asked.

"Piste. It's French for a 'fencing strip', most of our terminology is spoken in French."

There was a group of people off to my right who were opening their bags and rummaging through them, pulling out their long, sharp weapons. They looked like they were about the same age as me. One of them wore red track pants with a set of white stripes running down the sides and a jacket in the same color with a maple leaf logo on the front. He looked up and saw us, got up and walked over to Ethan. He gave both of us an enthusiastic handshake with his left hand. I was puzzled by that, and made a mental note to ask Ethan if he was left handed.

"Hey, Ethan! It's great to see you man. It's been what…a couple of weeks since you've been here, eh?"

When he spoke, I could've sworn that he had an accent, but I wasn't sure if it was just me trying to decipher a new voice. It had a bit of a rumbling bass to it, which made it harder for me to hear. His dark brown hair was cut short along the sides, except in the front where it swooped up like a little wave. He was a stocky guy and almost as tall as Ethan.

"And who is this lovely lady?" he asked, smiling broadly.

"This is Jessie," Ethan replied.

"Nice to meet you, Jessie," he said as he inclined his head. "Are you going to join our club?"

"I don't know, maybe?"

"We would love to have you here. We could use more fencers."

"You mean fresh blood, don't you?" Ethan said, narrowing his eyes at him.

"He's joking, of course," the other guy said then paused for a moment and added, "sort of."

Ethan rolled his eyes. "This is my coach, Patrice. Gotta

warn you, though, his sense of humor is a bit skewed."

I was already getting that impression.

Patrice glanced at the large clock on the wall. "We'll be starting soon." He looked at me. "Did you bring long pants and a shirt to wear?"

I nodded.

"The locker room is over there," Ethan said, gesturing to a small hallway on my left. "It's the door on the right."

"Okay." I carried my gym bag over to the room and quickly got changed. I pulled on a purple T-shirt and black yoga pants. I tugged on my white socks and purple running shoes.

When I walked out onto the floor, I found that Ethan had already changed into a red T-shirt, white pants that ended at the knee, with one white sock on the right leg and a red sock on the left. He was bent over doing up his shoelaces when I stood by him. I noticed that the rest of the group also wore their socks the same way.

"Um, what's with the socks? Why are you guys wearing them like that?" I asked Ethan.

Ethan looked down then back up at me. "It's our team colors. It's a tradition, we always wear the color sock on the left leg."

I gave them a big smile. "That is a wicked style. I like it!"

Ethan introduced me to the guys. "Jessie, this is Neal, Brandon, Tristen, Stephane, and Chris." He went around the group, gesturing at each one as he spoke their names. They reached out and eagerly pumped my hand, also with the left side.

"This may sound like a weird question but is everyone left handed here?"

"Heh, no. We always shake with our left hand after each bout. It's a habit for us."

"Oh, cool."

Ethan gestured at Tristen. "Don't worry about him, he may seem odd. He's just gay."

Tristen snickered. "Yep, it's true."

I smiled then noticed that they all had armbands on their sleeves beneath a logo of a red shield. The colors of their bands were green and blue.

"Wow, you guys must be experienced fencers."

"Yeah, I guess. We've been fencing for a long time, several years actually," replied Tristen. He had short and wavy blond hair with a sleek oval face. His eyes were a shade of chocolate brown. He was tall and slim.

"Although not as long as our coaches," remarked Neal, who looked striking with clean, chiseled features and a strong chin. He had black tousled hair and bright blue eyes. He had broad shoulders and looked like an Abercrombie and Fitch model.

"That's true," Tristen said. "Coach Patrice has been fencing for over fifteen years."

"No. Seriously?" I said.

They all nodded. "Yep. He's a Provincial and National Coach."

I balked. "No way. He's the coach for Team Canada?"

I was blown away by this neat trivia. To be in the same gym with a national coach was a very cool bonus.

"Yep," Ethan said, raising his eyebrows and giving me a quick nod.

Super. That made me even more nervous.

Within the next minutes, several more fencers joined us.

Coach Patrice walked over to a large white board on the wall and gestured at us to join him. "Okay, folks, gather around."

We all lumbered over, standing in a semi-circle around him.

"Before we start, please give a warm welcome to Jessie who will be joining us today. Be nice." He gave some of the guys pointed looks and I wondered what that was all about.

They gave me a brief applause and waved their hands at me to say hello.

Patrice uncapped a marker and began writing a list on

the board. He quickly explained the order of today's activities and drills that we were going to do after the warm up.

"Any questions before we start?" he asked, looking around the room. "Great. Go ahead and start running around."

Ethan touched my arm. "Just follow me, do what I do."

"Okay."

As we started our run, Patrice went into the middle of the room and started yelling out commands. I really struggled to hear what he said. His voice bounced off the high ceilings, and I couldn't lip read him while I was in motion. I could only hear snatches of what he said, just bits and pieces of the words.

He suddenly clapped his hands three times. Startled, I looked around at what everyone else was doing. Sit ups. I promptly sat down and copied them. I didn't know how many to do so I just kept going until Ethan got up and continued running.

Patrice clapped once and everyone suddenly sprinted forward. We kept going until he clapped twice when everyone slowed down to an easy jog. I could feel the frustration creeping in, the anger rising through my chest. Not being able to follow him made me feel left out, like an idiot. I was beginning to realize just how much harder it was to hear in a place like this. I felt very much out of my element, even though I had done these kinds of warm ups before. I was having a hard time following a new instructor and working hard to maintain my dignity with this group.

After what seemed like long time of running, he gave us a break to get a drink of water. I went over to my bag and picked up my pink water bottle, taking a lot of thirsty sips.

"Hey, you doing okay?" Ethan asked as he grabbed his water bottle.

"Yeah. I guess so. It's hard keeping up with these guys."

"Don't worry about it. We've been doing these drills for a long time and are used to it."

"I feel like an idiot sometimes when I'm left standing

there while everyone changes directions or goes down to the floor," I said, feeling a flush of hot anger creep up into my face.

Ethan put his hand on my shoulder. I could feel the intense heat radiating through my shirt. "Really. It's okay, you're doing fine," he said.

I took a deep breath and another swig of water.

"Besides, we're not done yet with the drills," he added.

"Huh? What do you mean?"

He jerked this thumb over his shoulder, where I spotted Patrice and another fencer laying down a rope ladder on the floor. There were also hula hoops and large wooden boxes in various places around the gym.

After we finished our drinks, we strode over to Patrice where he stood beside the ladder. "Okay, you're going to follow me as we go around the gym."

He proceeded to do stepping drills on the rope ladder, moving his feet in and out of the spaces, then ran over to the wooden boxes where we jumped up on top of them then back down then over to another box a few feet away. We followed him as he leaped from one circle to another, like frogs jumping across lily pads. It was intense and I was working hard to keep up with them. We ran around the gym and repeated all of the drills until he called halt. I was dripping sweat, and I could feel my muscles straining from the exertion.

Patrice stood in the middle of the floor facing us "Everyone line up along the wall and go into the en garde position," he bellowed.

I stood beside Ethan and copied his stance, turning my left foot out and placing my right foot in front, bending my knees and lowering my weight. Instantly, I felt my legs burning.

"Do what I do," Ethan said, as he watched me adjust my feet. He gave me a quick wink to reassure me.

Patrice was holding on to one of the weapons by the tip, letting the metal handle touch the floor. "When I tap the floor, start moving forward. Two taps means to go backward."

He tapped the floor once, and all of us proceeded to move forward. I moved my right foot then my left, as if attached by an invisible magnet. I could feel the muscles in my thighs working hard. Patrice banged the floor twice. Everyone immediately started to retreat, shuffling backward with practiced ease. He continued to do this several times, going back and forth.

"This time, at three taps, you're going to do a lunge. Don't forget to really bend your front leg and extend your back leg. I want to see a good thrusting motion with your arm. By the time your front foot lands on the floor, your arm should be fully extended. I want you to focus on hitting the target before you finish the lunge."

I blinked then looked Ethan, who proceeded to demonstrate the technique in slow motion. He did a little kick with his front foot as he thrust out his right arm at the same time. It looked like his arm was pulling his body forward. As I watched, I was praying that I wouldn't twist my ankle and fall flat on my face. I gingerly copied his moves, feeling rather clumsy compared to him. It felt odd since I was so proficient in karate. Going from being an instructor in martial arts to a beginner in fencing felt very strange to me.

While I practiced the motions, Ethan reached over and fixed the position of my arm and adjusted my legs. Once I got the gist of it, I followed along with the rest of the group while Patrice banged on the floor. I had sudden and vivid image of Puss N Boots from Shrek doing his Zorro impersonation with his sword and bit my lip to stifle a giggle.

"Excellent! All right, everyone, go put on your electric gear."

I looked at Ethan, puzzled.

"He's referring to the lamés that we wear, metal jackets that go over top. That's what those wires are for," he said, gesturing upward.

Patrice came over to us, "Ethan, did you want to show

Jessie how to use a foil and do a quick bout with her?"

He nodded. "Sure coach."

I raised my eyebrows in surprise at both of them. "Uh…bout? So soon?"

"Of course!" Patrice said, giving me hearty slap on my shoulder.

"Okay, but I don't have any equipment."

"No problem, we have our own supply here. Let's get you suited up. Follow me."

Ethan went over to his bag and began pulling out his white jacket, glove, wires and mask. I followed Patrice over to a wall that was lined with lockers, bins full of medicine balls, a stack of blue mats and a large cage full of jackets on hangers and shelves with masks.

"Let's see, you'll need this," he said as he grabbed a white plastic chest protector and handed it over to me. "This should fit you."

He continued to rummage around in the cage and pulled out a long sleeved white jacket, glove, and a mask.

"Ethan will help you put these on, if they don't fit, we can try a different size. Once you're ready, I'll help you pick out a foil."

I nodded, headed back to Ethan, and put everything on the floor. "So, I need to put this on first?" I said, holding up the chest protector.

"Yep. Trust me, you'll need it."

I slid the molded hard plastic shell over my chest, pulling the straps over my shoulders. I instantly felt like a Barbie doll. "I feel so stupid wearing this."

"The guys wear them too," he replied, tilting his chin at them.

I looked around and saw several of them had a smoother, flat version of my shield.

"Oh great, we look like Barbie and Ken dolls," I said snarkily.

"It will hurt without it. It's no different than wearing shoulder pads for hockey."

I rolled my eyes. "No, not really. This is really stiff. And embarrassing. It's like I'm wearing a bra on the outside."

He sighed. "Anyways, put this on." He held up my white jacket. I stepped through the looped strap at the bottom, slipped my arms through into the sleeves, and let him zip me up from behind. I pulled on the soft, leather glove which fit nicely.

"Here's your mask," he said, handing it over.

I grabbed it and noted that it was heavier than I thought it would be. The front of the mask was covered with tightly woven metal wires that crisscrossed the surface. There were two large Velcro straps across the back. He helped me angle the mask on, and I had to tell him to stop when my hearing aids squealed in protest. We pulled it off so I could lower the volume on the aids and tried it again. Once we got the straps tightened, I peered at Ethan.

"Holy cow, how can you see anything? It seems darker in here."

"Focus on me," he said. "That sensation will gradually fade."

I looked at him, watching his eyes come into focus. I noticed that when he spoke, his speech sounded muffled, and I suddenly felt anxious.

I took it off. "What about the foil?"

"Come on over here," he said, gesturing for me to go with him over to the metal cage where all of the weapons were stored.

"Some of these have different handles." He picked one up and showed it to me. It had a simple metal handle that resembled a very thick tongue depressor.

I held it in my hands. It was a strange sensation, like holding a long dinner knife.

"Now, try this one." He swapped that out for one that had a silver handle which looked a like a skinny gun. I tried it out. It sat nicely in my hand and was easy to grip. It was a natural fit that felt more balanced for me.

"What's this one called?" I asked.

"A pistol grip."

Of course, I thought. That made perfect sense.

"So, why is this handle different from than the other foils?"

"It was originally designed for a fencer with a physical disability."

"Cool. So does my hearing loss count?" I asked cheekily.

"No, nice try, though," he said. "So, are you happy with that one?"

"Yeah, I'll try this one."

We went over to one of the empty pistes since many of the other ones were full. The noise in the room was extremely loud and filled with long beeps and high-pitched alarms going off. I watched the fencers dart back and forth on the piste. They would lunge forward to deliver a strike then leap backward to avoid being hit. They wore silver vests and had wires attached to them at the back. The LED displays on the walls at the end of each piste would light up in red or green whenever a fencer scored a point. Whenever the light went off, it also gave off a piercing beep. I had to really listen to Ethan when he spoke, standing close to him so I could hear him over the mix of loud sounds. I put on mask and waited for Ethan.

He stood beside me and showed me to hold the foil. I held it in my hand like a gun and kept my elbow close to my hip. Ethan faced me, put on his mask and held his foil in front of me.

"I'm going to tell you where to aim while you're in the en garde position okay?" His voice was muffled.

I nodded and went into the correct stance, lowering my weight.

"When you fence, you need to hold your weapon in a threatening manner. This will give you priority. That's a good thing in bouts. Aim the tip of your foil slightly over your opponent's shoulder."

I moved the tip of the foil, correcting the position.

"Now, put the blade of your foil against mine."

I did as he said.

"I'm going to show you how to do some parries." He swiftly swept my foil aside like a windshield wiper. "This is called a parry four." Then he held up his free hand. "This move is a riposte, a follow up to the parry." He extended his arm and tapped my chest with the tip of his foil. Then he signed '*Okay?*' with his fingers.

I nodded. We started over again with me trying those moves on him. We went back and forth doing a parry and riposte, a simple block and strike. It reminded me of doing an arm block and punch in karate. After doing it several times, I was getting the hang of it.

"Good. Now let's do it moving up and down on the piste."

I gulped nervously. "Okay."

"Lower your stance a bit more," he said, holding his hand out and pushing it down, a visual reminder to adjust my position.

By now, my legs were beginning to scream.

Our foils clanged loudly as we worked on our parries and ripostes, going back and forth. Then he had me add lunges which made it easier for me to reach him, even though he had longer legs. We picked up the pace as I became more confident. I felt excited and terrified at the same time. It was exhilarating!

Ethan held up his hand like a stop sign then took off his mask. He came over to me and shook my hand from the left side. It felt weird to do that since I was right handed.

"Nice work, Jessie, you really got the hang of it. What did you think?"

"It was awesome!"

"You do realize that you have a big smile on your face right now?"

I tried not to blush when he said that.

He gestured toward the guys off to his left. "I'm going to fence with those guys. Did you want to fence with anyone?"

"Sure."

Ethan went over to a couple of them standing beside their bags, sipping on their water bottles. They looked at me and nodded. One of them waved me over. It was Neal. I noticed that he wore a green armband, a sign that he was an experienced fencer.

When I joined them, Ethan said, "Jessie, Neal will do a bout with you."

"Oh, thanks, I'll try my best to keep up with you."

He smiled. His face was flushed and sweaty which made his smile seem even brighter.

We picked a piste that was empty. "What have you learned so far?" he asked me.

I moved closer to him so that I could hear over the squawks and squeals of the various alarms all around me.

"Just the basics, en garde, lunge, parry, and riposte."

"That's good. We'll keep this simple. First, we will start on the en garde line just past the center line." He led me over to the second line that was taped on the floor. "This is where we begin our bouts." He marched over to his line, faced me. "We raise our foils to salute our opponent." He proceeded to bring it straight up, pointing skyward not far from his nose then did a quick flick downward.

I copied his motions.

"When I tap my leg, it means to begin," he said.

We put on our masks and I waited, watching his hand. Once he did a tap, he began moving forward. My stomach did a weird, watery flip. I began to feel intimidated, even though he wasn't that much taller than me. He exuded confidence. Lots of it. He was marching toward me like a soldier, determined to nail his target.

He kept striding toward me, hitting my foil occasionally. I realized that it was a scare tactic and a distraction. I started doing the same thing to him. Suddenly, he lunged at me. I managed to do a parry. He quickly parried back, did a circle around my foil, and thrust it into my chest. I felt the sting as it hit me.

He held up his hand. "Halt! Since I got that point, we go back to our starting positions."

"Okay," I said, trying not to let my voice betray me.

I was starting to get shaken up, which was ridiculous since I spent years competing in martial arts tournaments. I became more driven, determined to go after him harder and faster. As soon as he tapped his leg, I started to move down the piste toward him, hitting his foil to tease him.

He calmly parried my attempts while moving backward with ease. Then he switched tactics and suddenly changed directions, moving toward me aggressively. I had to scoot backward, quickly parrying as fast as I could. I tried to do a lunge but misjudged the distance between us and ended up on the floor.

"Oops!" he said, chuckling as he helped me back up. "Don't worry, I've done that too."

Somehow I couldn't fathom seeing him doing that. He was so smooth and flawless with his moves.

We started over again, our foils clanging loudly as we darted at each other while I madly tried to get a point. I focused on his chest, aiming the tip of my foil at his heart, determined to win a round. No matter how hard I tried, he calmly and swiftly flicked aside my strikes and struck me in the chest with the tip of his foil. He was like a duck in a rippling pond, staying afloat regardless of how rough the water was. He smoothly bobbed and weaved with his foil, just like Ethan.

I was beginning to feel exhausted, the fatigue creeping into my legs. I was immensely grateful when Neal stopped the bout. We took off our masks, saluted each other, and shook hands. I was panting hard, gasping for air.

"Whoo! That was quite a workout," I exclaimed.

"It is, isn't it?" he said, giving me a broad smile. His face was even more flushed now, his wet hair plastered to his forehead.

"How long have you been fencing?" I asked him.

"About three years," he replied.

I shook my head in amazement. "Wow, you are good."

He blushed. "Thanks."

"Do you only fence in foil?"

"No. I fence in sabre too, like Ethan."

"Sweet! Do all of you fence with both weapons?" I asked him.

"Not necessarily. We always train in foil first to learn the basics of fencing. It takes time to acquire the proper skills. Once we achieve those goals and feel comfortable with it, then we can switch to sabre," he said, ruffling his hair with his fingers.

"Oh, okay. So how did you get interested in fencing?"

"Through Ethan, actually. We go to the same school. I come here to practice against other fencers."

"Oh, wow! You're one of his first classmates I've met so far."

"Well, it was a pleasure to meet you."

"Thank you," I replied.

We strode over to our gym bags, grabbed our bottles, and gulped down the water. I watched Ethan who was fencing against another blue-armband fencer. They were moving back and forth quickly, their weapons a blur in the air. I couldn't even keep up with their strikes. Their motions were hard and fast, whipping in the air like snakes striking their targets. Several minutes later, they did a salute, shook hands, and unhooked themselves from the wires. Ethan came over to me, his face dripping with sweat. His cheeks were red and his chest was heaving from the exertion.

"So? How did it go with Neal?" he asked, bending over to pick up his water bottle and giving it a squeeze.

I gave him a thumbs up. "I didn't win but he was fun to fence against."

"Yeah, he is fun. I like fencing with him too," he said, nodding. He turned to look at Neal and bellowed at him, "Hey, Neal! Want to fence?"

"Sure!" Neal replied eagerly.

The two of them walked over to the piste and attached

wires to the clips on their silver vests and masks. They stood on the en garde line, faced each other, saluted to each other, then turned to the side where Coach Patrice stood and saluted to him. It looked like Patrice was refereeing this bout. He held out his arms with his palms facing down, reminding me of Ironman when he was trying to fly. "En garde!" he shouted. Then he turned the palm of his hand to face the fencers and bellowed out another command which I couldn't understand. He moved his hands together and shouted at them again.

Ethan lunged at Neal, scooting forward quickly, testing and teasing him with his foil. He attempted to do a thrust then circled his foil under Neal's blade and hit him in the shoulder. A green light promptly appeared on the display and a high-pitched alarm blared.

Patrice held up his hand like a stop sign. "Halt!" He did several gestures with his hands, saying words like "Attack" and "Point." I was having a hard time hearing what he was saying and not familiar with the referee signals. His held up his hand at Ethan. "Point."

They began again, this time Neal darting at Ethan more aggressively. The two of them of raced up and down the piste, doing circular moves and quick flicks with their foils. They were going so fast that I couldn't see who was getting hit first. There were a lot of stops and starts with Coach Patrice saying "No score," and letting them continue on.

It was then that I realized how talented Ethan and Neal were and how slow I obviously was in comparison. I became more intimidated when I figured out how much they held back while fencing with me. A shiver of fear ran through me as I watched them, seeing how strong and powerful they were.

I wondered if I would ever reach their level of skill and talent. They possessed incredible finesse, and it was a finely tuned ballet with their hands.

Coach Patrice ended the bout and declared Ethan as the winner. Neal and Ethan saluted to their coach then to each other, shook hands, unhooked themselves, and sat on the floor beside me, panting.

"Whew!" said Ethan.

"That was awesome! And terrifying at the same time," I said.

"Heh," Neal said. "It's not that scary when you're used to it and right in the middle of it."

"True," added Ethan. "I like the speed. It makes me work harder."

"I couldn't even see your moves, they were so fast!" I exclaimed.

They both grinned at me. "It takes practice," Ethan said.

"Lots and lots of practice," said Neal.

Ethan nodded. "It's like a game of chess. There's moves and countermoves. You're trying to anticipate what your opponent's going to do and try to fake them out."

"Sometimes you have to think several moves ahead, waiting for them to make a mistake," added Neal.

"So that's why you sometimes go slow at first, to test them?"

Ethan nodded again.

"Cool."

Ethan glanced at the clock on the wall. "It's time to go. We've been training for two hours already."

"Two hours? No wonder my legs feel so rubbery," I replied.

He snorted and pulled off his vest, gloves, and jacket. I struggled out of mine since it was sticky with sweat. It was like trying to take off a wet bathing suit. I noticed that I had some pinpoint bruises on my arms from being hit with the tip of the foil.

"What did you think of this class?" Ethan asked.

"Very cool. Although I have to admit that I feel like a human pin cushion."

"Ha!"

I shook hands with the some of the fencers before we left.

"I didn't know that Neal went to the same school as you."

"He's a good guy. Works hard too," Ethan said.

He grabbed my hand and pulled me into a hug. We were both still hot and sweaty from fencing. I blissfully sank into his warm chest.

Chapter 6

I staggered into my room, feeling exhausted and dizzy with sleep. My world went silent as soon as I took off my hearing aids and placed them into a small plastic box on the dresser beside my bed. I took a shower, pulled on my blue pajamas covered with glittering gold stars, and walked back to bed. Parker and Serena were curled up beside each other like furry caterpillars on top of the covers. I glanced at the lights in the shape of stars that hung above the window beside my bed. They gave off a soft, warm glow. They were a gift from Ethan, who knew how much I loved stars and that they represented hope. He had surprised me one day by decorating my room with these lights.

I snuggled under the covers, trying not to disturb the cats. Parker raised his head, blinking his eyes at me. I reached over and stroked his furry forehead. "Sorry, munchkin. I didn't mean to wake you."

He squeezed his eyes shut and gave me a smile, twitching his whiskers. Serena covered her face with her paws, snuggling closer to Parker.

I loved seeing the two of them together like that and wondered what would've happened if we hadn't rescued them. Both of them had been abandoned and left for dead. I shuddered, thinking how easily their fates could've changed.

Pulling the sheet over my shoulders, I looked at the glowing stars in the window. They began to fade, as if a misty cloud shrouded my vision, growing darker.

I could still hear what the girl in the dojo said to me, like an echo in my mind. It rattled me to the core to think that anyone could be so cold-hearted like that. My chest felt hollow and I shivered. It kept bouncing around in my mind, getting louder and louder. Then out of the corner of my eye, something began to glow, twinkling and shimmering.

Tiny, golden stars swirled in front of me, forming into the shape of a man. He was a handsome figure with a muscular body and chiseled features. Strapped across his back was a shield and a sword. His skin shimmered and glittered in gold as he moved. This was Parker in the form of my spirit guide.

He spoke in deep tones. I didn't hear him but felt him in my head as if he was speaking inside it. "Something troubles you. Your mind remains turbulent."

"I know. I'm trying to understand why some people hate me so much. Am I a selfish person for thinking like that?"

He inclined his head, giving me a slight bow, his skin shifting like golden sand. "You are most certainly not selfish. There will always be someone who cannot grasp the beauty of imperfection."

"What do you mean?"

His eyes crinkled at the corners as he smiled. He seemed to glow even brighter. I could swear that I felt him infusing me with his warmth, like I was being surrounded by immense joy. "It is a truly special honor for souls that contain a glowing heart such as yours. For those that cannot see it, they need to learn how to open their hearts to appreciate your gifts."

"Gifts? What gifts?"

He was being cryptic again, which was what he was good at, giving me a puzzle to solve.

"You are filled with kindness and empathy. You embraced us when no one else would," he said, referring to Serena and himself.

"It was an easy choice to make. I couldn't just leave you out there on your own."

He nodded, his body shimmering and sparkling in gold as he moved. "You are making on impact on everyone's lives, no matter how small it may seem."

"But what can I do to show them I'm a normal person? That I'm not that different from them?"

"Everyone is on a journey of discovery. They must follow their own path and find the truth about themselves. It's up to them to find forgiveness and kindness."

"Am I supposed to help them?"

"You already are, Jessie, by being yourself."

"I am?"

"Yes, my dear. The answer you seek will come in its own time."

He flickered for a moment which was unusual. That'd never happened before.

"You just flickered, Parker. Are you okay?"

He nodded, his face glittering. "Do not worry about me."

His voice began to fade. The golden, glittering orbs swirled and danced merrily around him, falling down like millions of tiny stars. I blinked open my eyes and saw Parker's fur glowing for a moment before I fell asleep again. I smiled, knowing that he kept me safe and stood by my side as my guardian.

Chapter 7

WONDer

I slipped on the soft pink dress, smoothing down the sides with my hands, and looked in the mirror. It felt so strange on me. It made me feel almost naked. I did a little twirl, feeling like a princess. Then I glanced down, wriggling my toes. They needed a touch of color. I headed over to the bathroom, rummaged through the cupboard, and found pink nail polish.

"Perfect." I sat down on the chair beside the desk in my bedroom and applied the first layer of nail polish. While I waited for it to dry, I opened the jewelry box and pulled out a pair of twinkling earrings and a glass necklace in the shape of a star. Tiny silver stars cascaded down a chain from the earring post, a gift from my mom on my sixteenth birthday. It was a potent reminder that she was there for me when no one else had shown up for my party that day. She had written me a note that said, "To reach the stars, all you need to do is believe."

Since then, I'd associated stars as a sign of hope. The glass pendant was a gift from Ethan. It shimmered with shades of pink and gold. I put them on and blew out a nervous sigh. I went to the bathroom and added a rosy pink blush to my cheeks. I applied pink lipstick, a swipe of black mascara, and shimmering gold eye shadow, a perfect complement to Ethan's necklace. I clipped my curly blond hair at the back, creating a fountain of cascading curls around my head.

Once the transformation was complete, I looked in the mirror again and realized how different I looked. It was a time of change, moving forward in my life. I suddenly felt a pang of sadness, not wanting to let go or grow up so quickly.

While I stood in the mirror, Serena came over and sat down at my feet. She looked up at me and meowed, reaching out with her paw, patting my dress. It dawned on me that the life I knew and grew up in was almost over. I felt scared, wondering how I was going to manage being on my own in college.

What if everyone hates me at school? I thought. *What if the teachers refuse to wear the FM system or don't want me in their class?*

My hands gripped the back of the chair as I tried not to panic with all of these thoughts swirling around in my head.

Then I heard Mom's voice bellowing from the bottom of the steps, "Jessie! Ethan's here."

I quickly snatched up my silver sandals, slipped them on, and gave Serena a pat on the head and kiss. It was then that I realized I shouldn't have done that. Her fur stuck to freshly applied lipstick. I was pulling stray hairs off my lips when I started walking down the stairs. I looked down and saw Mom and Dad standing side by side. Mom was holding onto a camera. My steps slowed and faltered when I saw Ethan. He took my breath away. He stood in front of the door, dressed in a sharply tailored black tuxedo with a crisp white shirt and pink bow tie. He was absolutely striking with his strong chin, dark blond hair, and hazel eyes. Ethan looked like a model straight of a magazine. There was a feeling of excitement in my chest. I wondered what I did to deserve someone like him.

"Oh, Jessie. You look so beautiful!" gushed Mom. She

raised her camera and pressed the shutter. The flash momentarily blinded me. I blinked several times.

As I got to the bottom step, Ethan reached out and helped me down. He gave me a broad smile that enhanced the dimples in his cheeks.

"I agree with your mom, you look stunning," he said, pulling my hand up to his lips and giving it a gentle kiss.

I suddenly felt very shy. "Thanks. So do you. I love your pink bow tie. We match!"

"And to complete the ensemble, I also have this," he said holding out a plastic box.

Inside was a wrist corsage adorned with a pink orchid. It was beautiful.

"Oh, wow," I said.

"Do you want me to put it on for you?" he asked.

I nodded. Mom took some more pictures of us while he did this. We posed for her as she took more shots. Ethan led me outside where a black limo waited in the driveway. I waved at Mom and Dad. Ethan and I headed over to the limo, did a few more poses for Mom then ducked into the car. It was my first time inside one. It was ridiculously spacious with a large bench at either end and enough room to stretch out and lie down on the floor. There were crystal glasses and a bottle of what looked like wine in the side pocket. There were flickering faux candles sitting in the side pockets, adding a warm glow around us.

I felt my breath catch in my chest. Sitting in here with Ethan made me feel loved. I gulped, trying not to cry. It was overwhelming.

I looked at Ethan who gave me a warm smile. He reached out and stroked my cheek with his thumb, his palm against my face. The heat of his hand very nice, soothing. It had a calming effect on me.

"So, what do you think?"

"You did this for me?" I asked.

"Of course," he replied.

I put my hand on my chest, holding on to the star pendant. "I'm speechless."

"Good. You deserve it," he said and leaned in, giving me a sensual kiss on my lips. He gently brushed some of my hair away from my eyes. His hand slid down my arm, lacing his fingers with mine. That's when I noticed that there was music playing. I listened to it and realized who was singing it. It was Michael Bublé singing "Sway."

I gasped. "No! That's our song!"

His smile broadened and he laughed softly. "I was hoping you would notice that."

That was the first song we danced to. He had signed it for me at the dojo. It was that moment that I knew that I was falling for him.

He let go of my hand and began to sign the words of the song, just like he did back then. I held my hand over my mouth, feeling overjoyed. This was a truly special moment for me. After he was finished, I held onto his arm and leaned into him, watching the city lights go by in the window.

The limo slowed down as it made its way through the waterfront, headed toward the pier. There were lights strung over the gangway leading to the cruise boat. We got out and walked over to the boardwalk. It was a warm evening with a gentle breeze in the air. I could smell hints of oily tar and fish nearby. There was a steady stream of sharply dressed couples in front of us. We held hands as we followed them on to the boat. I noticed several people staring at us, whispering to each other. Anxiety began to creep in when I saw that. I tried to ignore it and just focused on us. The music on the boat was loud. I could feel the bass thump in my body as we walked in. Hundreds of bright lights hung across the deck along the balcony.

While it wasn't overly crowded yet, there were still a lot of us, mostly seniors, and I recognized many of them. The majority of them were in my classes but we rarely spoke or interacted with each other. It was usually just a quick hello or reluctantly agreeing to work together for assignments.

I spotted Amanda who *was* a good friend and waved at her. "Amanda!"

"Hi, Jessie!" She came over to us, dragging someone I didn't recognize. He was dressed just as handsomely as Ethan.

"It's so good to see you!" I said as she came to a stop.

Her dress was a shade of peach, she wore high heels, and her long brown hair was done up in a slick bun at the back. She had on glittering crystal earrings that sparkled in the light. She looked very different, so grown up like this. I felt self-conscious about my earrings. They seemed dull compared to hers.

"Wow, you look amazing," she said.

"Thank you. So do you," I said. "You are so lucky that you can wear heels. And who's this?" I inquired, looking at her date.

"Oh! That's right, you guys haven't met. This is my boyfriend, James. He's here while on break from university."

I blinked several times, stunned by this fact. I didn't even know that she had a boyfriend or was dating someone older than her.

"Nice to meet you!" I said. Ethan and I reached out to shake hands with him.

"Ethan, right?" Amanda said. "We met in gym a few years ago when you and your dad taught self-defense at our school."

He nodded. "It's lovely to meet both of you tonight. And may I say that you guys make a great couple."

"Aw, thanks. That's kind of you," Amanda replied.

"Why don't James and I get some drinks for you?" Ethan said, looking at me.

"Sure," I said.

The two of them went inside the brightly lit cabin where it was full of guests. I could imagine how loud it would be in there. Amanda's smile was infectious. I hadn't seen her be this happy before.

"I didn't know you had a boyfriend," I said.

"We were keeping it quiet and, since we were both busy with school, we decided not to make a big deal out of it," she replied.

"You must feel relieved to finally be together, especially tonight."

She smiled even more. "Yes! That's so true."

"By the way, I love your earrings," I said. Whenever she turned her head, the crystals sparkled in the light like ice.

"Thanks, they were a gift from James," she said, reaching up to touch them. "I love your pink dress, it matches your hearing aids!"

"Oh thank you. It feels weird to wear it, though. I'm not used to being so formal."

"I know the feeling."

"You know what's funny?" I asked her.

"What?"

"How different we all look tonight," I replied.

"You mean so grown up?" she said.

"Yes! That's exactly what I was thinking."

Ethan and James came back carrying several tall, lean glasses filled with sparkling wine. As Ethan gave one to me, I noticed that it had a pink tint to it.

Curious, I asked Ethan, "What's this?"

"Pink champagne," he said.

"Oh wow, really?"

"Why not? The drinking age here is eighteen, which is pretty much everyone on this boat," he replied.

"That's true. Shall we make a toast?" I said.

We raised our glasses and I said "May our hearts remain strong and beautiful."

"Hear, hear!" Ethan said.

"Cheers!" said Amanda.

We merrily clinked our glasses and I took a tentative sip. The fizzy bubbles tickled my nose. It wasn't overly sweet and it tasted faintly like peach. I sipped it slowly, looking around the boat, admiring the view.

It was then that I noticed that several people were staring at me. I frowned, wondering what was going on.

Ethan saw my expression and laid his hand across my back. "What's wrong?"

"I'm just wondering why they're looking at me like that," I replied.

"It's because you're beautiful," he said.

"I agree," Amanda added.

"No, it's something else. I'm getting a funny feeling about this."

"Hey, why don't we go around introducing ourselves, get to know some of them?" James said.

"Yeah, let's do that. I like that idea. Come on." Amanda gestured for us to follow her.

We strolled over to the front of the ship, weaving past many elegantly dressed classmates. They were laughing and chatting merrily. Some of them stared slack jawed at me and Ethan. They elbowed their dates as we went past them. I began to wonder if I made a mistake coming here.

We stopped when we spotted some of the couples that we knew, exchanging hearty handshakes and exclaiming how nice they looked. By the time we got partway around, the music became louder. I looked up and belatedly realized that there were large speakers right above my head. The music was so loud that it sounded distorted, and I couldn't hear the lyrics, just the thumping bass against my body.

I turned around and saw a group of people crowded around each other, raising their glasses in the air and singing along to the music. I noticed Sandy, who was not only the most popular senior at school, she was also stinking rich. She was not afraid to flaunt it and relished the attention she received. We had never gotten along, and she often went out of her way to be deliberately mean to me. I never understood why she was so cruel, I'd surmised that I was an easy target to her. Whenever she was around me, I'd always felt underdressed and below her class, socially and financially. She had tried to trick me into dating her twin brother as a joke, and when I confronted her about it, she complete-ly denied it. As a result, I viewed her as a sadistic bully who enjoyed inflicting pain on others.

I noticed that Rick was amongst her group. It was a total cliché of prom kings and queens, jocks and bubbly cheer-leaders. I saw her eyes flick toward me. She waltzed up to me, grinning. She wore a sparkling satin dress in a deep shade of red that shimmered as she moved. It looked expen-sive. Her brown hair was done up at the back in a sleek do, and she wore large crystal earrings along with a dazzling necklace that celebrities often wore to the Oscars.

Oh crap, I thought.

"Jessie! I didn't expect to see you here," she said, letting her eyes roam over Ethan slowly.

"Sandy," I replied primly. "I see that you're having a good time."

She giggled. "And who's this?"

"This is my boyfriend, Ethan."

Her face momentarily froze as recognition dawned on her, "Ethan? From karate?"

I nodded.

Ethan reached out with his hand. "Hello."

She grasped his hand and held on to it as she stared at him. Her eyes flicked back and forth between us. "Oh my. You look very handsome tonight," she replied, giggling.

I was getting the impression that she was a bit tipsy, her drink was splashing over the rim.

"Why, thank you. You look lovely yourself," Ethan re-plied charmingly.

She was still holding onto his hand and leaned in close to him. "Isn't this dress amazing? I saw it on the runway and just had to get it for tonight."

Ethan gave her a tight smile. "May I have my hand back please?"

"Oopsie! Sorry about that." She was being syrupy sweet and putting on quite a show for him.

"No problem," he replied.

"You know, Jessie, when you said that you were dating Ethan, I thought that you making him up!" She began to laugh loudly, prompting the rest of her group to join in.

I began to blush, feeling the heat rush through me like a hot flame.

Ethan placed his hand on my shoulder and guided me away from them. I pressed my lips together, feeling the anger envelope me. I spun around and faced Sandy. "You know what? I feel sorry for you. You think that you're popular and have lots of friends. Wait until you need them the most, they won't be there for you. Money won't buy you the happiness that you so desperately crave. That hole in your chest? It's where your heart should be since you obviously don't have one!"

She abruptly stopped laughing, giving me a bewildered gaze. Her group was stunned in silence.

"Come on, let's go this way," Ethan said.

We walked around to the other side where it was quieter and stood by the railing, watching the scenery float by. I took a moment to admire the city lights reflecting in the rippling water as I waited to calm down. My hands were shaking from the anger.

"I'm sorry about that, Jessie. Am I correct to presume that was Sandy?"

"Yes," both Amanda and I said that at the same time.

"She certainly lived up to her reputation for being so mean," he said.

"I must say that you did a great job standing up to her tonight," James said.

"I just had enough of her crap," I replied, letting the cool breeze take the heat off my face. The anger was slowly dissipating.

"I agree, that took a lot of courage, Jessie," Ethan said, grasping my hand and giving it a squeeze.

"No, not really. My temper did most of the work. It took all of my strength not to hit her."

"You know what?" Ethan replied. "Same here. I had to restrain myself from speaking my mind."

"She is such a cold hearted, sociopath who only cares about herself. She's so manipulative and vile. I thought that she would get better by the time we were seniors, except that she actually got much worse. She created this outrageous persona to make herself appear beautiful and successful so that she could look down on others. That false charm is not going to last forever. Someone is going to see right through it, and she will be left all alone."

"That is so true!" replied Amanda.

James nodded. "You're right, Jessie. I've seen that happen at university, the students who were popular in high school became ordinary people. Nobody cared about how much money they had or what they wore."

I felt better hearing that from James. There was a sense of hope in that message.

"You know, Jessie, I wish that I was more like you," said Amanda.

I blinked, surprised by her remark. "Like me? Why?" I asked her.

"You're so brave and fearless. No matter what anyone says to you, you find a way to keep going. You're stronger than me," she replied.

"Gosh, no. I'm just being honest. All I'm trying to do is be more like you guys. In fact, I have to work to keep up with you," I said. "I always feel like I'm looking up to everyone."

She gave me a shy smile. "You taught me what it means to overcome challenges. You're the reason why I decided to become a school counselor for kids with disabilities."

I was stunned. That's the first time she told me that. She was so smart that she could've picked any field that she wanted and she chose this instead. I walked over to her and gave her a hug, trying not to cry.

"Thank you. That means a lot to me. I didn't know that," I said after we stood apart.

She sniffled than laughed. "Don't make me cry! I don't want my mascara to run."

I snorted then laughed. "Oh no! Me too."

Ethan grabbed our glasses and put them on a nearby table. He looked at me, placed his hands on either side of my face. I held onto his arms, feeling comforted by his touch.

"I'm so proud of you, Jessie," he said. We locked eyes and I could see that he meant every word. He leaned in and kissed my lips. His tasted sweet from the champagne.

"Why?" I asked him. "I was just being myself."

"Exactly. You're an inspiration. Not only to me, but to everyone else too," he replied.

I leaned into his chest, wrapping my arms around him. His hand caressed my back as we stood together for a while. Amanda and James leaned against the railing and gazed over the harbor, sipping their drinks.

"Did you want to go inside?" Ethan asked.

"Sure, why not?" I replied.

"Yeah, let's do that," Amanda said.

We emerged into the cabin where the volume of the music rose skyward, along with the noise of the crowd. I had to strain to hear the songs over the overlapping chatter. Some couples were dancing, others were sitting on the sofa along the wall, having animated discussions. There was a steady stream of people heading over to the bar.

"Wow! It's loud in here!" said Amanda.

I nodded, grateful that I could hear her say that. Well, I was kind of cheating and relying more on reading her lips.

"Want to dance?" Ethan asked me.

"Sure."

We went to the middle of the room with the other dancers. He grabbed my hand and pulled me in close, swaying to the beat. I laughed as he swirled me around and back into his arms. I shyly followed his moves, aware that I wasn't a very good dancer. I looked around the room for clues and watched what everyone else was doing.

I closed my eyes, feeling the beat of the thumping bass

in my body. I tried to hear the words to the song and couldn't make out the lyrics. It was much harder for me to understand music ever since I lost the rest of my hearing in my right ear. I had to rely on what was left in my other ear which wasn't very much. Sounds seemed more far away and muffled, especially voices, as if I was holding a pillow against my ear.

I looked at Ethan. "What music is playing?"

He gave me a quizzical glance, "Coldplay. You don't recognize it?"

I shook my head, feeling a pang of sadness for not picking that up. It was one of Ethan's favorite bands. He let go of my hands and began to lip synch and sign some of the words, his fingers dancing in the air like butterflies around each other. At first, I was embarrassed when I saw other people watching us, then I thought, screw it, I want to follow the music too.

It was the song, "Charlie Brown." Ethan's body became more animated as he pretended to sing, playing out the song with his hands, letting the rhythm flow through them. He was showing me the passion of the music and the lyrics. I could see several people watching us, delighted by his moves.

When we took a break and sat down on the couch, Amanda and James joined us. "Dude, that was awesome!" said James.

"What? The sign language?" Ethan asked.

"It was beautiful!" replied Amanda.

"Thank you, but it was for Jessie. She can't hear the words to the lyrics in here, it's too noisy."

"I know! I wish I could understand what you were saying," Amanda said.

"Could you show us some signs?' James asked.

I blinked, surprised by their curiosity and enthusiasm. Ethan and I nodded and proceeded to show them some basic signs. After several minutes, several more people came over to watch us. They too, were eager to learn. Ethan was the hit of the party. As the night wound down and the boat docked, we waved goodbye to everyone. Amanda and James walked alongside with us as we went down the boardwalk.

"It was so nice to finally meet you, Ethan. You guys make such a great couple," Amanda said.

"Thank you. We had a great time with both of you," Ethan replied.

"Well, you were definitely popular tonight," I said.

Once we were back in the limo, Ethan presented to me a long pink box wrapped with curly gold ribbon.

"What's this," I asked him.

"Something that will remind you of our love."

I narrowed my eyes at him suspiciously. He was being cryptic.

"Okay…" I opened the box and laughed. "Did you make this?"

He nodded.

I held it in my hands. It was a long wooden Scrabble holder with the tiles spelling out "I love you." I reached out and touched them. They were glued in place.

It was just like the first time Ethan spelled out those words to me during a Scrabble game. It was one of our memorable and passionate evenings together.

"This is perfect, Ethan! It means a lot to me."

He rested his hand on the back of my neck, his warm fingers caressing the skin. I grabbed the collar of his jacket, pulled him closer, and latched my lips onto his. We slowly exchanged sensual kisses. I could feel the intense heat between us. The feeling was electrifying, and I wanted more. I felt like I was falling into an abyss, the rest of the world fading away. My hands roamed over his chest. I undid his bow tie and pulled it loose. My fingers opened his shirt and I slid my hand onto his warm chest. I could feel his heart beating as fast as mine.

Chapter 8

I leaned my head against the window and watched the landscape blur past me as we drove on the highway. The fields were a vibrant green and lush trees swayed in the breeze. As we approached the city, it turned into thick, congested layers of subdivisions and condos, that rose higher the closer we got to the metropolis. Dad slowed the car down as the traffic became heavier, the roads snarled with many vehicles honking impatiently. Loud wails pierced the air as two large fire trucks sped past us, their red lights flashing.

This is what my life will be like soon, living in the city. I felt a chill, a sense of dread. I had gotten used to living in the quiet country, where it was peaceful, surrounded by a forest and fields of sunflowers and corn. Here, I felt very small and timid, an insignificant speck amongst thousands of people. Everywhere I looked, people were coming and going, a never-ending stream of activity. I wondered how I was going to fit in here. Living on my own and leaving my parents was terrifying. I felt like I was six years old again, going to school for the first time.

Mom and Dad chatted up front, arguing about which street to take. She was holding up a map, trying to give him directions. They decided to spend the day with me to help me search for off-campus housing since I couldn't get a dorm. We didn't want to wait until the last minute for an opening and decided to find a place ahead of time.

Dad drove through a narrow street filled with wall to wall townhouses, tightly packed together with tiny neatly clipped lawns. The houses looked the same, as if they were cut by the same cookie cutter, with a few variations such as the colors. Some had small porches, extra windows, or a balcony. He pulled into the driveway of a cheerful yellow house with white trim. There was a scattering of children's toys and a plastic slide under a maple tree on the miniscule lawn. We got out, stretched, went to the front door, and pressed the doorbell. Mom fussed with her hair while we waited and plastered on a big smile. I stood beside her, trying not to look terrified.

The door opened to reveal a large woman holding a baby on her hip. She wore black yoga pants and a pink T-shirt, which the baby was pulling off to the side that revealed her bra.

"Hello, dear, you must be Mrs. McIntyre," she said cheerfully.

"Yes! This is my daughter Jessie who is looking for a place to stay for school."

"Well, come on in!" she said, opening the door even farther to let us in.

"She's adorable, how old is she?" Mom inquired about the baby.

"This is Anna, she's almost a year old," the woman gushed eagerly.

Something twigged at the back of my mind. Curious, I asked her, "Is she, by any chance, named after Anna from Frozen?" I asked her.

"Why yes! You're a smart cookie to figure that out," she replied, giggling.

It wasn't all that hard to figure out since the house was covered in virtually every Frozen themed toy, book, poster, and various stuffed items strewn on the floor. Even the couch had a throw on it that featured a scene from the movie.

"I liked Sven, he was cute," I added.

She smiled more broadly and gestured down the stairs off to the left. "The apartment is this way."

Our feet creaked on the stairs as we followed her down the narrow hall.

"Here we go," she said, flicking on the light.

It didn't really help that much. I had to squint to see in the dim basement. There were two small, narrow rectangular windows above my head along the back, a couch against one wall, and a small coffee table sat in front. A small bed was at the far end and sliding doors on my right. It was a sparse room. There was nothing on the walls. A single overhead light was the only source of illumination. There were no additional lamps. Dad was walking around, giving everything a cursory look.

"Where's the bathroom?" I asked.

"Oh! It's over here." She gestured behind the closet doors.

There was a small hallway that led to a tiny bathroom, with just enough room for a toilet and shower. It was dark, even with the light turned on. Ironically, it reminded me of summer camp, with barely enough room to turn around in. I vividly remembered how I kept banging my head on the wall whenever I tried to bend down and pick up a bar of soap. I shuddered.

"No TV?" I asked.

"Sorry, dear. Just the one upstairs," she replied.

I nodded. "Okay."

"Want to see the kitchen?" she asked.

"Sure," I said politely.

We lumbered back up the narrow stairs, the floor creaking ominously beneath our feet. It was a typical kitchen with a small metal table in the kitchen, white cupboards and the fridge was covered in family photos and those colorful magnetic, plastic letters. There were several finger paints featuring tiny handprints which I surmised were from Anna.

Mom asked her some more questions about the house then they turned to face me. "Would you be okay with a baby in the house?" the woman asked. "Would her crying keep you up at night?"

I shook my head. "No. I'm deaf when I take out my hearing aids at night. I can't hear anything."

"How wonderful! It must be very nice to be able to shut out the noise like that," she gushed.

I shrugged my shoulders. "I guess. I never thought about it."

"Can you hear thunderstorms?" she asked.

"No, but I can feel the rumbles and see the lightning when it flashes."

"You know—you would be the perfect house guest since we wouldn't have to worry about noises!" she said cheerfully.

I nodded. "Uh-huh."

"We'll let you know what we decide," Mom said.

"Great! I hope to hear from you soon!"

She waved at us as we headed back into the car and pulled out. Mom turned around and asked, "Well? What do you think?"

"It seemed a bit dark, especially if I'm doing a lot of artwork."

Mom pursed her lips then nodded. "That's what I thought too. Nice lady, though."

"She seemed sweet," Dad added.

"And a big fan of Frozen apparently," I remarked.

He snorted and Mom smiled.

"She must really like kids," I mused.

Ten minutes later, we arrived at another townhouse, this one was on the outskirts of the city. It didn't look new like the others, although there were more trees and a spacious yard. It appeared more weatherworn and outdated. We got out and stepped onto the wooden porch. I noticed that the stain was faded and peeling. The door opened and we were greeted to an older lady with gray hair. She wore a knitted shawl across her thin shoulders. She had on a light blue blouse, and she wore black slacks. Her hair was done up in a tight bun, and her glasses were attached to a chain that hung around her neck, giving her the impression of a strict librarian. On her feet were black clogs.

"Why hello!" she said when she saw us. She gave us a gap-toothed smile.

Mom reached out and shook her hand, introduced us.

"Please come on in." She ushered us into her living room.

The walls were painted a dark shade of red and the floor was a decorated with an oval rug of the same color. It reminded me of red wine. The wooden furniture looked old, as if passed down from several generations. The walls held many framed photographs, going back several generations. There were knitted doilies scattered on various surfaces of the furniture.

The air in the room seemed musty and stale. I could hear dogs barking in the background.

"The apartment is downstairs, this way please," she said with an accent and I wondered where she was from originally.

We followed her down the carpeted stairs into a spacious room. It was painted a dark shade of green that appeared black in the dim light. It made it seem smaller and more claustrophobic. There were two couches and a coffee table in the middle. I noticed they had a bit of a shine to them. Curious, I walked over to them and touched the surface. They were shrouded in a thick plastic wrap. I had never seen anything like this before. It crinkled beneath my fingers.

"Do you take these off?" I asked her.

"No. It's to keep them clean. Please, have a seat," she replied, gesturing at them.

Alarms bells went off in my head. *Either she's an obses-*

sive neat freak or this is meant to keep the stains off it. Like blood. Lots of it.

We all gingerly sat on the couch. It crinkled loudly beneath my legs and felt uncomfortable and sticky. My butt squeaked whenever I shifted, and I grimaced.

"Would you like to see the bedroom?" she asked.

I eagerly got up and followed her to a small room. There was a twin sized bed and a white dresser that looked like it had been used by kids since it was still covered with stickers. I'd wondered if her grandchildren used this room. At least there were larger windows in this room that faced the backyard. She led me over to the bathroom, which was larger than the previous house, although it was still fairly small with a little white sink, toilet, and shower cubicle.

I noticed that the barking seemed louder here and I asked, "Do you have dogs?"

"Why, yes! I have two lovely German Shepherds. Do you like dogs?"

"Um—I'm more of a cat person," I replied.

I was terrified of dogs, ever since I was bitten by one when I was a little girl. Ironically, it was a German Shepherd. I saw the look on Mom's face and already knew that she was worried about the dogs.

We quickly went through the rest of the house and said our goodbyes.

Once we got in the car, I said, "Whew! I'm definitely not staying in that one."

"Because of the dogs?" asked Dad.

"Yeah, that and the weird furniture." I shivered thinking about it.

"I wonder why the couch was covered in plastic," Dad said.

"I don't know, vampires or zombies?" I replied cheekily.

"I think you're watching too much of *Supernatural*, Jessie."

"What? I like that show!"

"It seems ridiculous to have so many dark shows with

kids your age hanging out with hunters chasing supernatural creatures like Vampires."

"No, it's not. I love watching *The Vampire Diaries*, it's cool."

"Well, I think it's gruesome with all of those bloody scenes." Mom shuddered.

I sighed and rolled my eyes.

The next house on the list was in the other direction, closer to the industrial section. We went past more subdivisions and cookie cutter townhouses onto a road that had more warehouses and storage units. Dad drove the car onto a gravel driveway of a white two-story house with an attached garage. It looked old and worn, the paint peeling off in several places.

Mom looked at the print out of the description of the house then back at the property. She had a puzzled look on her face.

"Strange. This ad says they have a bungalow style apartment but I don't see it," Mom said.

"Odd," said Dad, peering out the window. "Well, let's go find out."

Dad introduced us when a man about the same age as him opened the door. He had thin blond hair that was receding. He wore a red and black lumberjack shirt, with a T-shirt underneath, torn jeans, and construction boots. I wondered if he was a carpenter or worked in construction. We shook hands with him.

"The apartment is separate from the house," he explained while we walked over to the garage. "It used to be a garage that we converted into a studio apartment."

"Okay," Dad said. "Great."

The man opened the door and ushered us in. It was a wide-open space with no walls in the middle. There were large windows along the sides and at the back. A small kitchen was situated at the back on the right. Mom started looking into the cupboards and the fridge. On our right side was a small worn out sofa and a wooden coffee table. There was a flat screen TV sitting on a dresser against the wall. A washer and dryer sat at the far left of the room.

"Where's the washroom?" I asked.

"Ah, it's over here," he said, gesturing at the back of the wall.

There was a glass partition and behind it was a shower. I could see the copper pipes running along the wall. The toilet was tucked off to the side behind a smaller partition. There were a couple of pots with ferns hanging overhead, creating a virtual jungle.

"When you want to take a shower, you can simply pull the curtain closed," he said.

"There's no door?" I asked him.

"No, it's an open concept," he replied.

"It's very much like a bachelor pad," Dad remarked.

"Yes, that's right."

"Did you do all of the work here?" Dad asked him.

He nodded. "Yes, I did."

"All right, well, thank you very much for showing us this apartment," Dad said and shook his hand. "We'll let you know if we decide to rent it."

"No problem."

"Wow, that was ridiculous," Mom said as we stepped into the car and headed back on the road.

"I don't even think that shower was legally safe with all of those pipes being exposed like that," Dad said.

"What did you think, Jessie," asked Dad.

I shook my head. "I didn't like it very much. It didn't feel safe."

"I agree, there was something off about that guy," he said.

I was beginning to think we were never going to find a place to rent. The more houses we looked at, the more anxious I became.

"Mom?" I asked. "Did you guys go through this with my brother?"

My older brother, Ken, was a teaching assistant up north at university in Outdoor Recreation.

"No, actually, he got a dorm," she said.

"Wow, he's lucky."

"That's what he thought at first then he quickly realized how hard it was to do his homework with people yelling in the hallways, pulling the fire alarm, and constantly interrupting him. He said it was an absolute zoo, and he found it hard to focus sometimes," Mom said.

"So, in a way, I'm better off renting an apartment?"

She nodded. "At least, you'll have more privacy and your own room."

"When we find one," Dad added.

We went to several more houses, and I began to feel like a trick or treater at Halloween, from ringing so many doorbells. After a long day of searching, I was growing super tired and at the point of giving up, when we pulled up to the last one on the list. It was a duplex, half of a townhouse. It looked weird with one side painted in gray, and the other side in navy blue.

We were let in by a young woman who seemed to be in her late twenties to early thirties. She was short and stocky, her long red hair was tied back into a ponytail. Her face was dotted with freckles.

"Hi! I'm Shirley," she said, greeting us at the door.

It was a long and narrow building, the skinniest house I'd ever been in. The stairs were slightly off to the right, on the left was the living room, and down the hallway was a small kitchen. The house smelled fresh and everything was clean. The furniture looked modern.

I had a good feeling about this place. She showed us the bedroom upstairs which was about the same size as mine, maybe a little smaller. The walls and carpet were white, and there was a medium-sized window beside the twin-sized bed. It was a bright and airy room. We went downstairs and walked around the tiny living room. It had a large flat screened TV with a DVD player and stereo system on top of a dresser. There was a white couch, glass dining room table, and metal chairs. I looked out the sliding glass doors and noticed that there was a fenced off backyard with a single tree in the middle. The kitchen was white—no big surprise there—with simple cupboards, sink, fridge and oven.

We said our goodbyes and drove out. "I think that would work!" Mom said. "What do you think, Jessie?"

I nodded. "Yeah, sure. It was fine," I said, feeling like there was no turning back now. I was totally committed to going to college, and that scared the crap out of me. *I'm leaving home,* I thought.

On the way back home, I watched the sunset, the clouds changing from lavender to indigo blue then twilight. I thought about the first house we stopped at today, recalling the lady saying that it must've be nice not hear anything at night. I closed my eyes, trying to remember what it was like before I lost my hearing. Mom said that I was about six years old when I got really sick with meningitis, and it took away my ability to hear sounds. I tried to remember what the world sounded like then. I felt like I was stumbling around in the fog, lost in the faint memory of my childhood. It was cloudy in my mind at first then it became crystal clear as I zeroed in on my younger self beside the Christmas tree. It was a bright red gift with a big bow of curls that tumbled down the sides. I ripped open the package, eager to see what was inside it. I reached in and pulled out a pink teddy bear. Mom reached out and pressed the heart shaped logo on its chest. I gave her a quizzical look then looked back at the bear, wondering what she was doing. She gestured at the bear then to her ear as if she wanted me to listen to it. I pressed the teddy bear to my cheek and listened. There was no sound. I shook my head and held up the bear. It was one of those electronic toys that spoke several phrases. I didn't know what it was saying. Mom clapped her hand over her mouth and started crying. I kept trying to listen to the bear, holding it to my ear, pressing the heart, over and over. Then I gestured to my ear and said it was broken.

I felt like I was punched in the chest when I realized that was when everything changed. I couldn't do the same things I did before. The lights on the trees twinkled then blurred out of focus. I blinked awake, looking out the window at the lights streaking past us.

When we got home, I showered then changed into my pajamas. I sat on the bed and held Serena in my arms, snuggling into her fur and feeling her rumbling purrs. I didn't have my hearing aids on and couldn't hear her purring. I wondered what it really sounded like, how different it would be if I had normal hearing.

Chapter 9

Deja Vu

When I woke up in the morning, there was a line of small toys on the floor, courtesy of the cats. Parker loved the stuffed birds that made chirping sounds and would often carry them around the house. Mom said that she would hear them warble at night everywhere he went. She said that I was lucky that I couldn't hear it. The felted bean-bag mice on the floor were Serena's favorite toys. They must've resembled the weight and shape of a real mouse, since she carted them everywhere. The two of them had gotten into the habit of leaving gifts like these for me to find every day.

I giggled when I saw them, following them as they led out into the hallway and along the stairs. Parker and Serena jumped off the bed and followed down the stairs and into the kitchen. They sat down and watched me make their breakfast, swiveling their heads back and forth, anxious to eat. I placed their plates in front of them. Serena wagged her crooked tail side to side while Parker wriggled his rump eagerly. Even though they had distinctly different personalities, they were equally adorable. Mom and Dad joined us shortly afterward, grabbing a cup of coffee and sitting at the table. Dad opened the newspaper and began reading it.

Since I didn't have my hearing aids on, Mom waved at me to get my attention. She signed to me, her fingers moving like tiny puppets doing a merry dance. '*Do you have karate today?*'

I nodded. "Ethan and I will be teaching the kids class before noon, then after that, we have our own class with Sensei Jonas."

'*Your father and I will be shopping for groceries and doing some errands. We should be back later this afternoon. You can take my car,*' she said.

"Okay."

She signed to me. '*Don't forget to fill it up with gas.*'

I rolled my eyes "I know Mom."

After breakfast, I got changed into blue track pants and a pink hoodie. I put on a little bit of makeup, braided my hair, and put on my pink sneakers. I grabbed my gym bag and headed out the door. I drove through the countryside on the back roads then turned onto the paved city roads, going deeper into the center of the city. Fifteen minutes later, I pulled the car into the parking lot. It wasn't full yet and I spotted an open slot. I parked the car in it and got out. The dojo was part of a long industrial building, located in one of several units. A large portion of the wall was glass, where everyone could see the students training. Along the front, beneath the window, was a line of trophies, some as tall as five feet. I walked over to the door, went in, and strolled past the gym that had a variety of training equipment, including punching bags. Sensei Jonas's office was stationed off to the side, and I waved at him as I headed over to the locker room. I quickly pulled on my white uniform, tied on my black belt, and bowed into the dojo where Ethan was getting ready. I placed my sparring gear along the wall on my left and walked over to Ethan, who gave me a big hug.

"Morning, Jessie," he said.

"Good morning to you too. How did your graduation go at your school?" I asked.

He shrugged his shoulders. "It was okay, nothing spectacular."

"Hmph. Mine was particularly memorable," I said.

"What do you mean?" he asked.

I blushed, feeling the heat burn on my cheeks. "I, um, stepped on the hem of my gown and fell on the steps."

"You did not!"

I nodded.

"You've gotta be pulling my leg," he said.

I crinkled my nose at him and shook my head. "It's true."

"Aw, sorry about that," he said then snorted. "At least no one will forget you."

"Ethan!" I gave him a playful punch on his shoulder.

He watched the students come in to the dojo, checked the time, and had everyone line up at the front. Ethan and I stood side by side, facing the kids.

"Keske!" shouted Ethan.

Everyone stood at attention.

"Rei," he said.

We bowed in unison.

"Today Sensei Jessie be doing the warm up, follow her instructions, okay?"

"Okay, everyone follow me!" I said to them.

I led them through a series of warm up drills and exercises. Once that was done, I had them all stand in a circle while I stood in the middle, holding on to a long pink pool noodle.

"I'm going to sweep this under your feet, you're going to jump over quickly. Are you ready?"

They bobbed their heads up and down, eager to play this game. I swept the pool noodle along the floor, going around the circle of kids who giggled and shrieked as they tried to avoid it.

I went back and forth, changing directions. Then Ethan came over, wearing a mischievous grin.

"Okay, now it's my turn!" he said, merrily cackling.

"I'm going to sweep this over your heads, you'll need to duck."

He took my place in the middle and eagerly swung the pool noodle like a baseball bat over their heads. They screamed with delight as they ducked and weaved while he changed directions unexpectedly. Then he had them switch to doing high blocks as he tried to whack them over their heads. After that drill, we split them up and worked on their katas, getting some of them ready for upcoming belt tests. Once we were finished, we had them line up and bowed them out.

Sensei Jonas came onto the floor and took over the next class, which was for the higher belts. This time, Ethan and I stood in line with the rest of the group, since we were students in this class. Most of them were about the same age as us, plus a few older adults. Sensei Jonas had us go through our warm ups and more demanding drills that left us panting with exertion. Then we worked on our katas as a group with him, our moves flowing in sync, a symphony of white as we followed his motions, snapping out our punches and kicks. At the end, we all did a loud kiai that reverberated throughout the dojo.

"Everyone, go put on your sparring gear," he said.

I went over to my bag and pulled out my equipment. I strapped on my shin pads, padded footwear, gloves, mouthguard, and put on my helmet. When I was ready, I stood up and waited for everyone else.

"Okay, we're going to rotate sparring partners as part of your endurance training to strengthen your aerobic skills."

I've been through this before. It meant that it would be a very exhausting match. My first partner was a slim teenager with long brown hair. I had sparred with her before. She was one of the most timid fighters here and seemed shy.

"Hi, Jessie," she said, giving me a big smile.

"Hey, Hannah. It's been awhile since we sparred, eh?"

She nodded. "I like sparring with you. You're more easy going than the other guys."

With her, I had to hold back since she wasn't as aggressive as them. "Cool. Are you ready?"

She nodded and tapped her glove against mine.

"Okay everyone, bow to your partner and go into your fighting stance."

Sensei Jonas blew the whistle and everyone immediately went into action. I darted toward Hannah, throwing a punch at her, testing her reflexes. She slapped it away and tried to do a back fist at my head. I leapt out of the way and delivered a quick kick, then stepped to the side, not giving her a chance to hit me. She was getting better with her timing and showing more confidence. I was having fun with this match, enjoying our casual pace. I did a punch to her ribs, faked her out, then brought it up to her head. We bounced around, exchanging kicks, slapping them away, and following up with more punches.

There was a sharp blast of the whistle, halting our match.

"Bow to your partners and switch places," said Sensei Jonas, watching us move around.

In front of me was Mike, a short muscular guy with blond hair who worked in the military. He was a serious competitor and had many patches on his sleeves that displayed his achievements. He was on the demonstration team, highly skilled with the Bo staff and Nanchuku, and was also a black belt. I didn't see him very often since he came on different nights because of his schedule. I reached out and did a fist bump with his glove.

"Hey, Mike," I said.

He inclined his head. "Jessie"

We bowed and went into our positions, holding up our hands near our faces. Sensei Jonas blew the whistle. Mike began prowling around me, staring at me fiercely. I gulped, suddenly feeling very intimidated. I wondered what he was like in the military. I could easily see him holding a gun and not afraid to use it. He lunged at me with a quick punch to my head. He was fast! I nearly got hit in the face and managed to leap out of the way at the last second. I amped up my speed and strength. He swiveled his hips and attempted to kick me in the ribs then raised it upward to my head. I quickly blocked it with my arm then followed up with a sharp front kick to his midsection. I pulled it back and immediately switched to a round house kick to his head. He deftly skipped out of the way. He didn't look like he was working hard, and he seemed to be in his element, obviously comfortable with fighting. I noticed that his kicks were slower than his punches. I watched him raise his right leg and swiveled his hips to do a roundhouse kick toward my ribs. I took that opportunity to dart in close to him and delivered two punches to his stomach.

There was a sharp whistle in the air. "Halt! Bow to your partner."

"Thanks," I said to Mike and bowed to him.

He clearly wasn't much of a talker. Not with me, anyways.

We went several more rounds with various partners. The next person standing in front of me was Ethan. I was beginning to feel weary from doing so many fights. My body felt drained, and I hoped that I had enough energy to keep going.

"Ha! Now it's my turn," he said, grinning. He seemed pumped, as if he wasn't as tired as I was.

I narrowed my eyes at him and tried not to say anything snarky. I touched his gloves and bowed, clenching my fist. I drew in a long and deep breath, gathering what was left of my dwindling strength. At the blast of the whistle, we both darted at each other, delivering a flurry of punches and kicks. I could feel the sweat pouring down the side of my face and back of my neck. He was moving fast and hard. I threw a series of kicks then jumped away. He did the same. It was like fighting a mirror. My strikes weren't getting through. He did a round house kick to the side of my head, and I raised my arm to block it.

The force of his kick was enough to slam my arm into the side of my face. I stumbled a little, caught off guard by his strength, then regained my composure. He kept going, faster and harder with his hits. Then he attempted to kick in the midsection but rapidly changed directions and aimed it at the side of my head.

I raised my hand to block it, but it was too late. His foot collided with my helmet, and I felt the impact. I could swear I heard a loud clang, like a bell going off. The room suddenly spun around. I momentarily staggered. The figure of Ethan swayed in front of me. I dimly heard him calling out my name. The room began to fade from my vision. I fell heavily to knees and everything went black.

When I opened my eyes, I saw Ethan cradling me while Sensei Jonas knelt on the floor beside me.

"Jessie. Jessie? Can you hear me?"

I blinked, wondering for a moment what just happened.

"Um, yeah. What's going on?"

"You passed out," said Sensei Jonas.

"I did?"

"You need to go to the hospital," he said.

"Why?" I asked him.

"This is serious. You've had a concussion before. We can't take any chances this time," he replied.

I looked at Ethan whose face was white. He was staring at me in shock. I reached up and touched his cheek. Tears welled up in his eyes.

"I'm so sorry, Jessie. I didn't mean to hit you that hard."

I struggled to get up. I didn't feel comfortable laying on the floor with everyone standing over me. Ethan held on to my hand and helped me stand up. I moved slowly. The room felt like it was tilting.

"I don't want to see any more doctors. I'm so sick and tired of them," I said.

"I'm taking you to the hospital, Jessie, it's not an option," said Sensei Jonas.

I sighed, feeling defeated. Ethan helped me take off my sparring equipment and put them into my bag. I leaned into his chest, feeling absolutely exhausted. He wrapped his arms around me. His hand moved in slow circles on my back.

It was a blur of activity going from the dojo, to the car, and into the hospital. Ethan held on to my hand, the warmth of his touch comforting me. I was sitting on the gurney in the ER, letting the nurse take my blood pressure when a tall, lanky man wearing green scrubs and running shoes walked in. He wore glasses and his short hair was raked back like tiny mountains. He had ropy arms, which was a sign that he was physically fit. A blue stethoscope hung around his neck.

Both Ethan and his father stood on either side on the bed with me. It was an eerie sense of deja vu. I had been through this before.

The doctor flipped through the chart he held in his hand then looked up at me. "Jessie?"

"Yes."

"I'm Doctor Hadfield," he said and reached out to shake my hand. "I see that you've had a similar injury previously?" he remarked while flipping through the sheets on the clipboard.

Sensei Jonas nodded. "Yes, she had sustained a concussion at a karate tournament two years ago."

"Ah, I see. Are you her father?" he asked.

"No, I'm her instructor, Jonas, and this is my son, Ethan. She was sparring and took a hit to the side of her head. After last time, I thought it would be prudent to bring her in."

"You did the right thing, Jonas, it's better to be safe than sorry," the doctor replied. "What happened last time? Did you pass out?" he asked me.

"I lost my memory that day, most of it did not come back," I replied, suddenly feeling very scared.

"How about today? Did you lose any memory?"

"No. I just passed out," I said.

"Does it feel different this time?" he asked.

"Yes."

"Do feel anything unusual? Any tingling?"

"I could've sworn I heard a loud bell."

"Okay. Any ringing in the ears?" he asked, running his fingers along my neck.

"No."

"Any pain where I'm pressing?"

"No."

"Tell me more about the hit," he said.

"I felt the impact of the hit, stumbled, then everything went black."

He narrowed his eyes at me. "You stumbled? Did you fall?" he asked as his fingers pressed against my cheek and jaw.

"The room seemed to sway, and I went down on my knees," I replied.

"Okay, let's focus on that. Is there any pain or tenderness anywhere?"

"Just on the side of my face."

"Anything else?"

"I just feel very tired, like I want to fall asleep right now," I replied.

"Follow my finger without moving your head," he said as he held up his finger.

He moved it from the tip of my nose then farther, then side to side. The room suddenly tilted and I began to feel nauseated.

"That's making me feel sick."

"Have you had any balance issues before?" he asked.

"Not that I know of. The only thing different is that I went deaf in my right ear last year. Can that affect it?"

"Possibly, although that's not always the case. I'm going to order a CT scan to make sure there is nothing else going on."

"Again? I already had one last time," I replied.

"That's actually a good thing since I can do a baseline comparison," he said then left the room.

I sighed, not really wanting to go through this again.

"I'm going to call your parents, Jessie, and let them

know what's going okay?" Jonas said and walked out to the lobby.

I leaned back into the pillow and looked at Ethan. He softly stroked my forehead with his hand then slid it down to the side, letting his thumb brush my cheek.

"This is ridiculous," I said. "I don't want to be here."

His brows creased together. "I think Dad was right to bring you here."

I sighed, feeling irritated and tired of being poked and prodded by doctors.

"I'm sorry, Jessie, this is my fault," he said.

Before I could respond, the technician came in, helped me into the wheelchair, and took me to the CT room. Since I'd been through this before, I knew what to expect, and this seemed to go much quicker than usual. By the time I got back, Mom was waiting for me.

"Oh my, Jessie." Mom's voice trembled as she spoke.

"I know, bad luck seems to follow me everywhere."

Doctor Hadfield came in a while later.

"Ah, you must be Jessie's mother," he remarked upon seeing her and gave her a handshake.

"Yes. Did the result come in?" she asked.

"I'm afraid it looks like she has had another concussion," he replied in a somber voice.

I suddenly felt cold.

"Jessie, after looking at your chart, the latest CT scan, and your previous head injury, I'm concerned about potential brain damage. I'm going to have to tell you that you need to stop participating in contact sports."

"Why?"

"You've already lost some memory from the previous concussion, and since you passed out today and are having balance issues along with nausea, the risk is much too high. You could end up with motor issues later on. One concussion was bad enough, to have two concussions is quite disturbing."

My voice began to crack and tears welled up in my eyes. "Does that mean I can't spar anymore?"

"I'm sorry but that means no more sparring. You can't afford to take any more hits to the head," he said, wearing a serious expression that meant his decision was final.

I was stunned. I looked at Ethan. His features became a watery blur. Hot anger rose through me like fire. "It's your fault that I can't do karate anymore," I said as tears rolled down my cheeks.

He looked bewildered then his face began to crumble as tears fell from his eyes, "I'm so sorry, Jessie."

He leaned in toward me. I held my hands out and pushed him away.

"Get away from me!" I yelled, sobbing.

Stunned, he backed away. "But, Jessie—"

"No! Stay away. Don't you talk to me!"

Ethan's father grabbed him by the shoulders and walked out of the emergency room.

Mom took me home after I was discharged. I stared out the window, numbly watching the lights of the city rush past us in streaks of colors. When we got home, I went upstairs to my room and sat on the bed, holding onto my graduation cap. It should've been an ordinary day, instead everything changed.

The doctor's voice still echoed in my mind. There was a big hole in my chest that felt icy cold. Ethan took away my identity, the part of me that I was growing to accept. My hands shook and fresh tears fell as I sobbed. It felt as if my black belt just vanished, all that hard work and years of training gone. I didn't know what to do. My world had suddenly shifted, and I felt lost.

I curled up on the bed, my body feeling utterly exhausted. I sank my head on to the pillow, gradually, my eyes grew tired and I fell asleep.

Later on, I blinked open my eyes, getting the sense that someone was with me. The room seemed to glow in shades of gold as if doused in late afternoon sunshine.

Parker's spirit form stood beside my bed, his golden skin shimmering. I could hear his voice in my head when he spoke, it was a low, baritone rumble. "Your mind seems scattered and your soul appears broken," he said.

"Why does this crap keep happening to me?" I said.

"It's part of your search for your identity," he replied.

"I just lost my sense of identity, how does that help?"

He kneeled down. His handsome features glistened and shifted like tiny grains of golden sand. His eyes were the same color as Parker the cat. "You must find your true purpose and discover what brings you great joy."

Super. He was being cryptic. Again.

The corner of his lips curled up in a smile. I had forgotten that he could read my mind, which, in hindsight, made perfect sense.

"I thought it was being a black belt and competing in tournaments. All of that hard work is completely gone. Poof! Like smoke."

He shrugged his muscular shoulders. "Maybe it wasn't meant to be. Perhaps you need to search deeper from within."

I stared at him, feeling exasperated. "It's not fair that I face more obstacles than everyone else!"

He inclined his head. "It's always the strong ones who will rise up to the challenge and become stronger in the end."

I narrowed my eyes at him, trying to make sense of his remark. It was like I needed a decoder ring to decipher it.

"I feel like I'm falling to pieces here. I'm so alone and lost."

"Do not worry, whenever you feel lost, always remember that I will be your compass." His image began to fade and flicker. I had a strange feeling about that. He reached out with his hand, his skin shimmered in the golden light that surrounded us. I held onto his hand as he began to dissipate, the glittering facets swirled in the air and bathed me in joyful light like a warm blanket.

Chapter 10

ORDINARY

I jerked awake to discover that I was holding onto Parker's paw as he slept curled up beside me. He stirred, popping his head up and blinking at me. He got up, stretched in a big arch, and walked up to my chest, touching his nose to mine. His whiskers tickled my cheeks. Then he reached out with his paw, touching my face.

"Aw, thanks, Parker for the kisses." I loved it when he did that. It was one of his endearing traits.

Serena was asleep on the couch beneath the window, enjoying the beam of sunshine that shone through it. When I tried to get up, the room suddenly spun around. I waited until it passed and got up. Both cats jumped down and padded after me. We went downstairs to the kitchen where Mom and Dad were having breakfast.

I filled Serena and Parker's dishes with cat food and got a bowl of yogurt topped with Mom's freshly homemade granola for myself. I sat down at the table and began munching on it.

Mom signed to me, her fingers spelling out the words, *'How are you feeling this morning, Jessie?'*

"Okay, I guess." I shrugged my shoulders. "My head feels a bit foggy."

'No dizziness or nausea?' she asked.

"If I move too fast, the room will spin. It's not as bad as last time," I replied.

She frowned then looked at Dad who was watching us.

'Your doctor said that your balance might be affected,' Mom said.

"I know, I can feel it. I'm not as steady as I usually am."

'He also said that you may develop other symptoms,' she said.

"More symptoms? Like what?" I asked her.

'A shorter temper, difficulty making decisions, head-aches, feeling overwhelmed or even depression,' she replied.

I gaped at her. "Seriously? I don't think I can handle any more symptoms."

'I know, it's frustrating. He did say that it may take your body longer to heal this time,' she said, concern etched on her face. *'We're here to help you, Jessie. Please let us know if you are struggling with anything, okay?'*

I nodded. "Okay."

'He also wondered if there was a connection between your previous concussion and you losing the rest of your hearing in your right ear,' she said.

I paused, trying to make sense of that. "What does that have to do with getting kicked in the head?"

'He seemed to think that since you've had so many health problems that it's taking a toll on your body. You may be more susceptible to injuries,' she signed, showing the emotions on her face.

"Health problems? It feels more like bad luck. I don't get it, why does this keep happening to me?"

'Jessie, you've been through so much, more than most people will experience in their lifetime. The fact that you remained strong is truly remarkable,' she said.

"Strong? I don't feel strong. I'm totally lost now that I can't compete anymore. Ethan ruined my life! I worked so hard to get my black belt." My voice cracked.

'Oh, honey, I'm so sorry,' she said, doing a circular motion on her chest with her fist, the sign for sorry.

"Why don't you take a couple of months off from karate to recover and focus on getting ready for college," Dad said, enunciating his words carefully so that I could lip read him.

It seemed very strange to consider that option after being in the dojo every week for the last three years. The dojo felt like my other home, a place where I felt comfortable. It was surreal, like an abrupt ending.

"So, how does it feel to finally graduate from high school?" Dad asked.

When I missed what he said, Mom signed it to me.

"A bit weird actually. I can't believe it's over," I replied, remembering how it felt when I walked through those doors for the last time.

I was officially an adult now, responsible for myself, and that terrified me. It was a similar feeling when I left home to start kindergarten, walking into a new and unfamiliar territory.

"I just find it hugely ironic that when I finished high school, I also lost karate at the same time. It feels like my life is over, that there's this huge void in me. I don't know what to do," I said, sniffling.

I got up and left before I started crying again.

Serena and Parker followed me outside where I went to sit on the porch swing. Parker tried to jump into my lap, and he struggled to reach me. *Odd, that's the first time he's done that*, I thought. I picked him up and held him in my arms while Serena jumped up and joined us, nestling beside me. The warm fur beneath my fingers was a comforting feeling. I could feel his purrs resonate through me. We sat together for a while, enjoying the warm sunshine. The cats eagerly watched the chipmunks and squirrels scamper around the yard, swiveling their heads around to catch the action.

I sighed, trying to ease the tension in my neck and shoulders, replaying what happened yesterday. I began to doubt myself and wondered if I stumbled or lowered my guard. What should have I done differently?

After some time, I went back in the house and got changed out of my pajamas. Standing in the room, I took a long look around and realized that a few months from now, I wouldn't be sleeping here anymore.

A message popped up on my iPod, I picked it up and read the message, it was from Ethan. *Hi, Jessie, are you doing okay?*

I sat down on the bench by the window and thought about what to say. I was angry. I was beyond mad about what he did and devastated that everything changed so quickly. With shaking fingers, I typed back to him: *No, not really.*

What's wrong?

I just about lost it when I saw his response and held on to the iPod tightly so I wouldn't throw it at the wall. After a long moment of thinking, I typed back: *You ruined my life, I can't do karate anymore!*

I'm sorry, he said.

That's it? I'm sorry? I thought.

After a lengthy pause, he added: *Will you forgive me?*

No.

He replied: *Dad wants to come over and talk to your parents, is that okay?*

I said tersely: *Fine.*

Later that afternoon, I saw a car on the driveway. It was Ethan and his father. I was sitting on the bench under the window, reading a book when Ethan walked into the room, carrying a bunch of purple lilacs. The fragrance was overpowering, filling the room with its sweet scent. Ethan wore black jeans and a dark blue denim shirt with the sleeves rolled up to his elbows. He looked tired and I wondered if he didn't get much sleep. Before he came in, I put on my hearing aids so that I could hear him.

"I got these from the backyard," he said as he came over to me and handed them to me.

"Thanks," I said softly.

He sat down on the opposite end of the bench, lifted my feet up and put them across his lap. He rested his hand on my knee. "How are you feeling?"

"Tired. Little bit dizzy. I can't move too fast, or I'll get nauseated." I took a deep breath and added, "I'm also angry. I'm not the same person anymore. You took that away from me."

He looked hurt. "I'm sorry Jessie. I didn't mean to hit you that hard."

I gritted my teeth in anger, feeling the heat rush through me quickly. "I thought that you had more control than that. My life is over because of what you did. Do you really understand that?"

"It was an accident, Jessie," he said, looking out the window for a moment then back at me.

"I have to live with that mistake for the rest of my life," I replied.

"What can I do to help fix this?" his said, his voice cracking.

It was obvious that he was holding back tears.

"That's just it, you can't fix it! I'm not a toy that can be repaired. I'm broken. Forever," I said.

"You are one of the strongest people I know. You can overcome this. I can feel it in my heart," he replied.

"Really? That's your response?" Fresh tears rolled down my cheeks and I hastily wiped them away with shaking hands. I took a deep breath, gulping back sobs. "As you once said so memorably to me, I think we need to spend some time apart."

The expression on his face was overwhelming. His lips quivered as he tried to hold back his grief. He nodded, got up, and gave me a gentle squeeze with his hand. Then he leaned over and gave me a kiss on my forehead. "Okay." Tears welled up in his eyes.

He let go of my hand and walked out of the room. The air suddenly felt very cold and empty. I leaned my head against the window and let my mind wander. I asked myself if I had moved faster and did a better job blocking the moves, would I still be in this position or did fate have a reason for this? Doubt filled my mind from every corner until I wanted to scream in agony.

Then I saw Ethan and his father, step in to the car. I watched it lumber down the driveway until it reached the end and drove away. It felt like my heart shattered into a million pieces. It was as if a part of me had died. It was truly over.

When I went downstairs for supper, Mom and Dad kept staring at me, giving me pitying looks which only made it worse.

"Honey, Ethan's father suggested that you focus on teaching classes, instead of doing any more sparring. He also mentioned that you can do katas and weapons in competitions," Mom said.

"He agreed with us that you should take some time off to let your body heal. You've been working so hard for so long and you need a much-deserved break," added Dad, who leaned across the table and patted my hand.

A headache was rapidly forming from the tension in my neck, and I was feeling physically drained. My mind was becoming more foggy, and it felt like my head was disconnected from my body. It was an odd sensation, as if everything was distanced from me. I turned my head to the side and the room started to spin. I gripped the edges of the table for balance and gulped back the nausea.

"Fine. I'll take time off. Geez, does that make everybody happy?" I replied, feeling irritable.

"There's no need to snap at us like that, Jessie," Dad said tersely. "We're just trying to help."

"Well, I'm so freaking sorry. I'm more broken than ever before, and now Ethan is gone!"

"Gone? What do you mean gone?" Mom said as she looked at me sharply, her eyes wide with alarm.

"I told him that I needed space from him."

Mom took a sharp intake of breath, clearly taken by surprise. "Oh, honey, I'm so sorry," she said then got up and gave me a hug.

My throat clenched painfully, feeling too small whenever I swallowed. I tried to hold back my tears as they welled up quickly, turning Dad into a watery blur.

"Just to let you know, Jonas can put you in other classes where you don't have to worry about Ethan," said Dad, putting his hand on my shoulder.

I nodded, too afraid to speak.

"We'll take everything one day at a time, okay?" Mom said.

"Just another ordinary day for me, right?" I said. My voice sounded raw.

"Jessie! I really wish that you weren't so hard on yourself like this," Mom exclaimed.

I shrugged my shoulders. "Well, it feels true. I'm like a freak that can't get anything right!"

Dad gave out a long sigh and shook his head. "You're not a freak, Jessie. We're proud of you for everything that you've accomplished so far. In fact, you've done more than many of my students. You've faced more adversity than them and defied those odds. You're an inspiration to them."

I stared at him. "What do you mean?"

"When I tell them that you have a black belt, teach karate classes, and taught at summer camp, despite the severity of your hearing loss, they're astonished to see how far you've come and done so well. Your accomplishments put them to shame," he said.

I tipped my head to the side. "Then why haven't you learned sign language for me?" I asked him bluntly.

He seemed stunned for a moment, blinking his eyes at me. Then he sheepishly raked his fingers through his hair, "I guess I was too scared."

"Scared? Of what? Me?" I asked him.

He shook his head. "No, not you. I was scared of my ability to communicate with you."

Feeling bewildered, I said, "That doesn't make any sense, Dad."

"At the time when you lost your hearing from meningitis, it felt like I had failed in taking care of you. That I didn't do a good job as a father," he replied, placing his hands on the table. "I didn't want to admit that you had a disability or accept the fact that your life would be forever changed. I was too afraid to take the next step and learn sign language. To me, it meant defeat. I had no idea that you would prove us wrong. You became a tenacious tiger. Once you put your mind to something, you were unstoppable."

"I'm just an ordinary person Dad, all I did was try to keep up with everyone else," I said.

"No. You're extraordinary," he said, giving me a timid smile.

That did nothing to quell the simmering anger within me. Then I suddenly felt more exhausted than before. All I wanted to do was go to sleep.

"This is too much for me. I'm going to take this upstairs," I said, grabbing my plate, and headed to my room.

I couldn't understand how my own father could be afraid of my hearing loss. I was just a little kid when my world suddenly went silent. I was still the same person, nothing else had changed. I puzzled over this while I ate my supper, not really tasting the food.

Chapter 11

renew

After several weeks of resting, the symptoms began to fade. The room no longer tilted whenever I got up or turned my head. The headaches receded, and the fogginess was pretty much gone. I felt stronger and closer to my old self. The emptiness in my heart still weighed heavily and, once in a while, I would find myself thinking about Ethan, which hurt even more.

The closer we got to college, the more I started gathering items that I thought I would need. Parker and Serena sat down on the bed, curiously watching me go back and forth, their heads swiveling side to side. I glanced at the list of required items. Paintbrushes? Check. Canvases? Check. Sketchbooks? Check. Acrylic paint? Check. I was mildly disappointed that the list wasn't as cool as Harry Potter's. I really wanted to check off items like a wand, owl, and cauldron.

I glanced at the clock beside my bed and realized I was going to be late for karate. When I grabbed my gym bag, I felt a pang of sadness and anger when I saw my sparring gear in a box beside it, equipment that I would never use again.

I marched down the stairs and snatched up a homemade

muffin from the kitchen counter. Mom turned around and glanced up from making cookies.

"All set for class?" she asked.

I nodded. "I think so. A bit nervous. It feels so strange not to be bringing my sparring gear."

"At least you can focus on the kids for now. Think of it like summer camp," she replied.

"I know, I'm trying. It isn't easy. It was such a big part of my life and my personality. I loved sparring. I think it was because I finally found something that I was good at and comfortable with."

"Well, you always did enjoy sports," she said.

"It was something that I knew that I was good at." I sighed. "I'm already missing it."

"Sensei Jonas mentioned that he wanted you to learn some new skills. He has something planned for you."

"Oh, cool. Guess I'll find out soon," I said. I had to admit that I was very curious about that. And super scared.

Mom stopped what she was doing and looked at me. "Don't worry about Ethan, okay? It may be awkward for a while though."

"I know." That's the part that I was dreading, coming face to face with him. "Making cookies for a client?" I said, gesturing at the counter.

She nodded. "I'm trying a new recipe. Shortbread with lavender. Want to be my official taste tester when you come back home?"

I smiled. "Sure!"

I munched on the banana muffin while I walked over to the car, dumped my bag on the floor, and stared at the key. My hands began to shake, and I gripped the steering wheel, trying to calm down. I took several deep breaths and turned on the engine. I drove down the gravel lane, past rows of maple trees, and turned right at the red mailbox.

I focused on the drive, determined to enjoy the scenery as I went past the farmland and rolling hills dotted with sheep and cows. The closer I got to the city, the more anxious I grew. My stomach tightened into painful knots. I drove into the parking lot, turned off the ignition, and leaned my head on the steering wheel, feeling over-whelmed. *Did I make a mistake coming here?* I wondered.

I didn't want to regret coming all this way then turning back without dealing with my fear. I needed to face it today. I grabbed my bag, got out, and headed into the dojo.

"Hi, Jessie!" Sensei Jonas greeted me as I came in and gestured for me to join him in his office. "Perfect timing."

I walked over and stood nervously in front of him, look-ing over my shoulder for Ethan.

"How are feeling?" he asked.

"Better. Bit nervous," I replied.

"I'm sorry about what happened Jessie."

"Thank you," I said shyly.

"Just to let you know, Ethan was suspended from spar-ring for several weeks. Even though it was an accident, I don't tolerate anyone using full force like that. Unfortunate-ly, it got out of hand that night, and it affected you."

"Oh, I see."

"He does feel badly about that," he said, sitting on the edge of the desk.

"I realized that. But it doesn't change anything. I can never spar again," I replied, trying to keep my anger in check. One of the things that I'd noticed since being hit, was how easy I became angry, my temper was worse than usual.

"Ah. Speaking of which, I have a special guest coming in today, and I would very much like to have you join that class."

"Sure." I had to admit that I was rather curious about that.

"Are you okay with teaching the kids class with me? I will be going in and out during the class while I talk to some of the parents and need to have someone on the floor while I do that," he asked.

I nodded and gave him a thumbs up. "I'm good."

He reached and shook my hand. "It's really nice to have you back, Jessie."

"Thanks."

I quickly got changed and went into the dojo, bowing at the entrance, then walked over to left to do some leg stretches. I spent that time trying to ease my tension. One by one, the kids came in, eager to start class.

Carrie, the little girl with long brown hair done up in two braids, spotted me and came running over to greet me. "Sensei Jessie, you're back!"

I smiled. "Hi, Carebear."

"I missed you," she said.

"Aw, I missed you guys too."

"Want a hug?" she asked me.

"From who?" I replied cheekily.

She giggled. "Me, silly!"

"Of course!"

I got on my knees so that she could give me a hug. Then she sat down beside me, cross legged. Several more kids came over and sat down around us, forming a semi-circle. Sensei Jonas came in, spotted us, and came over.

"Did I miss something? Did class already start without me?" he said.

The kids began to snicker and giggle and replied in unison, "No!" Carrie gestured at me then said, "We're doing our stretches with Sensei Jessie."

"Uh huh. All right, let's go line up then."

They all jumped up and scampered to the front of the class. I stood by Sensei Jonas and we bowed them in.

"Sensei Jessie will be doing the warm ups and helping you with your katas today," he said. He put his hand on my shoulder. "I want you guys to do what she says, okay?"

They bobbed their heads and grinned.

"Go for it Jessie," he said.

"Okay, everyone! Follow me," I said and started to run around the room.

As we went around in circles, I saw Ethan approach his

father. The two of them stood side by side, talking to each other. I wondered what they were talking about. He glanced at me when I went by him. He inclined his head and waved at me. Sensei Jonas gave me a thumbs up and mouthed, "Keep going."

I nodded and the two of them walked out of the dojo.

I took the kids through the warm up and had them form a circle around me. I held on to a large kicking pad and randomly darted back and forth toward the kids, letting them kick it.

"Don't forget to add kiais! I can't hear very well, so make sure it's loud!"

They snickered when I said that. One boy who was smaller than the rest of the group, raised his leg when I approached him the pad. He scrunched up his face, held up his fists near his face, and kicked with all of his might. He kicked so hard that he abruptly fell to the floor with a surprised thud.

"That's okay, I've done that too. Try again!"

He scrambled back up with a fierce determination and kicked it again, giving out a loud yell.

Sensei Jonas came in, watched us for a while then said "Keske!" Everyone brought their legs together sharply and stood at attention.

"We're going to work on your Katas, spread out and make sure you have enough room around you," he said.

I put the kicking pad away and joined him at the front.

"Since most of them are yellow and orange belts, can you take them through their katas?" he asked me.

"Sure."

"You're doing a great job, Jessie," he said.

"Thanks," I replied shyly.

I led them through their katas together as a class, going through each step, block and kick with them. It was a sea of white uniforms as they snapped out their arms and legs, an elaborate dance of moves in synch.

"Ichi!"

As I counted out the order, they changed direction.

"Ni!"

They did a block over their heads with their arms.

"San!"

They swiveled around and faced the opposite direction.

"Shi!"

And repeated the same move with the other arm.

I continued on, carefully watching their moves. Sensei Jonas came back in a while later. I bowed to him and turned to face the students.

"Good job, guys. Let's thank Sensei Jessie for helping us today!" he said to them.

In a loud chorus, they said, "Arigato, Sensei Jessie!"

It was then that I realized that I was meant to be here, that this was my place. I felt right at home.

We bowed them out and the next group of students came in, chattering amongst themselves.

"Jessie, I have a feeling that you will like this class," said Sensei Jonas.

I narrowed my eyes at him. "Why? What do you mean?"

He gave a big grin that was eerily like Ethan's. "You'll see."

I looked around and noticed that many of them were higher belts, blue, brown, and black and carrying a long, thin wooden shaft resembling a giant toothpick.

Sensei Jonas and Ethan walked over to the front of the class with another black belt instructor. I had never seen him before. He also carried a long wooden shaft. He looked a few years older than me with long brown hair that reached his shoulders. His features were lean and chiseled, looking a lot like a movie star. He walked with confidence with his shoulders straight back. There was something about him that struck me as being very sure of himself. He wore black pants, a bright red Gi with many patches on the sleeve and a large white dragon adorned the back.

"Keske!" bellowed Sensei Jonas.

We all stood at attention.

"Rei!" he barked out.

We bowed to him in unison.

"Welcome to today's class, everyone. We have a very special guest from Los Angeles joining us today. This is Sensei Michael. He's an expert in weapons, particularly the Bo staff. He's a world champion martial artist and has won many, many national championships. He has also been featured in several movies."

Aha, that explains his demeanor and good looks.

"Oh, stop it. You're making me blush," he said jokingly.

"Treat him with the same respect that you treat me, okay? The floor is yours Sensei Michael," said Sensei Jonas and walked over to the back of the class.

That was the first time I had seen him join us as a student.

Sensei Michael clapped his hands together eagerly. "Before I start, has anyone used a Bo before?"

Several hands went up in the air.

"Good! I'll work with you guys later and teach you some more advanced moves," he said, looking at them.

"Any Jackie Chan fans here?" he asked.

Almost everyone raised their hands.

"Awesome!" he said, laughing.

"Have any of you seen my movies?" he asked us.

Maybe half of the class raised their hands.

"Cool. By the way, I'll be doing autographs after class."

He seemed very laid back and very much at ease with our group. I already liked him.

"I'm going to do a demonstration for those of you who have not seen a weapon kata. Trust me, it will blow your socks off," he said, giving us a very white smile. "Can everyone spread out to the sides along the wall so that I can use the center of this room? Some of the moves that I do are very fast and totally wicked."

Once we were safely out of his way, he calmly strode over to the middle carrying the Bo staff nestled in the crook of his right arm. He stood still, his face darkened and became serious like a warrior ready to fight. He bowed then slowly raised the staff. His breathing became faster, and his face was set with a fierce determination. It was a complete change from his calm demeanor. He quickly looked in one direction, as if seeing an opponent. Then he suddenly flicked out the Bo in a punching motion and snapped it upward. He swirled to one side, the Bo making a loud snapping sound against his uniform. Then he rapidly switched to the other side, as if attacking an invisible opponent on his right. He did a quick mini circle near the floor then swirled the Bo around his body and raised it above his head, spinning faster and faster. He abruptly stopped, did a loud yell, quickly changed directions, and continued a myriad of fast paced strikes, hitting unseen opponents all around him. He delivered a final blow with a mighty yell.

My heart was pounding and my jaw dropped as I watched him.

As soon as he finished, there was a loud applause. His face changed back to a sunny disposition, a complete opposite of the battle mode he was just in.

I stood staring at him in absolute awe. He looked at me, came over and stood in front of me. "Don't worry, I'm a nice guy," he said, giving me a broad grin. "I won't bite."

I suddenly felt very shy, "That's was awesome! And scary too."

He laughed. "Good! And I'm going to make you just as awesome. Have you used one of these before?"

I shook my head. "I've never seen a Bo kata like yours."

"Sensei Jonas has some more Bo staffs at the back. Do you want to grab one?"

"Okay. By the way, I can't hear very well. I might miss some of what you say," I told him.

"No problem. Just copy everything I do," he said, giving me a wink, and went to the front of the class.

I went to the back, grabbed one of the slender staffs off the rack. It was almost as tall as me yet felt light and balanced. The ends were tapered to a slim point.

"Everyone spread out and make sure that you have enough room around you," said Sensei Michael. He watched us move around. "Great! Let's start with a basic kata."

He moved slowly yet sharply, flicking the Bo with great strength and precision. We did a series of moves, poking at imaginary opponents on either side of us, various blocks and strikes. He taught us how to spin the Bo around our bodies and over our heads.

He had us practice some of the moves on our own, trying them out. He approached me, watching me do part of his kata. "That's great, Jessie. You're a natural. Have you thought about doing Bo katas in tournaments?" he asked.

"Do you think I should?"

He nodded. "Yes," he said in a husky voice.

I gulped.

The more we practiced the moves, the more exhilarated I became. It was an incredible feeling and something clicked in me, like a light bulb turning on. I looked over my shoulder at Sensei Jonas who was working on his kata. He saw me and gave me a knowing wink. It suddenly dawned on me why he wanted me in this class. He must have known that I would like this.

There was a sense of renewed hope in me, once I realized that there were new possibilities.

After class, I went into the office where Sensei Michael sat doing autographs. There was a stack of glossy posters, postcards, and photographs of him holding the Bo in mid-strike. They were impressive. He clearly looked like a movie star.

When I approached him, he gave me a dazzling smile. "Hey, how's my favorite star?"

I blushed and looked down, feeling shy, "Good. I loved using the Bo. Thank you for showing us your kata, it was awesome."

"Gosh, thanks. I'm glad you liked it," he replied earnestly.

"Do you get nervous when you perform the kata in front of large crowds?" I asked.

"Yes, sometimes."

His response surprised me.

"Really? It was flawless," I said.

"Practice. Lots of it, until it's a reflex. It has to be second nature so that I don't get distracted," he replied.

"Cool, I gotta remember that," I said.

"The secret is that it doesn't have to be perfect or super fast. You just need to emphasize the moves so that they appear lethal. Sharp and precise."

"So, basically it means being totally confident?" I asked.

"Absolutely! The judges can see that. If you believe in yourself, they will believe you," he replied.

"Okay."

"Would you like me to autograph something for you?"

"Yes, please."

He picked up a large glossy photo, signed it, and handed it to me. I looked at it and saw that not only did he sign it, he added: *Be awesome, Jessie*.

"Thank you so much, Sensei Michael," I said.

"You're welcome, Jessie," he said and reached out to shake my hand. When I gripped it, he placed his other hand over top. "Believe in yourself, you can do it."

"I'll try," I replied.

"Awesome!" he said.

When I turned around to leave, I was face to face with Ethan. I froze and sucked in a quiet gasp. "Ethan," I said.

"Hey, Jessie."

He looked a bit down, not his usual self. His expression seemed guarded and lacked the normal, happy disposition. I wondered if I was too hard on him and momentarily, felt a pang of sympathy.

"How are you?" he asked me.

"Okay, I guess."

"Feeling better?" he asked.

"Yeah." I nodded. "I'm still trying to come to terms with

these new changes. It's a lot to process," I told him.

He looked crestfallen. "It's tearing me to pieces that I can't be there for you."

"I know, but right now, I need to figure how to move forward in my life," I replied.

He grabbed my hand and held it to his chest. I could feel his heart beat beneath my fingers. "I'm sorry for everything you're going through," he said.

I gulped, my throat painfully tight. "Thanks," I said quietly, holding back tears.

"Please let me know if there's anything I can do for you," he said.

I tried not to cry when I pulled my hand away from his chest. He slid his hand down my arm, a familiar gesture, and gave my hand a squeeze. I reluctantly released his grip, turned around, and walked away.

Chapter 12

I stood and surveyed the room where several cardboard boxes and plastic bins sat on the floor. Parker and Serena were on the bed, watching me move around while I packed. I felt a sudden pain in my heart when I looked at them. It was hard leaving them and, for a moment, there, I didn't want to go.

Dad came into my room. "Is this everything?"

I nodded. "Yeah, I think so."

He looked at me. "Nervous?"

I gave him a smile. "Heh, yes. I'm more worried about Parker and Serena," I said, casting a glance at them.

"They'll be okay," he replied. "Actually, you know what? I have an idea. Do you have any old sweatshirts?"

I gave him a quizzical stare. " I can look in my closet, why?"

"Something I remember reading about that cats like having a familiar scent of the person and clothes work well. If you leave your sweatshirt on the bed or bench by the window, they might snuggle up to it so that they don't feel so anxious."

I loved that idea and began rummaging through the closet. After a few minutes of searching, I found a light blue one and placed it on the bench beside a pillow in the sunshine. Serena jumped down off the bed, padded over to it. She pawed at it for a moment, turned around, and promptly curled up on it.

"Aw!"

"See? It works," Dad said, giving me a smug look. "All right, so all of these boxes go in the car, right?"

"Yep," I said, picking one up and giving it to him.

I hefted another one into my arms and marched downstairs with him. We headed over to the van where the side door was already open. My duvet cover and pillow sat in a clear plastic bag on the seat. A drafting table lay flat on the floor at the back. There was a toolbox full of paint, brushes, pencils, pens, and erasers, most of the items that were on the list. Dad and I placed the boxes beside them and went back in to get the rest of the stuff. Twenty minutes later, and after a last minute search, I gave Serena and Parker a kiss on their soft, furry foreheads. "I'm going to miss you guys so much."

Parker said, "Murrup?" a mix of a meow and loud purr.

I blinked back tears and went downstairs into the kitchen. Mom had packed two large boxes worth of food—her version of care packages.

"I think that's the last thing to go in the van," she said.

We picked them up and went outside. The box was surprisingly heavy, and I suspected that she put cans of soup in it. We placed it at the back with the other boxes. It was a tight fit but we managed to get everything in the van. I managed to squeeze into the backseat while Mom sat up front with Dad. I noticed that Mom brought a box of tissues with her. I was hoping that I didn't have to use them. As Dad drove the van down the gravel road, I looked out the window toward the house, watching it grow smaller as we left.

I watched Mom and Dad converse on the way to college, enjoying their casual banter. I was going to miss that too. After a nearly two hour drive, which felt a lot longer, we arrived at the blue and gray duplex. We pulled into the driveway, got out, and began unpacking the van. Mom carried the care package into the kitchen while Dad and I placed the boxes in my new room. He helped me assemble the drafting table, set up the desk and floor lamp.

Ironically, it was much faster to unpack everything. Mom helped me put the sheets on my new bed. Once we were finished, we stood in the room and looked around.

"Well, it looks like you're all set. Is there anything else you need?" asked Dad.

"No, I don't think so," I said, feeling apprehensive.

Mom seemed sad but she put on a brave face for me and took a deep breath. "I think it's time for us to go and let you get settled in."

She walked over to me, opened her arms, and gave me a big hug. We went downstairs and I stood by the van.

Dad gave me a quick hug. "I hope you have a good time at school!" he said before hopping into the driver's seat.

I waved at them as they backed out and drove away. I could imagine Mom going through those tissues already. It felt so strange to be the one waving at them, since this was now my home, and usually it was the other way around. I went back inside and went through some of the boxes, putting my clothes in the dresser drawers. I sorted through the art supplies and books, getting them ready for class on Monday. The house was eerily quiet, there were no pets, none of the usual sounds of Mom and Dad, or the aroma of Mom's cooking.

After a while, I became uneasy and got up, curiously peeking into the cupboards and doors around the rest of the house. I discovered that the master suite had a mini chandelier that hung over the large bed, along with a huge Jacuzzi, and giant flat screen TV. My jaw nearly dropped when I saw that. It was the classiest room compared to the rest of the house. I went downstairs and checked out the television, DVD player, and stereo system. There was quite a collection of DVDs, featuring popular movies and shows. Off to the left was a large circular glass dining room table. It was big enough for at least six people.

I headed over to the kitchen and looked around. It was small and narrow, with two long counters on either side. The fridge was mostly empty except for a moldy jar of salsa. The shelves had been divided into sections for us, my shelf held a variety of fresh fruit and vegetables, slices of meat and cheese, eggs and juice, all courtesy of Mom. I took a peek in the oven, it looked sparkling clean as if it was rarely used. There was some food in the pantry, mostly crackers, canned soup, pasta, a bag of chips, and nachos.

The house felt very different than home. Here it seemed empty, devoid of any personal touches. It was more like an empty hotel room. Even though it was fairly new and modern, I got the impression that the owner wasn't here very often. I knew that she traveled quite a bit since she was in sales and marketing for a local company, helping them distribute their products. I looked around the room. It was missing the usual lived in look. Everything was neatly organized and stacked, as if no one touched them. I noticed that there were very few books around here, virtually no magazines or newspapers anywhere.

I felt a pang of sadness as I stood alone in this room. The house felt too big for me, and it made me feel more alone than ever before. I went over to the glass sliding doors and pulled the curtains shut then headed to the front door and locked it.

This is ridiculous, I thought. *I should be behaving more like a grown-up and celebrating my freedom and independence.*

Determined to act more like an adult, I decided to make my own supper by reheating some left overs in the microwave. I poured myself a glass of iced tea, waited for the ping when the food was ready, took out the hot plate, and was about to sit down at the dining room table. I changed my mind and went to my room instead.

While I munched on my supper, I opened the laptop,

courtesy of Dad, clicked on Netflix, and started watching *Supernatural*, my current addiction. It was Ethan's fault that he got me hooked on to this series. I tried not to think about how we used to snuggle together to watch it.

My iPod pinged, displaying a message. I picked it up and noticed that it was from Mom. She asked me how I was doing. I typed: *Okay. Eating supper, watching* Supernatural *on Netflix.*

Mom typed back: *I swear, you watch too much of that show.*

I smiled, then replied: *At least I know how to fight off monsters.*

She responded: *Uh-huh.*

I asked her how the cats were doing. She said that they sitting beside her on the couch.

She texted: *I think they miss you.*

That broke my heart. I said: *Aw. Please give them a hug and kiss for me.*

She replied: *Will do. Dad says goodnight.*

I texted back: *Goodnight, Mom and Dad.*

After I finished watching Netflix, I took a quick shower, put on my pajamas, and went around the house checking all of the windows and doors, making sure they were shut and firmly locked. I slid under my covers and held on to my pink plush bunny, trying to relax. The room seemed awfully bright from the streetlights outside. I felt very small and ridiculously scared. I yanked the covers over my head, closed my eyes tightly, wishing that I was back home with Parker and Serena sleeping beside me. I missed their comforting purrs.

જીજીજી

I bolted upright, suddenly awake in the middle of the night. It wasn't morning yet. I checked my alarm and noticed that it didn't go off. There was a sudden flash of bright light from the window, and I flinched so hard that the alarm clock nearly flew out of my hands. It took me a moment to realize that it was a thunderstorm and a strong one from the looks of it. Even though I couldn't hear the thunder, I could feel the rumbling which shook the bed. I began to tremble with fear and wriggled even deeper under the covers.

When morning came, I opened my bleary eyes at the soft light coming through the window. It felt so strange to wake up by myself in a completely different room. I was momentarily confused, thinking that I was still dreaming and back at home. It was Sunday which meant I didn't have to go to school. I sat up, looking around the room, expecting to see Parker and Serena jump up onto the bed. It was odd not to smell anything cooking, no strong scent of coffee or bacon in the air. It was eerie. I got up, swung my feet onto the floor, stood up, and stretched. I went over to the window and peered out. The view was visually uninspiring. All I saw were rows of houses and small, fenced in backyards. Some had plastic playhouses and swings for the kids, others had picnic tables and umbrellas.

It wasn't like home, where I often saw a variety of critters like squirrels and chipmunks running around, birds fluttering around, and deer in the field. Here, it was quite sparse in comparison, devoid of any wildlife.

I'd wondered if Shirley was home yet and curiously opened my bedroom door. So far, I didn't see anyone and headed downstairs to the kitchen. I gave out a big sigh. It was so odd to the only one in the house, and it felt very lonely. I grabbed a bowl, added cereal and milk, poured myself a glass of orange juice, and sat down at the small, empty kitchen table. Without any distractions or anyone to talk to, I quickly ate breakfast and went back upstairs. I was tempted to use the big Jacuzzi in the master suite then thought better of it. I didn't want to be caught red handed if she came home today. I went to the other bathroom, which was considerably smaller and very plain, and ran the water to take a bath. After a few minutes, it turned into a frothy mini pool and I eagerly sank into it, letting the warm water envelope me. I blissfully closed my eyes.

I had no idea how long I was in there when I suddenly noticed a shadow beneath the door. I sat up with a jolt, splashing soapy water onto the faux marble floor. Was there an intruder?

Reaching over to the rod on the wall, I snatched off the plush gray towel, quickly got dried off, and pulled on my jeans and hoodie. My hearing aids were in the bedroom so I had no idea who was on the other side of the door. I looked around the bathroom for a potential weapon to defend myself. There was nothing, except a loofah on a stick. I grabbed it, took a deep breath, yanked opened the door, and shrieked when I came face to face with a tall man. He wore black jeans, a black T-shirt, and black leather jacket He was ridiculously good looking with long blond hair at the front and a square jaw. He jumped backward and held up his hands.

I could only assume he yelled too. His eyes slid over to my hands, and he started laughing. Puzzled, I stood there wondering what was so funny. He gestured at my hands, I followed his gaze and belatedly realized that I was still holding onto the sudsy loofah. I snickered at the scene before me. He stepped forward and reached out with his hand.

I put my hand up "Just a second and I'll put this away."

I hurried back into the bathroom, put the loofah in the tub, turned around, and shook his hand. "Hi, I'm Jessie."

He started speaking to me and I couldn't lip read him since he was talking too fast. I waved my hands at him. "I can't hear you. I'm going to put on my hearing aids."

I dashed over to the dresser by my bed, snatched up my hearing aids, and put them on. When I turned around, he was standing in the room, curiously watching me with his hands in his pockets.

"Sorry about that. I'm deaf without them. Literally."

"Oh, cool. I think you're the first person that I've met with a hearing loss. I'm Jackson, by the way."

Cool name, I thought. "Are you with Shirley?" I asked him.

He gave me a bemused stare then his eyes widened as it dawned on him, "Oh!" He laughed. "No, good lord, no. She's definitely not my type."

"Oh. Okay."

"Besides, I already have a boyfriend," he added.

I wanted to give myself a mental slap on my forehead. *Of course you do*, I thought.

"Are you attending college too?" I asked.

"Yep! Illustration," he replied, beaming.

"Sweet! So am I!" I said.

"Oh, hey, we probably have the same classes together," he said, casually leaning against the door.

"We should compare our schedules to see if we can co-ordinate rides together," I remarked.

"Actually, I have my own car," he said, then gestured at me. "Although it would be nice to have you come with me, keep me company."

"Sure. That would be great."

He tilted his handsome chin at me. "So, when did you arrive here?"

"Yesterday, my parents dropped me off," I replied.

"How far did you have to travel?"

"Couple of hours, not too far," I said, sitting on the edge of my bed. "How about you?"

"About three hours. There was quite a bit of construction to get through."

"There usually is on the highway, it never seems to end. Where are you from?" I asked.

"Outskirts of London."

"Oh, hey, that's a great city. I'm not too far from Strat-ford which is near there," I replied.

His eyes lit up. "I've been to Stratford. I love going to see the plays."

"Which one is your favorite?"

"I would have to say *Twelfth Night.* Maybe it's because

of the tight pants the actors wear." He gave me a playful wink and sly grin. When he smiled, he became even more attractive.

I snickered when he said that.

"Speaking of which, don't you find it distracting when they do that?" he asked.

I was momentarily sidetracked. "What?"

"Wear those pants? I mean, how do you pay attention, especially with your hearing loss?" He gestured toward his ears for emphasis.

Holy cheese and crackers, he was amusing. "Oh! I'm usually too focused on lip reading and paying attention to what they're saying. I also read the script and memorize it ahead of time so I can keep up."

"Seriously?"

I nodded.

"Isn't that a lot of work?" he asked, grabbing the chair, turning it around, and sitting in it. He rested his arms across the back.

"Not really. I'm used to it," I said.

"That's so freaking cool! Have you noticed any actors forgetting their lines?"

"Yeah, actually, it's happened a couple of times," I replied.

"Don't they have devices you could wear?" he asked.

"It depends on which ones they provide. Some of them have headsets that go in your ears which I can't do because I can't take out my hearing aids. The other ones are often full of static and not strong enough for me. It's for people with a mild hearing loss. Mine is just too severe."

"Were you born like this?"

"No. I lost my hearing from meningitis when I was a kid. I recently went deaf in my right ear from antibiotics."

He placed his hand on the side of his face in awe. "My dear, you are doing superbly. If I hadn't seen your hearing aids, I wouldn't have known that you had a hearing loss. Your speech is so clear," he remarked.

I didn't know why so many people said that. It was like they assumed that I was supposed to sound different because I couldn't hear. "Thanks, I had a lot of speech therapy and good hearing aids."

He shook his head in consternation. "Well, I'm impressed. It paid off."

It just occurred to me that he was probably still in the process of bringing his stuff into the house or unpacking. "Did you need any help carrying your things up to your room or unpacking?" I asked him.

He blinked for a moment. "Oh! I was so distracted that I totally forgot! Yes, by all means, come on down and you can help me carry them upstairs."

I followed him to the living room where several boxes sat on the floor. He picked one up and passed it over to me then grabbed another one for himself.

"Follow me, dear."

I juggled the heavy box as we went up the stairs and into his room on the right. Mine was at the far end of the hallway. I placed the box on the floor and headed back downstairs to grab another one. We went back and forth until the living room was back to normal.

"Whew! That the last one," I said, feeling the sweat roll down the back of my neck.

"Thanks, dear."

I looked around the room. "Wow. That's a lot of boxes."

He placed his hands on his hips. "I didn't think I would be going home very often, it's a bit too much traveling."

"True. But what about your boyfriend?"

"Wesley said that he would try to come for a visit. He would love to meet you!"

I gave him a smile. "Okay, I'll let you unpack."

"Thanks, Jessie," he replied, opening a box and pulling out some books.

I went back to my room, turned on my laptop, placed it on my bed, and clicked on Netflix. After an hour of binge watching *The Vampire Diaries*, I could smell something burning. Alarmed, I darted out of bed. Jackson's door was open, and he wasn't in his room. I hurried down the stairs and into the kitchen. Smoke billowed out of it.

I coughed. "What happened Jackson?"

He looked at me sheepishly and gestured over his shoulder with his thumb at the microwave. "I was trying to cook some popcorn," he said then did a muffled cough and waved his hand in the air to dispel the smoke.

I gave him a bemused stare then started giggling. "Popcorn?"

He nodded then began chuckling.

"I didn't know you can burn popcorn!" I said, laughing.

Jackson guffawed, placing his hands on his knees. "I didn't either!"

Chapter 13

COLLEGE

Jackson and I hefted our artist's toolboxes and portfolios into his car, sat down in the front seat, and backed out of the driveway.

It was our first day at college. I hadn't felt this nervous about school in a long time.

"This is great, Jackson, thanks for the ride."

"It's no problem, dear," he said, giving me a quick smile.

"I'm amazed that you've come all this way for college. What made you choose this one?" I asked him.

"The program and reputation, of course," he replied.

"Did you meet any illustrators before?" I asked, leaning my elbow against the window.

He nodded. "Yeah, a couple of them. They worked for an advertising agency and did a lot of posters for them. Their stuff was pretty cool. I hope to become as talented as them."

I knew what he was talking about. "Same here, I collect children's books because of the art, I think they're beautiful."

Jackson glanced at me while we sat a stoplight. "Were you always interested in art?"

I nodded. "Yes, I loved sketching. It's funny, for me it was an outlet, a form of escapism from the bullying and teasing I endured at school."

"I know what you mean, Jessie. I've been through that too," he said, drumming his fingers on the steering wheel.

"Really?"

He nodded, flicked his eyes at me then back at the road, "After I came out, I took a lot of flak for it. I became a huge target at school. My locker was often written in marker and lipstick with rude slang and nasty notes were slipped in it. It was awful. After a while, they became bored and went after someone else from a new school. They just wanted a target to pick on and I happened to be an easy one for them."

"Oh, I'm so sorry about that," I said, feeling his pain. I couldn't believe that we had been through similar situations, even though the circumstances were quite different.

"Thank you, darling. You know—it's such a shame that we didn't know each other a few years ago. We would've been best friends," he said, giving me a big smile.

"And gotten into a lot of trouble, I suspect."

He snickered, eyes beaming.

"I'm curious, how did you meet Wesley?"

"Ironically, at the principal's office. We were both sitting on the bench in the hallway and started talking. That friendship grew into a relationship. I guess it was fate."

The college was around the corner, a monstrous glass building surrounded by manicured green lawns, a pond with white swans, and pathways through the trees on the property.

"How about you, Jessie? Do you have anyone?" he asked, giving me a quick glance.

"I did, but we're taking a break right now," I said, looking out the window then back at him.

"Oh, dear, that's a shame."

"It's just as well since we're going to different schools. I guess it was meant to happen."

He pulled up to the main gate and showed the guard his

ID tag. Then he turned to face me, "Do you really believe that?"

I shrugged my shoulders. "I'm not sure. Right now, it feels weird."

He gave the guard some money then proceeded into the parking lot. I tried to give him some change but he wouldn't take it.

"How so?" he asked as he looked for a parking spot.

"Um—there were a lot of changes happening at once. It was too much for me, like the final straw."

"Hmm, from the sounds of it, there must have been a trigger or underlying issue," he said, deftly pulling the car in open slot. Even though we were on time, the parking lot was nearly full.

"Holy cow, we arrived in the nick of time. There's not very many spots left," I said.

"Yeah, we may need to come sooner next time."

We got out, grabbed our equipment, marched into the building, and approached the front desk.

"Hello! We're first year students in Illustration, where do we go?" Jackson asked the man at the desk.

The security guard looked up from his monitor. "Main auditorium, down the hall on your left." He gestured in that direction with his hand. He sounded extremely bored and I wondered how many students had already asked him that question today.

"Poor guy," I said to Jackson once we started walking down the hallway. Bright light streamed in from the large skylights above us.

"Huh? What guy?" He seemed momentarily confused.

I jerked my thumb over my shoulder toward the front desk, "Him. He's probably repeated himself hundreds of times today."

"Oh! Heh. Yeah. Can you imagine having that job?"

I shook my head. "I wonder how much it pays?"

"Not sure," he replied. "Probably not enough."

We found the auditorium, pulled open the large, heavy

doors, and had to squint to see inside. Compared to the brightly lit hallway, it was extremely dim in here. The overhead lights did very little to help us see where we were going. We picked an aisle and proceeded down the steps near the front. It was a large room in the shape of a semicircle, the seats sloping downward like a bowl. It was like a mini version of a football stadium.

Jackson gave me a quizzical look. "Are we sitting in the front row?"

I nodded. "It's so I can see the teacher's face and lip read."

He did a face palm. "Oh right, sorry, darling."

"It's okay. You don't have to sit with me if you don't want to," I said.

"It's fine," he replied.

"Doesn't this remind you of Stratford?" I said, gesturing around the room.

"I was just about to say that! Guess that's the stage, eh?" he said, pointing at the long table in front of us.

A slim gentleman came through the doors on the lower level, just off to the right of the table. His entrance brought in a sudden burst of bright light. He was carrying a laptop, couple of books, and a binder and placed them on the table. He spent a few minutes hooking up the screen. I rummaged through my large purse, pulled out the FM system, and walked over to him. I'd always dreaded this part. I never knew how a new teacher would react to being asked to wear the listening device.

I held out my hand. "Hi! I'm Jessie McIntyre."

"Oh, hello," he said, giving me a broad smile. He reached out and gave me a hearty handshake. "I'm Professor Charles. How may I help you?"

"Um, yes. I'm hard of hearing, and it would help if you could wear this for me."

"Ah. Yes, your counselor mentioned that you would need assistance," he replied.

I nodded. "This is part of the FM system, yours is the

microphone." I held it up for him to see. It was a small white box with a loop around the top. It looked more like a trendy necklace. "You just loop it over your head. I've already turned it on for you," I said, gesturing toward the on/off button.

"Super. Remind me to give it back to you, otherwise I will end up walking all over the place with it," he replied.

"I will."

That was easy, I thought.

I went back to my seat, grabbed the receiver, a small white box attached to a rubber wire, and placed it around my neck. It was very light in weight and the sounds would be transmitted wirelessly right to my hearing aids. I pressed the button on the top, waiting for the green light to turn on and, within seconds, I heard Professor Charles rustling around.

"What's that you're wearing?" asked Jackson.

"A receiver, it's so I can hear my teachers."

"Neat. Does it get loud?" he asked.

"Yeah, it can actually. It comes with a volume control that I can adjust."

"So, you can turn it off when they go to the bathroom?" he said, raising his eyebrows.

I grimaced. "Yes, a much-learned lesson."

"Okay, folks! Welcome to first year Illustration. This will be your art history class, however, today will be orientation." He looked at me. "Is this on?" he asked, gesturing at the FM system.

I could see everyone turning their heads to look at me and could sense more gazes from around me. I nodded and gave him a thumbs up.

"Awesome. By the way, this is a microphone that I'm wearing for Jessie who has a hearing loss."

My face burned from the embarrassment. I wanted to shrink into my chair. I raised my hand and waved at everyone meekly.

"I'm Professor Charles Newman but you can call me

Charles or Professor, whichever suits you. We are quite casual here at college. Speaking of which, there are no bells or alarms to indicate when class is over. Everyone is an adult here. This is the real world, and just like a job, you are expected to be on time. Okay?" he said, looking around the room, watching us nod our heads.

"A point of interest, this is not an easy program and is, in fact, one of the most difficult and intensive programs here. Only half of you will graduate. Think about that for a moment. Now, all of you will need to wear ID tags from here on in to be able to access various classrooms and the computer lab. The photographer will be here today. Report to the office and you'll have your picture taken. A badge will be issued to you. Do not lose them. Keep them visible. I know they're tacky but that's technology for you today."

The giant screen came on behind him, and I assumed he was using a remote. "Bear in mind, that this will not be your typical classroom. You will be working primarily in studios with easels, which leads me to the next point. Keep anything of value such as wallets, purses, expensive art supplies, with you or in your locker at all times. Things can and will be stolen. I'm sorry to say this, but it does happen."

The screen featured a list of book titles. "You will be needing these books for this semester for this class. They can be purchased at the bookstore here on campus."

I opened my notebook and started writing down the titles. Professor Charles waited for a few minutes then continued. "All right, let's begin art history."

After nearly an hour of historical trivia, I was ready for my next class. When he was finished speaking, I went up to Professor Charles and stood waiting beside him. He was gathering up his books when he saw me.

"Yes?"

"I need the FM transmitter," I said, pointing at his chest.

He frowned momentarily, looked down, and recognition dawned on his face. "Oh! I totally forgot," he said then looped it over his head and handed it back to me. "Don't be afraid to ask me any questions okay?" he said kindly.

I gave him a shy smile. "I will. Thanks."

Jackson was waiting for me, and we marched up the stairs to our next class, which was down another level in a different wing. We emerged into a large, spacious room with floor to ceiling glass windows and walkways overhead. It was an open concept that reminded me of an airport terminal. I looked up at the walkway and saw several people watching us. On my left was a glass wall on the upper level, where more people were walking by, some stopping to look down on us. I felt like a specimen, a bug caught in a glass jar, much to the amusement of everyone else. There were easels scattered throughout the room, a table sitting on a podium in the middle of the room where a collection of squash, Indian corn, and corn stalks sat artfully displayed on top.

I looked around and noticed that there were no chairs or desks to sit on. There were wooden stools lined up against the wall. I walked over to one of them, placed my toolbox and portfolio against it, and sat on top of the stool. It wasn't particularly comfortable but at least I didn't have to stand around, looking like a bumbling idiot. I already felt insecure enough as it was. After a few minutes of waiting, a tall man with a shock of red hair cut in a buzz and large beard strode in. He was carrying a black portfolio and wore a blue denim shirt with the sleeves rolled up to his elbows. Over top of his shirt was an orange knitted vest along with dark indigo blue slim jeans and shiny black shoes. He looked young, maybe no more ten years older than me.

He placed his portfolio on the floor beside one of the easels, rummaged through it, and pulled out a large sketch pad. It was placed on the easel along with several pencils and erasers on the skinny shelf at the bottom.

"All right, folks, welcome to my drawing class. I'm Professor Kurt White but you can call me Kurt or Professor, it doesn't matter," he said, giving us a big smile.

I walked over to him, held up the FM system, and explained what it was and how it worked. When he draped it over his head, he remarked, "Wow! This is so light, I can't even tell I'm wearing it. Technology is amazing, isn't it?"

I nodded and gave him a smile.

"Place your portfolios along the wall for now and gather around me." He waited until all of us formed a semi-circle. He picked up a pencil and began to sketch some of the objects on the table in the middle. "Today, I want you to focus on capturing the shape of any object on the table. You can pick one, two, or even three items if you wish. Then once you decide which one interests you, you're going to work on the composition, finding the most pleasing balance, particularly with the negative and positive space. You need to determine how much negative space, namely the background, that you want around the object. Do you want to focus just on the squash or include the corn beside it?"

He held up an old slide from a 35 mm camera, like the one Dad used to have when he was younger. There was no film in it, just the white plastic frame around it. "You can use these to help you decide what to focus on and how much of the subject matter you want to draw."

As he spoke, he held up the slide, looked at the table, and quickly sketched in the objects, lightly at first, on the pad. I was beginning to see what he was talking about.

"Concentrate on the angular lines and remember how perspective works—objects that are closer to you are larger. Think of the corn like a long, skinny rectangular box and the squash like a square box. Round it out, removing the sharp corners. Use your pencil to find the right angle, hold it out in front to the object then bring it back to the pad. Okay?"

We nodded, watching his eyes flick back and forth from the display to the easel, adding more details and shading. He was good, capturing the essence of the food with quick gestures and strokes.

He put down his pencil and turned to face us. "Walk around the room, think of yourself like a camera and find the vantage point that you like, grab an easel and place it near the table. There are extra sheets of paper on the table at the back wall for you to use. However, you will be required to bring your own materials from now on."

We all scrambled over to the display, curiously observing it from various angles. I walked around it, found the most pleasing angle, grabbed an easel, and placed it on the floor. I brought over my portfolio and toolbox. I saw Jackson across the room, doing the same thing.

I chose to sketch the squash and stalks of corn around it. I pulled out my sketch pad, clipped it to the top of the easel, and placed several pencils and erasers on the ledge beneath it. Peering around the pad, I began sketching out the general shape, adding angular lines for the stalks. Then I gradually added some shading. Professor Kurt came over to observe me. It was unnerving to have someone watch me.

"That's good, Jessie. You clearly have a knack for this kind of style. You have a good eye for sketching."

"Oh, thanks," I said shyly.

"If you don't mind, may I offer a suggestion?" he asked.

"Sure," I replied.

"Try not to go too dark, too quickly. Watch the tones. It helps to think of it like a black and white picture. In fact, do you have a camera phone?"

Then he looked at my hearing aids and recognition dawned on his face, "Oh my, I'm truly sorry. I didn't realize that you may not be able to use a phone."

"That's okay. I have an iPod, would that work?"

"Yes, that would be great. Would you mind getting it?" he asked.

While I searched for my iPod in my purse, he said to the class, "Okay, everyone. Come on over here for a moment. I'm going to show you a trick that can help see objects from a grayscale point of view."

Everyone peered around their easels to look at us, then there was a loud sound of scraping stools on the floor as they got up and walked over. I instantly felt embarrassed at the attention and suddenly became really nervous.

I turned on the iPod, thumbed on the camera mode, and gave it to him.

"Perfect," he said. "Okay, for those of you who are having trouble with the shading, particularly in regards to how dark you want to go, it helps to take a black and white photo of the subject you're drawing. This way, you can determine which areas are the darkest and which are lightest. Once you go super dark, it's difficult to go lighter, and the overall sketch can appear too muddy. You want to highlight the objects so that they pop out."

He held up my iPod, selected the mono tone setting, snapped a photo of it, and placed it near the sketchpad. He quickly added darker shading beneath the squash and along the edge of the stalks. His strokes added more definition, making them seem more realistic.

He looked at me. "Does that make sense for you, Jessie?"

I nodded.

"Go slowly, gradually going darker until you get the shade that you want, okay? Here you go." He handed me the iPod and earnestly said, "Good work."

Twenty minutes later, we took a break and stood up, stretching our arms and necks. I could feel the tension in my muscles between my shoulder blades.

Jackson came over to me, rolling his neck. "Whew! That's a lot of drawing," he said, rubbing his arm.

"I know and we still have several more classes this afternoon," I said, wriggling my fingers. "My fingers are going to go numb by the end of the day."

He squinted his eyes at me. "Speaking of which, you do realize that your hand and forearm are turning black?"

"What?" I glanced at my arm, the white sleeve was filthy. I was mortified.

He gestured at my clothing. "I think white is a bad idea here, gets dirty too quickly."

I sighed. "You're right. Is that why you wear black?"

He scoffed. "Heh, no. It's because I look good in it."

I rolled my eyes at him.

A slim guy with blond, shaggy hair and blue eyes approached us. He was wearing a ratty gray hoodie and light denim jeans with holes in them. I couldn't tell if they from being worn so much or if they were designer jeans. Jackson turned to face him, said hello, and asked what his name was.

"Hi! I'm Randy," he said, inclining his head.

"Hi, Randy, I'm Jackson and this is Jessie."

"Hey, nice to meet you folks," he said, giving us a nice smile. He kept his hands in the pocket of his hoodie.

I got the impression that he may be a bit shy.

"Where are you from?" Jackson asked Randy.

"Up north, near Sudbury," he replied.

"Cool. My cousins live up there. I've been to Science North," I said. "That's a fun place to visit."

"Yeah. My uncle helped design it. It's one of his favorite buildings."

"That's seriously cool!" I said.

His eyes fell on the FM receiver and he gestured at it with his hand.

"What is that?" he asked me.

"Oh! I'm hard of hearing. This is part of an FM system that helps me hear the teachers. Professor Kurt is wearing the microphone."

"Oh neat. How does it work?" he inquired.

"It amplifies the teacher's voice, reduces the background noise, and sends it wirelessly to my hearing aids through this box," I said.

"Oh! Like a Bluetooth," he said, raising his eyebrows as he figured it out.

I nodded. "Yep."

He peered at my head and looked at my ears. "Love the colors and bling on it."

"Thanks." I couldn't believe how down to earth he was. It was at that moment that I realized how different college was from high school.

"Wish Grandpa had one of those," he mused.

"Hearing aids?" I asked him.

"Yeah, he's having trouble hearing us but he won't get one," he replied.

I blinked. "Why not?"

He shrugged his shoulders. "Stigma. He doesn't want to admit to defeat."

"That's ridiculous. I've been wearing hearing aids since I was a kid. How's that any different?" I said.

"He seems to think that it would make him look older and look more like a handicapped person," he replied.

It felt like a blow to my stomach. Did that mean I looked like an old person?

He must've seen the expression on my face and quickly added, "Oh, don't worry. I didn't mean that it made you look handicapped in any way or, you know, old…" He trailed off.

"Now you can tell him that you have a classmate who wears hearing aids and see if that will change his mind," I said.

"I'll do that. Hope it works," he said, grinning.

After our break, we spent another thirty minutes finalizing our drawings. Professor Kurt went around the room, selecting some of the sketches and putting them up on the wall. I was surprised when he came over to my easel, grabbed the sheet, and added it to the collection.

"I put these sketches up here to show you what I'm looking for. It's a good example of composition, shading, and overall balance. They all have an interesting personality and a sense of uniqueness. I will be doing critiques and can go into more detail about what can be improved. You can collect your sketches next week. Good job, everyone, on your first attempt!"

Jackson came over to me as I was picking up my microphone from Professor Kurt. "We have a break, want to get our student ID's now?"

"Yeah, sure."

We went down a long hallway into a small office where there was already a long line up for the photo IDs. While we waited, he turned to face me. "I'm curious, do your hearing aids fix your hearing the way glasses do? You know, when you put glasses on, you have normal vision while wearing them."

I blinked, momentarily caught off guard. "Sadly, no. My ability to hear speech has been damaged so a lot of those sounds are gone. The hearing aids can only amplify a small amount since I don't have much residual hearing left. It's a very narrow band of sounds and frequencies that my hearing aids can pick up. I'm very lucky that I can hear this much, actually."

He nodded while he listened. "So, if we were to switch bodies, what would it be like for me to hear things from your perspective?"

I thought that was a very cool question, "Wow, that's kind of hard to explain. The best I can tell you is that it would probably sound very muddy or muffled, as if you had pillows covering your ears. With music, it would sound far away, as if you were sitting outside of the auditorium. When people talk, you would hear just a few words out of an entire sentence. You would miss a lot of information."

"Oh my. I had no idea," he replied.

"I don't think anyone truly gets it. It's not until they lose their hearing that they realize how much they took it for granted. It doesn't come back. It's gone, poof! Forever. Nothing will ever sound the same again."

"I'm sorry that it happened to you, Jessie. I can't even imagine being in your place. I don't know how you do it," he said solemnly.

"I think because it happened to me when I was a kid, I was able to adapt to it. I learned what worked for me. In a weird way, I cheated by growing up with it."

"Oh, okay. Yeah, that kind of makes sense when you put it that way," he said.

"It's still not easy but I do the best I can," I said, smiling.

"Well, from where I stand, you're doing an awesome job," he said.

"Thanks, Jackson."

We had our pictures taken and grabbed some lunch. Afterward, we had two more classes, painting and graphic design. By the time we got home, we were exhausted from our first day at school.

"At least we don't have homework," Jackson said.

"Yet," I said, sitting on the couch.

"True," he said. Then he padded over to the kitchen. "Guess it's time for supper, eh?"

I let out a heavy sigh, pushed myself off the couch, and followed him. Opening the fridge didn't reveal a lot except for left over mac and cheese. "Ooh! Want some of this?" I asked, pulling out the plastic container.

"Sure, we should add some vegetables. I think there's a microwavable bag in the freezer."

He rifled through the frozen shelf in the freezer, muttering to himself. "Aha! Let's see…cook on high for eight minutes," he said, squinting his eyes at the tiny instructions. "That's easy." He placed it on a plate, put it in the microwave, and pressed the buttons.

"I'll start heating this in the oven while we wait," I said and turned it on then began setting the table with plates and utensils.

It was beginning to feel more like home, and I felt comfortable having him here. After a few minutes, I began to have a nagging thought.

"Hey, Jackson?" I called out.

He came over to the table. "What?"

"Did you remember to put holes in the package?"

"Holes? What on earth for?"

Just then I heard a loud pop. We both ducked and Jackson said, "Was that a gun?"

We went into the kitchen. I closed one eye and gingerly opened the microwave door. There were bits of corn, carrots, and peas plastered all over the interior. I opened the door all the way to show Jackson. "That's why. They explode."

"Oops."

I snickered for a moment then grabbed a plastic spatula and began scraping it off the walls of the microwave. "You know, I'm sure it's fine to eat."

When we sat down, I cautiously tasted a spoonful of the mushy vegetables. It was a colorful collection that looked unappetizing but was still edible.

Chapter 14

GESTURES

A week later, I finally got a locker, grateful to have a place to put my stuff. The only thing I couldn't put in there was my portfolio. It was just too fricking large. Most of us left them in the classrooms, tucked away at the back.

We finished eating lunch and stepped into the next class. We hadn't met this teacher yet, it was a woman with a massive head of curly, gray hair. She wore a loose flowing shirt and denim skirt.

Ironically, she reminded me of Professor Trelawney from Harry Potter, who was equally as eccentric in terms of her personality and style.

When I gave her the microphone to wear, she didn't appear at all surprised. "Oh, yes, I've worn one of these before." She slipped it over her head. "Hello, dears. It's so lovely to see you today," she said as she did a broad sweep of the room then clapped her hands together. "Welcome to gesture drawing. Before I begin, did everyone pick up their required items for this class?"

Oops. I had forgotten to get some of them since the bookstore was closed yesterday.

She gathered up a stack of sheets and handed them out to

us. "Here's the complete list of books, as well as my personal recommendations."

As I perused the list, I'd idly wondered when I was going to find the time to read them all. Then one of the items caught my eye.

I raised my hand. "Um…Professor Murphy?"

She turned around. "Yes, dear?"

"Is this right? Grey's Anatomy? I'm not a medical student."

She gave me a level stare. "In order to draw people, we need to have a profound understanding of the human body." She took a deep breath. "Therefore, yes, we do need it."

"Okay," I whispered.

I saw Jackson, who was standing on my left, trying to hide a smile behind his hand. Then he looked at me and mouthed "Profound," obviously getting a kick out of the way she emphasized it.

She continued to explain the rules for this class. "Since we are studying the human body, we will be learning how to draw nude models."

The room suddenly went quiet. Everyone gave each other nervous glances.

"To protect the models privacy, you are strictly forbidden from taking any photos, and that includes your cell phones and various mobile devices. Is that understood?"

She looked around the room, giving us all a stern glare. I gulped loudly.

"I want everyone to grab an easel and clip on your sketch pads. I will bring in the model."

The room came alive once again as everyone began unpacking their gear, the wooden easels scraping across the floors and a general murmur of people talking.

A few minutes later she came back in with a young man who was just a few years older than me. He looked like a model for Abercrombie and Fitch. He had long blond hair in the front, shorter in the back. He had strong cheekbones, square jaw, and green eyes. He strode in wearing a blue bathrobe and flip flops. She placed a chair in the middle of the raised platform in the center of the room and gestured for him to sit in it. He stepped out of his flip flops, casually peeled off his bathrobe, and sat down. His skin was tanned and his muscles rippled as he moved. I got the impression that he was an athlete.

Professor Murphy grabbed a bright halogen lamp on a freestanding pole and moved it around to face the model. She stood in front of an easel and clipped on a sheet of paper. "Gather around me everyone."

I saw Jackson flick his eyes at me then at model, back at me. His grin grew wider. It was evident that he was happy with this class and gave me a thumbs up.

We all formed a semi-circle around her. Some of the students looked awkward, crossing their arms on their chest or placing them in their jean pockets, rocking back and forth nervously.

"Today, we're going to do use charcoal sticks. A rule of thumb is to use a lighter shade first to capture the feel and gesture of the figure then gradually adding more shading with a darker color." She glanced at the model then back at the paper, quickly doing broad strokes. A simple gesture of the model's body began to appear. "Don't forget about composition, otherwise you may run out of room. Decide if you want to capture their entire body or perhaps focus on the upper body and face. It's up to you and what you feel comfortable doing."

While she spoke, she demonstrated how to do perspective and general shapes of the body. Several minutes later, we all went back to our easels. I walked around the model, trying to decide which angle interested me, picked the spot I liked, and set my easel there. I took a deep breath, with my hand poised over the sketch pad and looked at the model. It was almost as if he was staring right at me, and I suddenly became shy and felt uncomfortably warm. I hoped that I wasn't blushing. This was my first time drawing a nude person, and the last thing I wanted to do was end up with a horrible sketch. My eyes roamed over him while I tried to decide how much to draw, my gaze slowed down to just beneath his torso and lingered a bit too long in that…ahem…area. I quickly blinked my eyes and diverted my attention elsewhere for a long moment. I did a very quick gesture the way Professor Murphy showed us. After what felt like an hour, I took a step back and scrutinized it. I realized that the proportions were off. His head looked too small and his legs were huge in comparison to the rest of his body. I was disappointed with my sketch and wanted to crumble it up and throw it away.

Thankfully, Professor Murphy called a break, and everyone put down their charcoal sticks. We all stood back and did some stretches, trying to ease the tension in our muscles. Several people began to mingle and chatter. I padded over to Jackson and took a look at his sketch. It was gorgeous. Everything was perfectly balanced and the proportion looked just right. He was a natural at this.

"Wow! Jackson, you are really talented at sketching people," I said.

He smiled. "Thank you, darling. He's so dreamy, isn't he?"

I snorted. "Yes, he is. Don't you already have a boyfriend?"

"Of course, but that doesn't mean I can't appreciate the finer things in life, like him," he replied, gesturing at the model who was putting his robe back on.

"Uh-huh," I replied cheekily.

The model was standing up and doing some stretches then began walking around the room, looking at the sketches. He would smile and nod his head as he went by the easels. When he came over to Jackson's easel, he stood for a long moment with a finger on his lips. "Wonderful work. You have an excellent grasp of the gesture of the human body. It's not easy to do, especially for first years."

"Oh my, thank you kindly. Are you an artist too?" Jackson asked him.

"Yes, I am. Third year in Illustration," he replied, not even remotely embarrassed about being practically naked and chatting with us.

"Really? That's awesome," I said.

He smiled. "I like doing this, helping out. Plus the money helps me pay for my art supplies. By the way, I'm Cole," he said, reaching out to shake our hands.

"I'm Jessie and this is Jackson," I replied.

"How do you hold a pose for such a long time?" inquired Jackson.

"As long as I have something to rest my arms and legs on, I'm okay. It's a bit like meditation, I have to zone out for a while. It takes practice," he replied earnestly.

"Doesn't your tushy get sore?" I asked.

Jackson gave me a bemused stare.

"What? I'm curious," I said.

"Ha! Sometimes, that's why I get up and walk around. I can get a bit stiff."

I saw the corner of Jackson's mouth curl upward in a devilish grin. His gaze slid downward at Cole.

I decided to divert Jackson's attention and change the topic. "How do you like Illustration?" I asked Cole.

He gave me a broad smile. "Love it. Mind you, it wasn't easy the first year and it was a lot of work. As long as you stay focused and disciplined, you'll do okay."

He put the emphasis on the word "lot," and that scared me for a moment. What did I get myself into?

"Any particular area that you like?" Jackson asked Cole.

"Um…painting. I find it to be an exciting challenge," he replied.

"I gotta ask you, how do you stay in such great shape?" asked Jackson.

That question didn't surprise me.

"Rowing," Cole replied. "There's a club in the city that I go to. Even though our professors discourage us from doing sports, I needed an outlet and time away from the heavy workload."

I blinked. "Wait. What? Why aren't we allowed to do sports?"

"They think it's too much of a distraction," he said.

I raised my eyebrows. "That's ridiculous."

"I know, but I do get their point of view. They're strict about having our assignments being handed in on time. Unfortunately, that doesn't stop people from partying." He shrugged his shoulders. "The professors are trying to enforce the importance of being on time, since missing advertising deadlines can be costly."

"Costly? What do you mean?" I asked him.

"When a business rents space for advertising, such as a billboard, the artwork needs to be available on the date they request it, otherwise they stand to lose hundreds or thousands of dollars for an empty space. All it takes is missing one deadline, and you'll never be hired from them again. As a freelance artist, we can't afford to do that. With jobs, it can be a bit of a hit or miss, and you may go for many weeks without a paying job. That's what they are trying to get us ready for, a tough job market."

I gulped, suddenly feeling more like a grown-up. "Oh, I had no idea."

"Neither did I until one of my professors told us about his experiences. They're trying to bring in more real world situations for us to go through. They will even give us the same assignments that they had for their jobs. It's pretty cool, actually."

"Holy cheese and crackers, now I'm scared," I replied.

"Don't be, you'll get used to it. And don't worry, the exercises are fun to do," he said with a smile.

"All right, folks, break is over. Let's get back to work," said Professor Murphy.

Not surprisingly, Jackson's sketch was selected to go on the wall at the end of class after we had our critiques.

On our way over to the next class, Jackson asked me, "Hey, want to go to a karaoke bar tonight? Some of the other guys are going."

"Sure, I've never done that. Sounds like fun," I replied.

After we got home, we changed into more decent clothes since we were covered in paint and smears of dark charcoal. My hands were literally black from doing so many sketches, and I had to scrub them clean. I stood in front of the closet, looking for a nice jacket to wear. I didn't bring very many clothes with me when I moved in and really didn't have much in the way of a stylish wardrobe. Jackson came in pulling on his trademark black leather jacket which suited him extremely well. It brought out his eyes and enhanced his already handsome features. He was ridiculously good looking.

"Are you ready to go yet?" he asked while adjusting the collar of his jacket.

I gave out a big sigh. "No, I can't find a nice jacket to wear," I said.

He came over, slid the hangers across my selection of clothes and pulled out a black and white scarf adorned with glittering, silver stars. He draped it around my neck. "Let's start with this." He took a step back, surveyed me. "Hang on a sec, I have an idea," he said and left the room. He strolled back in and handed me a dark gray leather jacket. "Try this on."

"Really? Are you sure?" I said.

He nodded. I grabbed it and shrugged it on. I was surprised at how comfortable it was. It felt like warm butter. "What do you think?"

"It suits you," he replied clapping his hands together.

"Do you really think so?"

"Yes, darling. Go look in the mirror in the bathroom and you'll see what I mean."

I went into the bathroom, glanced at the large mirror, and was pleasantly surprised at how different I looked. The leather jacket gave me a more sophisticated air.

"Wow," I said quietly.

"See? You look fabulous, dear," said Jackson.

"Thank you, that's very kind of you to lend me your jacket."

"Okay, let's go have some fun!" he replied.

We got into the car, drove out of the driveway, past the duplexes. It still felt strange to be living in the city. I missed being in the countryside where I could see the changes of the seasons and watch the animals stroll around on our property. The more I thought about it, the more I missed Mom and Dad, and Parker and Serena.

Jackson drove through the traffic at a speedy pace. He certainly drove faster than me, and I was trying hard not to stomp on the imaginary brake. The sky was growing dark, with shades of twilight blue and lavender. The clouds turned a dark purple shade as the sun disappeared behind the horizon. Lights blinked on in the buildings that reminded me of tiny, floating lanterns. The street lamps flickered on with an orange glow.

"Will you be going home this weekend?" he asked as he came to a stop at the lights.

I was grateful for the soft glow of the city lights since I was having trouble hearing him and struggled to lip read him in the darkening car.

"Next week, Mom and Dad got me a train ticket."

"Cool. I can drop you off at the train station, let me know when you're leaving," he replied.

"Sure, that would be great," I said.

"Will you be visiting your boyfriend?" he asked me.

"No, although we might see each other during class," I said.

"Class?" he said, giving me a bemused look. "Class for what?"

"Oh, you don't know. I have a black belt in karate, I'm one of the instructors."

He turned his head sharply at me, his eyes grew wide. "A black belt? Oh my! You can protect me anytime."

I snorted.

"How long did it take to get it?" he asked.

"About three years," I replied.

"Impressive! Is that how you met him?"

I wagged my head. "Sort of. His father was my self-defense teacher in high school."

"That is supremely cool. I think you're the first person that I've met who has a black belt," he said, flicking on the turn signal then turning right. "So, did you guys officially break up?"

"Not necessarily. Just taking time off."

"I'm sorry to hear that. Well, I'm here to listen to if you ever need someone to talk to," he said.

"Thanks, Jackson."

He turned left onto a large parking lot that was more than half full. We found an empty slot and pulled into it. As we got of the car, the air was crisp and smelled of exhaust and stale beer. We walked over to the main doors and pulled them open. We were immediately assaulted with loud, thumping music. I could literally feel the pulse, particularly the bass, pounding against my chest. My hearing aids squealed, the loudness creating a feedback in them. I quickly reached up and turned down the volume.

There were several round tables on our right, the bar was situated on the left, and I could see a couple of pool tables along the wall. At the back was a small stage with a microphone. Someone was already on the stage singing, watching a screen off to the side, I assumed they were following the words. Jackson's eyes roamed around the room, searching for his friends, then he spotted them. He waved at a group at the far end of the room near the stage. They waved back enthusiastically.

"There they are! Come on, let's join them," he said, grabbing my hand and pulling me along past a throng of people.

Once we reached them, Jackson introduced me to them and we all shook hands. We sat down and spent a few minutes watching a couple of people sing on stage. I narrowed my eyes at them and realized that they seemed a bit tipsy.

I nudged Jackson's elbow with mine, titled my chin at the karaoke singers. "Is it my imagination, or are they drunk?"

He glanced at them then back at me, nodding. "Yes. And out of tune. Way out of tune." He flapped his hand to convey distance and grimaced.

I snorted and gave him a thumbs up. "It's loud in here, eh?"

"Yes! Are you able to turn them down?" he asked, gesturing at my hearing aids.

"I already did," I replied, raising my voice as the drunk singers belted out a particularly high tone that was painful to hear.

"Man, I wish I could do that. They're killing me," he said.

We ordered our drinks and snacks. I tried to follow the conversation as it bounced rapidly around the table from person to person. I felt like a referee watching a tennis match as my eyes ping-ponged back and forth. I could barely hear what they were saying, the music overwhelmed their voices. As far as I could tell, they were talking about where they came from and how they became interested in their programs at school.

Finally, the drunken couple was ushered off the stage by someone who, I assumed, was the manager. He was tall and slim and wore jeans and a long-sleeved black shirt with a black leather vest over top. His long black hair was slicked back, and he reminded me of the actor Nicholas Cage. He stood in front of the microphone. "Okay, folks, now it's time for Comedy Hour! Please welcome our guests tonight. Let's give them a round of applause." He raised his hands and began clapping. "Stephanie is our comedienne tonight," he said, gesturing to a woman wearing a sparkly black tank top and pants. Her hair was held up with chopsticks. "The stage is all yours, darling," he said.

My heart sank when she began to speak. She had a heavy accent and spoke very quickly, which made it hard for me to understand her. I leaned forward on my chair, straining to hear her over the laughter of the crowd. I sighed deeply when I realized that it was futile. I was missing the punchline and not laughing along with everyone else. I smiled politely from time to time, unsure of how to react. My frustration was growing, and I was mentally cursing myself for agreeing to come here in the first place. This was one of those times when I really missed Ethan. He would've gladly signed to me or repeated the jokes clearly. I began to truly regret the decision to take time off from him. I had to accept that responsibility and learn to live with it. I didn't expect it to be this hard, and I realized that I had taken a lot of things for granted with him. It was a bitter pill to swallow.

By the third comedian, Jackson nudged my elbow and gave me a concerned look. "Not funny enough for you?"

I reached up and tapped my ear. "I can't hear what they're saying."

He reached out and placed his hand on my shoulder. "Oh. I'm sorry. I didn't think about that."

"Don't worry about it. It's my fault, I didn't know how hard it would be for me. At least I tried," I said, shrugging my shoulders.

"Do you want to go?" he asked, mouthing the words at me.

"No. I don't want to ruin this for everyone else."

"I think they're almost done, anyways."

He was right. Ten minutes later, they switched back to karaoke.

"Hey, Jessie, want to go up?" Jackson asked.

I was mortified and my eyes grew wide in alarm, "Seriously? No. I'm tone deaf. Literally."

"You're funny!" he said, "You should be a comedian."

I gave him a level stare. "I'm being honest, not funny." After a long pause, I said, "Hey, why don't you get on the stage?"

To my surprise, Jackson and one of the people sitting with us got up and dashed over to the stage. It turned out that Jackson sang better than most people. When he came back to our table, I gave him a playful punch on the shoulder. "You cheeky monkey! I had no idea that you were so good!"

"I was actually kind of rusty," he replied. "Come on, let's dance," he said, grabbing my hand and pulling me to the middle of the floor into the crowd of people. "Don't worry about the lyrics, just dance with me," he said, enunciating the words.

We danced for a while until I realized how it late it was getting. "I think we should go. It's getting awfully late," I said to Jackson.

"I think you're right, dear. We do need our beauty sleep," he replied.

We went back to the table, said our goodbyes to everyone, then walked outside into the cool night. It was suddenly so quiet that I wondered if my hearing aid batteries died.

"Wow! That was loud," Jackson remarked.

We walked through the maze of cars, trying to remember where we parked. A strange feeling crept over me and the hair on the back of my neck stood up. I was getting the feeling that we were being followed. Jackson was moving at faster pace and was already ahead of me. I could've sworn I heard something. I tried to listen but didn't hear anything, except the noise of the traffic and sirens throughout the city.

Suddenly, someone grabbed my shoulder and jerked me backward. I turned my head and saw a man wearing a red plaid shirt that was untucked, slouching jeans, and construction boots. He was pulling on my jacket, trying to get me closer to him. "Hey, honey," he said, slurring his words. "Want to come home with me?"

"No, thank you," I said and shrugged away from him.

I started to walk away from him when he grabbed my shoulder again, more aggressively this time. I quickly spun around, pinned his arm to my ribcage, grabbed his throat with my other hand, and slammed him into a nearby car. "I said no!" I told him in a firm voice.

He gave me a stunned look then relaxed and continued to grab at me with his other hand.

"You want it rough? That's fine with me," I said, feeling my anger rise.

I let him go and gave him a disgusted sigh, backing away from him. He lurched at me again. This time, I sidestepped him, grabbing his outstretched hand in the process. I gave it a sharp twist and flung him to the ground. He gave out a yell as he landed with a thud. That seemed to wake him up a bit. He appeared more sober after the impact.

Angrily, I said to him, "Walk away from me right now." I let go of his hand.

He nodded in scared, jerky motions, then scampered to get up, stumbling as he walked away holding onto his injured hand.

I noticed that Jackson was standing beside me. "I think you left your manhood on the ground here, honey!" he yelled at the man.

I snickered then realized that my hands were shaking. The adrenalin was coursing through my body like lightning. I was amped up.

"Oh my, that was so Jackie Chan of you," Jackson said.

I burst out laughing, grateful for his presence.

Chapter 15

FELLOWSHIP

I was in the hallway, practicing one of my katas, going through the moves when Jackson approached me from the kitchen, carrying a tall glass. I was in warrior mode, feeling strong and powerful, doing sweeping blocks, hard punches, and fast kicks. On the last punch, I gave out a loud shout, a strong kiai which startled him. He flinched and nearly dropped the glass he was holding, the ice cubes rattling in it. He scrambled to catch it, splashing the liquid over the sides.

I started laughing at his comedic timing then noticed that he was wearing a large apron that covered most of his body. All I saw were his bare legs peeking out from the hem.

I pointed at Jackson's legs and said in between laughs, "You look naked!"

He gave me a sultry grin. "Guess I'm just too hot."

The way he said it made it sound like a double entendre.

I laughed even harder when he said that, gasping in between in breaths.

As our laughter died down to a snicker, he asked me, "What in the name of all things holy were you doing?"

"Oh, that. I was practicing my kata. It's a series of moves that help refine our reflexes."

"It scared the crap out of me, especially when you yelled."

It was my turn to give him a sly grin. "Good. That means I did it right."

"Is it like meditation?" he asked.

"In a way, yeah. I do feel better afterward, more in focus."

There was a sudden, muted bang. Jackson had developed a reputation for his cooking, or lack thereof, and I gave him exasperated sigh.

"What are you trying to cook now?"

He slapped his palm over his forehead. "Oops," he said then went into the kitchen.

I was relieved to see that he was wearing shorts and was not, in fact, naked. He opened the microwave door to reveal that the walls were covered in lumpy bits of potato.

I turned to face him. "Ew. Did you poke holes in the potato before you put it in?"

"Was I supposed to?" he said.

I groaned. "Yes. Otherwise they explode," I said dryly.

"Oh, cool. I mean, my bad," he replied.

"No offense, but I thought gay people were good cooks?"

"No, not really. We do love a good dinner party, though. We're big on gossip and friendship and essentially having a good time," he replied, giving me cheeky grin.

"Uh-huh," I said and grabbed several paper towels. I started cleaning out the microwave. "Hot! Hot!" I exclaimed as I scooped out the potato and tossed it into the trash can.

We opted for a frozen pizza and heated it up in the oven. I went back upstairs to my room and finished working on my sketch of bones for Professor Murphy. She had us doing detailed pencil sketches of the skull, humerus, and the radius and ulna. I had asked her why we were doing these kind of drawings and she said that it was for those of us who were interested in doing medical illustrations. She went on to say that not everyone liked doing these and it wouldn't be until they tried it out that they realized it didn't suit them. I thought it was fascinating. It didn't bother me at all to be sketching bones but it didn't really inspire me to consider that particular field.

Not yet, anyways.

She told me that it would take time to truly figure what I liked and that the passion had to come from my heart. So far, I'd learned that I sucked at drawing models. It really intimidated me. I was more comfortable drawing inanimate objects and animals.

There was a sketch pad on my bed along with pencils and erasers. My laptop sat beside it, and I had Netflix on pause. I pressed play, picked up my sketch book, and went back to adding more shading on the skull.

I had no idea how much time had passed until Jackson came in and told me that the pizza was ready. He stood by the bed and gestured at the laptop. "Doesn't that hurt your ears? It sounds really tinny." He shuddered as he spoke.

"I know but it's the best I can do," I replied.

"What do you mean? Can't you just plug in your headset?"

"What headset?" I asked.

"The FM system you wear in class."

"I don't know, I haven't tried it," I said.

My purse was on the floor beside the bed. I bent over and lugged it up to me. After a minute of rifling through it, I found it and pulled it out. He came over, examined it, then looked at the laptop, putting them side by side, comparing the outlets.

"The headset plug on your computer looks like the same one on your receiver. Did it come with a wire that you can plug in?"

I pondered that, got up, went through the drawers in my desk, and pulled out a bag of wires.

"Would any of these work?" I said, giving him the bag.

"Let's find out," he replied. He rustled through the bag,

plugging in the wires, switching to another one, then re-marked, "Et voila!"

"It fits? No way," I said.

He nodded. "Turn on your receiver and see if it works."

I eagerly looped the cord over my head and powered it on. Instantly I could hear the show stream through my hearing aids. I was ecstatic.

"Oh, wow! Thanks, Jackson, for helping me figure that out."

He shrugged his shoulders. "Glad I could help."

"How did you know about stuff like this?" I said, pausing the laptop.

"My mom, she always has trouble figuring out to use electronics, especially with the wires. Guess it's a girl thing," he replied, smirking.

"Hey!"

I grabbed my pillow and chucked it at him. He ducked and it flew over his head.

"I wonder…can I see your receiver and iPod?" he asked.

"Sure," I replied and gave them to him.

He unplugged the jack from the laptop and plugged it into the iPod. "Hmm, they fit," he said, raising his eyebrows in surprise.

"Seriously? Sweet."

"Do you have any movies or videos on your iPod?"

"Yeah, I think I do. Want me to try it out?" I asked.

He nodded. "Go for it."

I looped it back over my head, scrolled through my iPod, and found a music video that Ethan had added. I pressed play and was thrilled when I suddenly could hear it in my hearing aids. I was in awe. "That's so freaking cool!"

"Awesome," he said. He tilted his chin at the iPod. "You should put some TV shows or movies on it for the train rides."

"That's a great idea, I'll do that for sure. I hope they're captioned, though."

"I hope so too," he replied, giving me a kind smile.

We went downstairs and ate our pizza while I scrolled through iTunes, looking for closed captioned movies and muttering, "Cool!" once in a while.

Jackson watched me, giving me a thumbs up.

When I reached for another slice of pizza, there was a sudden flash outside the window followed by a loud bang. The table rumbled beneath my fingers. I looked up in concern, flinching from the light.

Jackson saw my reaction. "Are you okay?"

"Yeah. I don't like storms."

"Oh. They don't bother me."

"Ever since we had a tornado at school a couple of years ago, I've been terrified of storms. I think it's because I couldn't hear my teachers or understand what was going on."

"Aha. Gotcha," he said.

The lights flickered, dimmed, then came back on. I had to suppress a groan and managed not to crawl under the table in fear. I gulped loudly, gripping the edge of the table so tightly that my knuckles were turning white.

Jackson's eyes flicked to the ceiling, then he looked nervously around the room. "Are there any flashlights around here?"

I got up and walked around the kitchen and dining room, pulling out drawers and rifling through them. There wasn't even a candle or matches anywhere. I was getting more nervous by the minute. There was another loud bang that made me freeze on the spot. The lights faltered and dimmed even more this time.

Jackson came into the living room, peered around the glass cabinet at me. "There might be a flashlight downstairs, we should go look."

I looked at him bewilderment. "We have a basement?"

He nodded. "Yeah, under the stairs."

Of course it's under the stairs, I thought. I wondered how dark and creepy it was and shuddered. I followed him out to the hallways and saw the door that he described.

"Weird, I've never noticed that before," I said.

"I was curious one day and happened to find it," he replied.

There was another flash and loud crash, I flinched harder this time and nearly screamed.

"Coming?" he asked, gesturing at the door.

I had a sudden thought. "Hang on a sec," I said and went into the kitchen. I quickly rummaged through the shelves and cabinets, found what I was looking for, grabbed it, and stood by Jackson.

He gave me a wry look and pointed at my hand. "What are you doing?"

I held up the large canister. "You know—just in case there's something spooky down there."

He snorted. "Really? Who are you channeling, Sam or Dean?"

I chose to ignore that comment and held it close to my chest. "It makes me feel better."

"Fine. Can we go now?" he said.

I nodded, waiting anxiously. He gripped the door knob and gave it a twist. The hinges gave out a loud, eerie creak as pulled it open. I gulped nervously and inched my way over to the threshold. I peered down the narrow stairs. It was so dark that I couldn't even see the bottom. We went down a couple of steps, gingerly feeling our way. There was a massive bang and rumbling throughout the walls. The lights suddenly winked out, plunging us into darkness. I reached out and grabbed onto Jackson's shoulder. I felt him move forward, taking a tentative step down. I could feel his shoulders shifting. He was reaching for something, touching the walls perhaps. I did the same, stretching out one arm to feel the side of the wall. We continued to go down the steps, more slowly this time.

Then something brushed against my face. I jerked backward violently, spluttering. "What the—"

I felt it again, that eerie sensation across my face. I reached up and touched my hair and felt something in it. I wanted to scream. My heart hammered like a drum against my chest. Then I felt something brush against me.

I jumped then yelled, "Recedo!" and sprayed the salt in the air in the shape of a cross. There was a loud scream then I was frantically being pushed backward out in the hallway.

Jackson and I landed in a tangled heap on the floor, he was muttering and cursing to himself.

Then I had a sudden thought. I turned on my iPod and clicked on the mini flashlight, shone it on Jackson. He had his hands over his eyes, obviously in pain.

"Gah!"

"What's wrong, Jackson?"

"You got salt in my eyes. Ugh!" he said then removed his hands, clenching them into fists. His eyes were bright red and he was furiously blinking them as tears ran down his face.

I grimaced and sucked in my breath. "Sorry about that."

He yanked the can of salt out of my hands. "Gimme that! No more *Supernatural* for you."

I offered my iPod as a peace offering. "Want to use this?"

"Grrr!" he growled at me between his teeth and snatched it away from me. "What didn't you think of this before we went down the stairs?"

"I don't know. I just thought of it now."

He gave out an exasperated sigh then turned around and aimed it at the door. He grumpily pushed himself up and headed over to the edge. The beam of light illuminated the steps. I gingerly followed him as he headed down the stairs. I peered over his shoulder, trying to see where we were going. The tiny cone of light didn't extend very far. We finally reached the bottom, and I nearly missed the last step, fumbling to feel the floor with my foot. I reached out to grab something and stumbled into Jackson.

"Sorry."

Jackson scanned the light across the room. The basement was filled with boxes along one wall, stacked right to the ceiling. There was a washer and dryer on the left and a small work bench on the far right. We headed over to it in search for a flashlight. We found a battery powered Coleman lantern and turned on the button. It flickered on, casting a cool circle of light around us. I grasped the handle and held it up in the air, looking around the room. There was a flashlight on the shelf above the bench, Jackson picked it up and tried flicking it on. Nothing happened. There was a flash in the narrow window above us followed by a dull rumble. I clenched my teeth and shivered, rattling the lantern. We continued looking around and didn't find any more flashlights or batteries.

"What kind of person doesn't have backup batteries or flashlights?" I remarked.

"City people," Jackson replied.

"So, can we go back up? It's getting super creepy down here."

"Guess so," he said.

I quickly paced across the floor and scampered up the stairs. The house was completely dark. I wasn't in the mood to eat any more pizza and put it into the fridge.

"Want to trade?" I asked Jackson.

We switched the lamp and iPod and headed upstairs, stumbling occasionally on the steps.

"It's a shame that we don't have a fireplace here. We could've roasted some marshmallows and traded ghost stories," he said, holding up the lamp near his face.

"I know! That would've been so cool. Oh, wait, I have something on my iPod. Hang on a sec while I find it." I swiped the screen, found the app, pressed play, and showed it to him. Flames flickered on the screen.

"You have a fireplace app? Sweet," he said. "Now we can chat by the fireplace."

I nodded. "Well, we definitely can't do our homework in the dark, anyways."

We sat on the carpet in my room, made a mini table with a stack of books, and placed the lamp on top. I put the iPod on the floor between us, turned up the volume to hear the crackle and pop of the fire. Jackson put out his hands, pretending to warm them. I snickered.

"You know, I just realized that if the power doesn't come back on, it's going to get cold in here."

"Oh yeah, you're right. We should wear warm layers when we go to bed," he replied.

"Just like summer camp," I added.

"Are you looking forward to going back home?" he asked.

"Yeah. It would be nice to take my mind off school."

"Have you thought about what to do with Ethan?" he said.

My heart clenched painfully and a cold chill went through me. "I'm not sure."

He looked at me in concern. "You know, sometimes the hardest thing to do is forgive someone, even if it means forgiving yourself first. I've had to learn to embrace myself in order to let everyone else accept me."

I thought long and hard about that and wondered if he was right, that I needed to find forgiveness.

"I know it's not easy," he continued when I didn't respond. "Believe me. It took my father a long time to accept me. And there were still some people who didn't want to have anything to do with me when I came out. I found out very quickly who were my true friends."

I heaved a deep sigh. "It's just that my life changed so quickly, and I'm having a hard time accepting it. I've been going through a lot of self-reflection."

I stared at the flickering fire, transfixed by the golden flames.

"You know, having someone there for us can give us the strength to move forward," he said.

I tilted my head at him. "How did you get to be so smart?"

"Experience. Lots of mistakes and good friends," he replied.

I smiled, my chest feeling lighter already. "I think that fate set this up for us, that it was meant to happen."

"That wouldn't surprise me in the least bit," he said.

"You know what's strange? I rarely see Shirley here."

"She said that she traveled a lot and worked long hours," he said.

"Oh, I didn't realize that."

"She said that she feels better knowing that we're here all the time," he added.

We talked a little bit longer and, when it became obvious that the power wasn't going to come back on anytime soon, we decided it was time for bed. I took a chilly sponge bath, which left goosebumps on my body, and quickly pulled on my pajamas. I scooted back into my room, shivering, and grabbed a pair of socks to put on. I snuggled under the covers, trying to maintain some warmth, and finally fell asleep.

I was rudely shaken awake a short time later. I blinked opened my eyes to find Jackson standing over me, holding the Coleman lantern near his face. He was frantically gesturing at my hearing aids that sat on the bedside table.

"What's wrong Jackson?"

He gingerly picked up one of them and handed it to me. I looked at him in confusion. He pointed to his ears and mouthed, "It's still on!"

I was mortified. I looked at my hearing aid, turning it over in my hand, and realized that the battery door was closed, this meant that it was still turned on. It would've given off a high-pitched squeal, like a shrill alarm. I quickly yanked open the battery door which would've shut it down, then checked the other one. "I'm so sorry! I didn't know it was still on."

He yawned, waved his hand at me sleepily, then slumbered back to his room.

When I woke up, the power was back on. I had no idea how long it had been on. I put on my hearing aids and got up. It was still chilly in the house, and I wrapped a blanket around me and headed downstairs. Jackson was in the kitchen, sitting at the table surrounded by several fashion magazines.

"Morning. What'cha doing?" I asked him.

He looked up at me and gave me a wicked grin. His eyes were bloodshot, either from the salt or lack of sleep. I'd surmised it was probably from both.

"I'm going to play a prank on Cody."

I blinked. "Cody? Why?"

"Because he deserves it," he replied.

I took a guess. "Is this because he's so good looking?"

"Yep," he said, smiling even more.

Cody was one of our classmates, a beefy guy with broad shoulders and thick forearms. He always wore a heavy, silver watch that looked expensive and he was a classy dresser, as if he belonged to a yacht club. He could've easily been a model and I wondered if he done that when he was younger. He walked with a confident strut and always seemed to be at ease, perfectly poised.

I loved Jackson's idea and immediately sat down and began clipping out half naked models wearing nothing but underwear or pajama bottoms. I found one in a provocative pose and showed it to Jackson.

"Ha! That's perfect," he exclaimed.

"So, where are you going to put these?" I asked him while clipping out another one.

"All over his locker, from top to bottom," he replied cheekily.

I began laughing, tears running out of the corners of my eyes. I could visually see that in my mind. After we were finished, we gathered all of the clipped images and placed them in a large envelope, snickering and chortling.

We had breakfast, got changed, and headed over to school early. We taped up as many of the cut outs as we could. It was quite a sight to behold, and we eagerly rushed down the hall and hid around the corner. While we waited, several of our classmates joined us, peering over our shoulders in curiosity. Cody came down the hallway, giving quizzical glances at the people walking past him. He came to a halt in front of his locker, completely dumbstruck, then ran his palm over his face. Several people walked past him, snickering.

He turned and saw us watching, raised his hand upward, and said, "Oh come on!"

We cheered, gave each other high fives, then headed over to our respective classes in good spirits.

Chapter 16

JOURNEY

I tried not to fall down the stairs as I carried the suitcase, eager to go home. Just as I reached the bottom step, the door suddenly swung open, and Shirley came in carrying *her* suitcase. Her red hair was done up at the back and loose tendrils fell across her face. She wore a dark gray business suit, black high-heeled boots, and a long black jacket over top. Leaning against the wall, she unzipped her boots and dumped them on the mat by the door, letting out a sigh of relief.

It had been a long time since I had seen her. We kept missing each other because she typically came home late at night, long after I had gone to bed, or left early in the morning, before I went to school. It was such a rare sight to see her that I was genuinely surprised.

She looked tired and her clothes were rumbled, the overall appearance making her look older.

"Hi, Shirley. Wow, it's been awhile since I've seen you."

"Oh, hey, Jessie. Sorry, I've been so busy lately. The company has me doing more traveling than usual," she said. Her eyes gave a quick, cursory glance around the room. "At least the house is still standing."

"So far," Jackson replied.

I smirked and bit my lip from saying anything else. I'd hoped that she didn't know about Jackson's habit of exploding things and the mess he left behind in the oven and microwave.

"Well, I'm going to take a long, hot bath," she said, edging past me.

"Okay. We're on way to the train station, maybe I'll see you when I get back?"

She nodded wearily and went up the stairs.

Jackson and I headed outside.

I hefted my suitcase in the back seat and climbed into the front. "I don't think I've ever seen her look that tired before."

"She did look rather beat didn't she?" he remarked as he slid behind the steering wheel and turned on the ignition.

"I hope that she doesn't have a fit about the kitchen," I said.

He snorted. "We did clean it," he said. Then after a beat, he added, "Many times."

Jackson pulled into the parking lot at the train station.

"Thanks, Jackson," I said. "I'll see you in a few days."

He winked at me and gave me a cheerful smile. "Have fun!"

"Try not to explode anything," I said, stepping out of the car and grabbing my suitcase.

He snorted, waved at me, then drove away. I turned around and went into the cavernous lobby. There were about twenty people sitting in the plastic chairs and benches, most of them reading newspapers or scrolling through their phones, their eyes cast down. There was a loud burst of static overhead then a jumble of unintelligible words. I had no idea what they said. They might as well be speaking elvish from *The Hobbit*. The large ceiling and glossy marble floors bounced the sounds all over the place, creating a strange echo.

I strode over to the monitor by the ticket booth and glanced up at the screen. I was relieved to see that the train was on time. There was a man behind the glass in the booth. I walked up to him. He looked up and gave me a polite smile. "May I help you?"

"I hope so. I can't hear the announcements, would you be able to tell me when it arrives?"

He gave me a perplexed stare. "What do you mean?"

I turned my head to the side and gestured at my hearing aids.

"Oh! You have a hearing loss. Gotcha. Um, the best I can do is wave at you just before it comes. Most of the trains are usually on time but don't worry, you won't miss it."

I wasn't entirely convinced that he would remember, but I appreciated his candor. "Thank you."

I sat down at the nearest bench where I could see him and pulled out my iPod. The station had free Wi-Fi so I texted Mom to let her know I was at waiting for the train.

Great! Text me when you get closer to home okay?
Will do.

I spent some time watching people, wondering where they were going and what their lives were like. Did they have children or grandchildren, were they on their way to meet them? Some of the travelers were my age, and I wondered if they were going home for the weekend, like me. I curiously watched them, noting their behavior and body language. After spending so much studying anatomy and drawing models, I became acutely aware of how people walked and the way their clothes fit as well as their facial expressions. I was seeing the world from a different perspective.

After a while, I realized that the ticket agent was waving at me. I went up to the window. He gestured toward the wide doors facing the tracks. "The train should be arriving soon. There is a waiting area outside."

"Thanks, I'll do that."

I grabbed the handle of my suitcase and pulled it alongside me, the wheels bumping against the bricked ground outside. There were already several people lined up by the tracks. I joined them, watching for the train. Within a few minutes of waiting anxiously, I saw a glimmer of light in my direction. It grew in size as it came closer. I could feel the ground beneath my feet vibrate. Soon after, the train roared up to us, sending a blast of wind in my face, sweeping my hair across my eyes. The sound of the engine was intense, rumbling against my ears. It slowed to a stop with a piercing shriek. Several station attendants stepped out of the cars, placed small step stools on the ground, and helped the passengers off. As I walked over to a line that formed at one of the cars, I came face to face with an attendant, a man close to my father's age. He wore a long overcoat with the train's logo, black slacks, and shiny boots. I told him the name of the city where I was headed.

"Turn to the right and go down the aisle when you get to the top of the steps," he said loudly then gestured for me to proceed up the stairs.

"Okay." I went up, stood at the top, and turned to the car on my right, going through a narrow hallway, past a mini kitchen, over to the luggage racks. I tucked my suitcase on the lower level, walked down the aisle to find my seat, and sat down by the window. A few minutes later, the train jerked forward, slowly at first, and then began to move at a quick pace. The landscape became a blur as we raced across the countryside, through the cities, and along Lake Ontario. The sun turned the tops of the waves into sparkling diamonds.

The service attendant came down the aisle, checking the passenger's tickets. I rummaged through my purse, found it, and pulled it out. When he approached me, I handed it over to him. He scanned with his mobile device and was about to leave when I asked, "I can't hear announcements, would you be able to let me know when we are close to my destination?"

He seemed momentarily perplexed until I pointed to my hearing aids. When he saw them, he said, "Oh! Certainly.

I'll try to remember, but I can't guarantee it." Then he saw my iPod sitting on the table in front of me. He gestured at it. "Can you access Wi-Fi on that? It's free here on the train."

I smiled. "Yes, I can."

"Great. There should be a GPS map on it that can show you a live feed of where you are."

I was surprised and creeped out, at the same time at the thought of how easily that information could be accessed. I swiped the screen to side, searched through the apps, found the one he was talking about, and selected it.

"Is that the right one?" I asked him, showing him the screen.

He knelt beside me. "See that blue dot that's pulsing? That's you."

I stared at the tiny dot as it raced across the map of Ontario. I was surprised at how quickly we were moving. "That's cool! Thanks," I said.

"That should help give you a better idea of how close we are, okay?" He gave me a thumbs up, and went over to the next passenger.

I plugged my iPod into the FM receiver, selected the video app, turned on the captioning, and started watching *Supernatural*. Every once in a while, I pressed pause, checked the progress of the train on the map, then went back to watching the video. I was on my second episode when there was a muted thump and the brakes suddenly screeched loudly in a high-pitched squeal. Bright orange sparks flew up on either side other side of the windows, and there was a heavy smell of burnt steel.

The train swayed momentarily, rattled violently, and came to a gradual halt. Black smoke billowed around us outside. I jolted upright, gripping the armrests, my knuckles turning white. The lights flickered above me and a staticky announcement burst out. I had no idea what they said. I turned around and saw that all of the passengers appeared alarmed and confused, standing up with their faces pressed against the windows. A couple of attendants ran down the aisles past us, their walkie-talkies squawking loudly. I couldn't make out what they were saying, which intensified my fear. My hands shook as I glanced at the map on my iPod. I had guessed that we were thirty minutes away from my destination. I was starting to panic. Several passengers were standing together and pointing out the windows, chattering back and forth.

Trying to quell the rising panic in me, I texted Mom: *Something's happened. The train stopped and there's smoke everywhere.*

What? Where are you?

I texted back. *Near Guelph I think.*

Another attendant ran past us from the opposite direction. He was using the walkie-talkie and stood between the cars, looking out the windows on the doors.

Is there smoke inside the train? Mom texted.

My fingers shook as I texted back. *No. It's outside but I can smell it. Something is burning out there.*

Oh my. Are you okay?

Yes. I replied. *Bit scared, though. I don't understand what is going on.*

I noticed that several of the passengers in front of me had crowded together, looking out the windows, exchanging worried glances. There was a sudden burst of static overhead then an unintelligible string of words. I glanced at the passengers on my side, pointed skyward, and asked, "What did they say?"

"They asked us to stay in our seats," the lady in the gray business suit with black high heels and her hair pulled back into a ballet bun, replied.

"Oh. Thanks."

She gave me a curt smile then looked over her shoulder, watching the attendants behind us. I followed her gaze. There were three of them, quickly gesturing at each other and pointing at the doors. I'd surmised that they were getting instructions from the walkie-talkie.

I leaned over to the business woman. "Do you know what's going on?"

She shook her head. "Not really, something about evacuation protocols and the police."

A cold shock of fear ran down my spine. Goosebumps erupted on my arms. I texted Mom. *Sounds like the police are involved.*

She responded quickly. *Oh, dear, sounds serious.*

After a lengthy wait of people looking around anxiously or talking to someone on their phones, an attendant came into our car and stood in middle, not too far from me. Fortunately, I was able to see her face and lip read her.

"Is anyone injured or in need of medical care?" she asked, her eyes scanning over us. When no one responded, she continued. "Okay, folks, we will be evacuating this train as soon as the buses arrive. They will take you to the next train station. Alternate transportation will be arranged for you at that location." She repeated this announcement in French.

A man on my right, a couple of seats ahead of me, stood up and waved his hand at the attendant. "Can you tell us what happened?"

"I can't provide much detail. All I can say is that we hit a vehicle on the tracks."

Several people started asking questions at the same time.

The attendant raised her hands in the air. "Folks, I'm sorry but that's all I can say for now. The police will be arriving soon to help escort everyone off the train." She repeated the statement in French then briskly walked down the aisle to the next car.

Flashing red and blue lights appeared in the windows. I stood up and saw several police cars zoom by us, coming to a stop on the road by the tracks. We were in a residential area, surrounded by fenced-in houses. I could see a large crowd of people already forming on the side of the road, holding onto their children, curiously watching the action. The police were setting up roadblocks at the intersection.

I texted Mom. *The police are here. Buses are on their way.*

Did they say what happened?

My fingers frantically typed back: *The train hit a car!*

Oh, dear, that's awful. Was anyone injured?

They didn't say, I texted.

I'm so sorry you had to go through this, she texted back.

I gulped, my eyes welling up. I sniffled loudly and tried not to cry. This was my first time on a train by myself. Last time, I went with Ethan, and I wished that he was here to help me understand what was going on. I felt very isolated in this situation. I was beginning to truly feel the impact from the lack of his presence. As I watched the police and attendants collaborating outside, I realized the enormity of what I had done by pushing him away. It would've been so much different if he had been here with me. He would've known what to do and calmed my fears. I began to wonder if I should reconsider talking to him.

A message came up on my iPod. It was from Mom. *Jessie, your train is already on the news!*

I typed back. *Seriously?*

I glanced up and looked out the window. Sure enough, there was a TV van parked on the side of the road behind the roadblock. A news crew was filming us. The business woman beside me gave me a quizzical glance. I gestured out the window. "We're on the news."

Her eyes widened. "Super," she said sarcastically.

Looking at the crowd of people and camera crew made me feel like a caged animal, trapped and helpless.

I held the iPod up to the window, snapped a picture of the TV crew filming us and send it to Mom with a note that said: *Yep. It's like a media circus out there.*

After what seemed like a long time, several buses appeared at the barricades, the police let them through and they trundled past the police cars and parked alongside the train.

I texted Mom. *The buses are here.*

Good. Where will they take you?
I messaged back. *To the next train station.*
We will meet you there.
Okay, I said.

The attendant came back into our car and announced to us, "Okay, everyone in this car will be going on that bus." She gestured out the window. "A police officer will escort you onto the bus. Do not worry about your suitcases. we will put them on the bus for you."

Everyone stood up and proceeded down the aisle, out the door, and down the metal stairs. A police officer wearing a bright yellow vest stood at the bottom, guiding everyone off. I followed the line of passengers outside. It was a sea of chaos with so many police cars, buses, TV crews, and a large crowd across the road watching us. It was the same thing on either side of me. Everyone was exiting the train out of each car, like ants following a sweet trail. There were loud squawks and sirens, people frantically gesturing at each other. I could see black smoke billowing out from beneath the front of the train and there were many fire trucks and ambulances surrounding that area.

There was sense of fear in the air, despite the efficiency of getting everyone off the train and over to the buses. I continued to follow my line onto the bus, anxiously watching the crowd. I sat down next to an elderly lady and nervously watched the attendants carry our suitcases over to the bus, loading them into the cargo hold, and I hoped that mine was one of them. It felt like an eternity, waiting for them to load all of the suitcases. The bus finally lurched forward, moving slowly past the throng of emergency vehicles, the crowd of onlookers, and the media. After a few minutes, the bus picked up speed and headed over to the highway. Within forty minutes, we arrived at the train station, following several buses, and pulled into the parking lot. I scanned the rows of cars, trying to find Mom and Dad. Panic rose in my chest when I couldn't see them. I wondered if they went to the wrong station. I got up and went outside to collect my suitcase. As soon as I spotted it, I grabbed it and went over to the platform, searching for my parents. After a while, I went into the station and sat down on the bench. My heart sank and I wondered if I made a mistake, was I supposed to stay on the bus or go to a different train station?

Feeling perplexed, I spun around, frantically searching for Mom and Dad. I went back outside and was about to ask the bus driver what to do, when I saw them. Relief washed over me. They were standing beside their van, waving at me. I quickly made my way over to them.

Mom promptly pulled me into a hug. "Oh, Jessie! It's so good to see you!"

My hearing aids squealed in protest from her tight grip. "Sorry," I uttered, feeling embarrassed by the feedback.

Dad came over, picked up my suitcase, and placed it in the back of the van.

"Thanks, Dad."

His eyebrows creased in concern. "I can't believe that you were just in a train accident. Everyone hears about them, but to actually be in one is quite a different experience. Are you sure you're okay?"

I nodded. "Yeah. It's a tough train. There was lots of smoke, bright sparks, and screeching of metal, though."

"I suspect that most of the damage and smoke was from the car," he said.

"Why would anyone do that? Park their car on the tracks?" I asked.

"Lots of reasons. Maybe their car broke down? Although I have a feeling that this was not the case," he said.

We got into the van. I sat beside Mom in the back so we could talk more easily as I could see her face.

I looked at Dad in confusion. "What do you mean?"

"The media is being tight lipped about the occupants in the car."

I sucked in a quiet gasp. "There were people in that car we hit?"

Mom nodded and reached out to touch my hand. "As far

as we know from what was on the news, the police are still trying to figure out what happened.

"So how's school, so far?" he asked, clearly trying to re-direct the conversation.

"It's hard and really busy. We're doing a lot of work, more than we did in high school, but more career focused. Does that make any sense?"

Mom nodded and laughed. "Yes, it does. Are you enjoying it?"

"For the most part, yeah. It's definitely more challenging. I'm learning that there are some areas where I'm not as good as the other students in my class."

"What do you mean? In terms of talent?" Dad asked.

"Yes. I'm okay with doing still life sketches but suck at drawing models and doing watercolors. There are a lot of talented artists in my class, and I feel intimidated sometimes."

"There's no shame in that, honey," Mom said, "it will take time to develop those skills. Everyone is naturally good at doing one or two things, and they focus on those. There's nothing wrong with that."

"I agree, there's nothing wrong in being stronger or weaker in some subjects," Dad said. "That's the beauty of college, it's about discovering what suits you and a great opportunity to find out where you really shine. Your style will flourish and blossom over time."

"Do you really think so?"

They both nodded at me.

"Which classes do you like so far?" asked Mom.

I took a moment to think about it, watching the landscape blur past us out the window. "I would have to say sketching. The design and typography class is neat in terms of coming up with cool logos. Painting is fun and I like art history."

"Is most of it practical skills, very hands on, or is there computer work too?" Dad said.

"It's both. We're learning how to use Photoshop and Illustrator as well as graphic design layouts for magazines. It's more technical but I like learning about balance and composition in terms of how to make things more visually appealing. That crosses over into everything else I do."

"Look at you, already sounding like a pro," Mom remarked proudly.

I smiled. "It's interesting, though, I'm looking at everything differently now and seeing it from a new perspective. It made me realize how much of an impact the overall design, colors, and compositions have on posters and ads. Before, I took everything for granted."

"Funny," Mom said. "I didn't think about it like that. I just know what I like when I see it."

"That's because you're aware of how well it's designed on a subliminal level," I told her. "It means they did a good job of attracting your attention."

"Interesting," Dad said, "you're already sounding like a professor. Who knows? Maybe you will continue the tradition and become a teacher too."

"Me? A professor? I'm not sure about that," I replied.

"Why not? You're already teaching karate," he said, slowing the car down and turning into our lane.

"True," I said.

The long gravel driveway was lined with maple trees that led up to the house. The leaves glowed in the sun in shades of bright red and amber, shimmering in the breeze. It felt good to be home. I didn't realize how much I'd missed it until we went inside and found Parker and Serena sitting in the foyer with a small collection of their stuffed toys, mostly felt mice and birds. It was obviously a gift for me.

"Aw! How cute. Thanks, guys," I said, kneeling down and giving them kisses.

They stood on their hind legs to bump their heads against me, purring enthusiastically. I could feel their rumbles beneath my fingers when I stroked their soft fur. Parker greeted me with a loud yowl and Serena talked to me in tiny, squeaky meows. I sniffed loudly, trying not to cry. I missed everything about being here, from the comforting smells of Mom's baking to the wood smoke from the fireplace. It was a country home, full of love and warmth. Living in the city wasn't the same. It didn't have the lived-in feeling. There was something special about being here, surrounded by nature. I felt more relaxed here. Dad took my suitcase upstairs to my room while I went into the kitchen with Mom.

She turned on the oven, pulled a chicken out of the fridge, and began preparing it for supper. "So, how are you enjoying life in the city?"

"It's completely different, very fast paced. I always feel like I'm on the go, that it's one thing after another. Don't get me wrong, it's exciting and new. There's so much going on, but I need a moment to slow down and breathe."

"That's what it was like for your father and for me," Mom said. "School was such a big part of our lives and it felt overwhelming at times."

I grabbed some place mats from a drawer and went around the kitchen to set the table. "I'm still trying to get used to the routine. Some of my classes are at night."

"Do you do most of the cooking at your place?" she asked.

"Pretty much. Jackson tries to help out."

Mom looked up. "Jackson? That's a strange name for a girl."

I snickered. "Jackson's a guy, Mom."

Mom froze with her hand halted midair. "I thought all of your roommates were women."

I sighed. "Don't worry, he's gay."

"He is?"

"Trust me, he's totally gay," I said.

"Hmph. Okay, that's a new one," she said, grabbing the tray with the chicken and placing it in the oven. "So what's he like?" she asked, chopping up the potatoes.

"He's nice and easy going. He knows what it's like to be bullied and ostracized. In some ways, he has a better understanding of what it's like to be unfairly judged by others. He just gets it, and that's rare," I said.

"You're right, not everyone understands that. He sounds like an interesting person."

"You'd like him, Mom," I said, leaning my elbow on the table and resting my chin in the palm of my hand.

"Can he cook?"

"No, not really," I replied.

"Oh, why not?" she asked.

"He has a tendency to blow things up."

"Oh, dear. He doesn't do that on purpose, does he?" she inquired.

"I don't think so. At least the meals are memorable," I remarked.

She laughed as she placed the potatoes in a pot of water on the stove. "Maybe I could give him pointers someday."

"Is that an invitation?" I said, raising my eyebrows.

"Sure, why not? He might like a break and want to spend some time in the country."

"That's a good idea," I said.

"Can you let your father know that supper will be ready soon?"

I stood up and went in search for him, I found him in the living room watching the news.

"Dad?"

H gestured at the television. "Jessie, that's the train you were on."

I stared at it in shock. The front of the train was covered in black scorch marks with pieces of charred, twisted metal scattered around it. Some of it was still smoldering. The firemen were busy hosing down parts of it along the tracks and grassy bushes nearby. If there was a car, it was virtually unrecognizable. No one could've survived that.

My knees suddenly felt weak and rubbery, and I abruptly sat down. A sickening feeling washed over me. I couldn't believe what I was seeing, that I was on that same train. Seeing it from this perspective was disturbing. The fact that

I walked away without a scratch was a miracle. The news showed additional footage of us being escorted onto the buses.

"Jessie, you okay?" he asked, placing his hand on my shoulder.

"No wonder Mom was so worried," I said.

"Yes, that's something no parent should have to go through. It really shook us up. It wasn't until we saw you at the train station that we knew you were safe."

My chest felt tight as I watched the horror of the wreckage on the television. I didn't realize how serious it was since we were shielded from the worst of it. As I saw Dad's reaction, the reality, of how close to being severely injured or, worse, sank in. It was a potent wake-up call for me.

Chapter 17

Fear

It was *sooo* good to be home. I felt calmer and more re-laxed than I had been for some time. Here, the routine was more familiar and even the cats seemed to appreciate having me back home. They followed me everywhere I went, padding along beside me. Whenever I sat down on the bench by the window or my bed, they would jump up and sit on either side, bookending me. They would lean into me, rubbing their cheeks against me, purring loudly.

When I woke up in the morning, both of them were sleeping beside me, curled up together resembling the shape of a ying, yang, with Parker's dark fur against Serena's lighter silver fur. I reached out to stroke them, they raised their heads and blinked their eyes sleepily at me. Parker rose, crept up to me, and leaned in, touching his soft pink nose to mine, tickling my cheeks with his whiskers.

"Thanks, Parker, I missed you too."

I really missed having them sleep on my bed and giving me sweet kisses in the morning when I woke up. I gathered him into my arms and climbed out of bed, heading down-stairs. Serena followed us, tagging along beside me, her crooked tail wagging side to side. I could feel Parker's purrs rumble against me. He was happily draped over my shoulder and leaning into my neck. I could smell coffee when I reached the bottom of the stairs. Mom and Dad were in the kitchen, sitting around the table. Dad was reading the morning paper, absentmindedly reaching for his cup, grabbing it, and taking a sip. Mom looked up and signed to me. *'Morning, Jessie. Did the cats sleep with you last night?'*

I nodded.

'They do seem happier now that you're home, especially Parker.'

I glanced at him then back at Mom. "What do you mean?"

'He hasn't been himself lately, sleeping a lot more than usual. I guess he missed you,' she replied, her fingers dancing as she signed the words.

I gave Parker a gentle squeeze and placed him on the floor beside Serena. The two of them gave each other nose kisses.

There was a plate of cinnamon rolls that Mom had made and I eagerly snatched one up. I munched on it, savoring the sweetness of it while I grabbed a can of cat food from the cupboard. When I opened it, the cats sat down near me, eagerly watching me. They gobbled up the food as soon as put it into their dishes. Rummaging through the fridge, I grabbed a carton of banana mango smoothie and poured myself a glass, then sat down with Mom and Dad. I grabbed another roll and took some bites out of it. "Do you really want Jackson to come for a visit?" I asked Mom.

'Why not?' she signed. *'I think he would like the company. Maybe you could introduce him to karate or fencing?'*

I hadn't thought of it. It was a great idea.

Dad flicked down the top of the newspaper, peering at us. "Who's Jackson?"

"My roommate. We go to the same school and classes."

He gave me a perplexed stare. "I didn't know they allowed co-ed roommates."

"Don't worry, he's gay," I said.

"Are you sure?"

I sighed. "Yes."

Out of the corner of my eye, I could see Mom smiling, and I had sneaking suspicion that she was snickering.

Dad narrowed his eyes at her.

'*Are you helping out with karate classes today?*' Mom asked.

I nodded.

'*Great. I'll drop you off and do some errands, then pick you up afterward,*' she said.

"Okay."

Mom's catering business kept her busy, and she would often drop off orders while driving around town. After breakfast, I went upstairs, got changed, and put on my hearing aids. I grabbed my gym bag and sat outside on the porch steps. Parker and Serena sat beside me, happily watching the birds and chipmunks. The ground was covered in golden yellow and orange leaves. There was a cool breeze in the air. I closed my eyes, enjoying the warmth of the sun on my face. I felt a tap on my shoulder and looked up to see Mom standing beside me.

"Ready to go?"

"Yep."

I gave the cats a kiss on their furry foreheads, grabbed my bag, and climbed into the van beside Mom. It smelled delicious, a mix of gingerbread and cookies. I glanced in the back and, sure enough, there were several boxes with the logo of Paige's Pastries on top. Mom's cookies were decorated with elaborate, colorful designs that were almost too pretty to eat. She often gave me the broken pieces, and I was happy to eat them.

"Ooh, looks like you got a lot of clients today," I said.

She beamed. "Yes, the fall cookies seem to be a big hit. I will have to start working on the Christmas cookies soon, since they're so popular."

"Really? Wow, it sounds like it's really taking off."

She nodded. "It's definitely a nice surprise."

As we reached the city, Mom headed over to the dojo

and pulled into the parking lot. I got out, grabbed my bag, and waved at Mom as she left. A couple of people were in Sensei Jonas's office, I waved at him as I went by then headed into the locker room. There were several girls already getting changed when I came in. They looked up at me and smiled.

One little girl with brown eyes and straight brown hair cut in a bob came up to me. "Hi, are you new here?"

I glanced at her belt and noticed it was white, which meant she hadn't been here for very long. "Hi. No, I'm not new. I'm one of the instructors."

"Oh. How come I haven't seen you before?" she asked curiously, bouncing on her toes.

"I go to college, it's in a different city. It's a long way from here."

"Oh. Okay. Will you be teaching today?" she asked.

"Yes. I'll be helping out."

"Cool! I like your pink hearing aids, they're pretty," she said, giving me a generous smile.

"Thank you. That's very sweet of you. I like them too."

Another girl came in and saw me. "Jessie! You're back!" She wrapped her arms around my waist and gave me a hug.

"Oof! Is it my imagination or you're getting bigger and stronger?" I asked.

She giggled and let me go. "I'm taller too."

"Wow, I think you're going to need a new uniform if you keep growing so fast."

She nodded briskly. "Mom said I can get a new one for Christmas."

I quickly got changed and joined the kids in the dojo. Ethan and a couple of other instructors stood in a circle by the wall where the kicking shields, Bo staffs, and boxing gloves were stored. All of them wore black belts and had numerous badges on the sleeves of their uniforms. They were about the same age as me, maybe a few years older, and were obviously very fit. The sleeves were rolled up to their elbows, revealing thick, muscular forearms.

Ethan looked suave as usual. The front of his sandy blond hair was styled with an upward flick. The other two had dark hair—one with a short, wavy style, and the other was much longer, nearly touching his shoulders. I glanced at the clock and noticed that the class was going to start soon. I waltzed up to the guys and stood near them. They gave me a nod.

Ethan smiled politely. "Morning, Jessie."

"Morning, Ethan," I replied.

They continued to converse, and I was close enough to hear some of what they were saying and read their lips.

"Then the camera panned over to the wreckage where the metal was bent and twisted beyond recognition. It didn't even look like a car anymore," said the guy in front of me with long hair. He spoke animatedly, using his hands for emphasis.

Something twigged at the back of my mind, and I had a suspicion I knew what they were talking about. I crossed my arms and tried to follow the conversation more closely. He went on to describe the carnage. "And the entire front section was blackened from the fire. The damage was unreal."

I narrowed my eyes, feeling the heat of anger rise through me. My cheeks grew hot.

He was getting more excited as he described the accident, "There were so many firetrucks and emergency vehicles. It was wicked!"

I stepped in. "Are you talking about the train accident?"

"Oh, yeah. Wasn't that awesome?"

I stood there blinking, stunned. "Seriously? It was awesome? I was on that freaking train. Someone died in that car."

All three of them stared at me in shock.

"Oh, man, I—I didn't know," he stammered. "I'm sorry."

I turned around and walked away, fuming.

Ethan reached out and grabbed my arm. "Jessie, wait."

I stopped but didn't turn around.

"Jessie, look at me, please." He walked around to face me so I could hear him. "I had no idea that you were on the train. None of us did. Why didn't you text me?"

It was my turn to stare at him in surprise. "Why? Was I supposed to?"

I saw sorrow in his eyes. "Yes, Jessie, you should've reached out to me."

"Why?" I asked bluntly.

"Because I still care about you," he replied.

"You do?"

He placed both hands on my shoulders. "Yes, of course I do. I never stopped loving you."

That hit me hard. I sucked in a quiet gasp and my chest tightened painfully. "Oh. I thought you would've hated me."

"Why in the world would you think that I'd hate you so much that you couldn't talk to me anymore?"

"I was mean to you. I pushed you out of my life," I replied.

"Jessie, you were upset and you had every right to push me away. If we had switched places, even I would've done that."

"Really?"

"I can be a jerk sometimes and dimwitted when it comes to understanding women. Dad had a long talk with me after that happened and made me see things in a different light."

"Oh, I see," I said.

Speaking of which, Sensei Jonas appeared in my line of vision behind Ethan. He coughed and cleared his throat loudly, and I suddenly realized that we had an audience.

Ethan and I sheepishly stepped apart. Sensei Jonas gestured toward the front by the mirror, miming that we stand in line with him. Ethan titled his head to the side, indicating that I should join him. Sensei Jonas watched us with amusement, wearing a smile.

I couldn't explain it but if felt like the ice around my

heart was beginning to thaw. Sensei Jonas bowed to the class then had Ethan and I run the warm up and do various drills with the kids. We had a lot of fun, chasing them, trying to outwit them with the kicking shields then a game where Ethan would do a particular stance, block or kick incorrectly on purpose. It was a test to see if the kids could see what he was doing wrong and learn how to fix the mistakes. In this instance, he was standing with his legs straight and held his arm in front of his face.

I stood by Ethan, pointed at him. "What is he doing wrong?"

They all chimed in, giggling madly. Ethan was overdoing it and making it look obvious.

"His legs are too straight!" said a chubby, little boy with freckles.

Ethan bent his legs in response. His pose was so comical that I had to press my lips together to stop myself from laughing.

"His horse stance should be lower!" remarked a thin, small girl with her blonde hair in two ponytails.

Ethan promptly lowered his stance.

"Good! What else needs to be corrected?" I said, raising my voice over the chorus of laughter and giggles. They were a cute bunch of kids, and their giggling was adorable.

"Um…his high block looks kinda funny," replied another boy with dark skin and short curly hair.

"That's right. What should he do to fix it?" I asked them.

"It shouldn't be in his face," replied another girl.

"Okay, where should it go?"

There was a mix of responses. "Higher!" and "Above his head."

Ethan adjusted his pose. "That looks much better," I said. "Thanks, guys. Now go grab your sparring gear."

They all scrambled over to the back wall to gather their bags and equipment. Much to his relief, Ethan stood up and shook out his legs. "Next time it's your turn to stay in that pose."

I snorted. "Aw, what's the matter? Out of shape?"

"Ha! You laugh now but wait until you try it, waiting in agony for them to figure it out."

"That's called patience, and it's a good virtue. Isn't that part of your club's motto?" I replied cheekily.

"Probably," he muttered.

"What's that? I'm deaf, you know," I jokingly replied, gesturing at my hearing aids.

"You are so going to pay for that remark," he said.

I squinted my eyes at him playfully then looked at the students, the majority of them were suited up and ready to spar.

"Ethan, do you want to be the referee and I'll help get the rest of the students with their equipment."

"Yeah, sure."

He called them over the side of the dojo where there was a large square taped on the floor which made up the sparring arena. I went over to the other kids who were struggling with their shin pads and boots.

I kneeled down beside them. "Do you want some help?"

They nodded. I helped the girl on my left pull on her gloves and helmet, then over to the other girl on my right, who was having trouble with the Velcro straps on the boots. As she pulled on her helmet, she said, "When I grow up, I want to be like you."

"What do mean, like a black belt?" I asked her.

"No, silly. Like a warrior," she beamed as she said this.

I snorted. "Me? No, I'm not a warrior."

"You are too!" she replied emphatically.

Okay, I think someone had a little too much sugar in their cereal this morning, I thought. "What makes you think I'm a warrior?"

"I've seen you spar."

"Is it because of the way I spar that makes you think I'm like a warrior?"

She pumped her head enthusiastically. "Yeah. You're so brave and strong too!"

"Oh, thank you. But you know what? I'm just like you. I get scared too. I just don't show it."

"Really?"

I nodded. "Yes. Some of the guys that I compete against are bigger and faster than me, and I get super scared. Even at tournaments."

"You do?"

"Even though I'm scared, I'll put on a brave face so that they can't tell. That's why I go into a fighting mode, to look scary to them."

"Ohhh, so it's like a warrior mask," she said, raising her eyebrows.

"Sure, it's like wearing a mask," I said.

All three of us stood up.

"Okay, show me your warrior faces. Try to scare the pants off me."

"Grrr!" They bared their teeth at me and held up their fists, like two determined baby tigers ready to pounce on a toy.

"Awesome! Now you're ready to fight, go join the rest of the group," I said, ushering them over to the ring.

Ethan cast a quizzical glance my way. I gave him a thumbs up.

When all of them had their chance to spar, Sensei Jonas came in and bowed the class out.

One of the girls named Tonya, who had long blonde hair, came running up to me and grabbed my hand. "My Mom wants to meet you."

"Oh, okay. Lead the way."

She tugged on my hand, eagerly pulling me out to the lobby where the parents waited during the classes. We came to a stop in front of a tall, slim woman with long blonde hair and blue eyes. Right away, I could see the resemblance between them. She held out her hand and I reached out, giving her a hearty handshake.

"Hi, I'm Sensei Jessie."

"I'm Tonya's mother. It's so nice to finally meet you. She is always talking about you."

I looked down at Tonya to see her grinning from ear to ear.

"You're her hero. She loves being with you in class and adores the fact that you don't let your hearing loss hold you back. I'm so glad that you're setting such a good example to kids like her. It means the world to both of us to have such a talented teacher like you."

I was almost speechless. "Really? Wow, I had no idea. Thank you, that means a lot to me."

Tonya looked up at me. "Can I give you a hug?"

I smiled. "Sure."

She promptly wrapped her arms around me.

"Aw, thanks," I said. "I needed that."

She giggled.

"Come on Tonya, it's time to go. Thanks again, Jessie," the mother said.

Tonya waved at me enthusiastically as they left. I waved back, still surprised by their remark.

I felt someone standing beside me and turned around to find Ethan leaning against the wall, watching me. "What's going on?"

"Tonya's mom just told me how much she appreciated having me here as an instructor," I said, jerking my thumb over my shoulder as I headed back in the dojo.

He raised his eyebrows. "And you're surprised?"

"Yes. I didn't expect that. She made it sound like I was a hero which I'm not. I'm just like everyone else."

"Some people have a hard time seeing past the disability, while others see the real person behind it. To them, it's a big deal when someone like you proves them wrong."

"I know what you mean, but I don't like the idea of sitting on the sidelines when everyone else gets to play. I've been through that before, and it hurt me deeply. I had to stand up for myself and go out there and do it. I learned that lesson a long time ago."

"And it shows, you're a stronger person now."

"Stubborn too."

"Yeah, I know," he said, playfully bumping his elbow against me.

We bowed in for the adult class and did our warm ups. After the workout, Sensei Jonas divided us up, half of us worked on our katas and the other half focused on weapons. I concentrated on my moves with the Bo. I held the long, slender staff in my hands, taking my time and attacking imaginary opponents in different directions. I swung it to one side in a crisp motion against my ribs then switched to the other side. I swirled it overhead quickly, the speed of the motion making a whistling sound. It felt good to be doing these moves, snapping it out and rotating the staff in my hands. I jabbed it upward several times then did a quick side sweep at the knees of my imaginary opponent. On the last strike, I delivered a loud kiai for emphasis, then bowed.

Ethan had been working on his Bo kata too, albeit one with more advanced moves. He came over to me. "Wow, Jessie. You are getting really good with the Bo."

"Oh, thanks. I like using it."

"I can tell. You're a natural at it. Have you thought about entering tournaments in that division?" he asked earnestly, his eyes shining brightly.

"No, I hadn't really thought about it. Do you think I should?"

He nodded. "Yeah, it suits you. I think this is what you were meant to do."

"Wait, do you mean like fate or serendipity?"

"Well, why not?"

Sensei Jones came over and Ethan told him how I was considering doing a Bo kata in tournaments.

"I agree, you do have a knack for it, Jessie," Sensei Jonas said.

I narrowed my eyes at him. I had a sneaking suspicion that he already knew this. "Is that why you wanted me to try weapons katas?"

"Let's just say that I had a good feeling about it," he replied.

My eyes flicked back and forth between them. Everything started to make sense, like pieces of a puzzle falling into place. "Sure, why not?" I replied, feeling more confident about it. It felt like I was finally headed in the right direction.

We continued working on the kata for a few more minutes, then Sensei Jonas bowed us out. I started to head out when I felt a hand on my shoulder. I turned around and saw that it was Ethan.

"I wanted to ask you if you were interested in going fencing with me tonight?" he asked.

"Not tonight, I think it's too much after everything, especially the train accident. Maybe next time?"

"Sure. Don't be afraid to send me a text when you want to go fencing."

"Okay."

"It was good to see you again, Jessie. College has definitely made an impression on you. You seem more sure of yourself," he said.

"Thanks. I didn't realize that. It has been a big change for me. What about you, are you doing okay at school?"

He nodded. "Yeah, I'm enjoying it, even though it involves a lot more work. You know what's funny? I thought it would be easier, not harder than high school."

"I know! I felt the same way. At first, I wasn't sure if I was talented enough, you know, compared to the other students in my class. Everyone is so gifted, and they all have their own unique styles. It's taking me a while to figure out where I fit in."

"Yeah, I know the feeling. Some of my classmates are really smart and intimidating. They seem so sure of what they want, in terms of goals. I swear, they're turning it into a contest. I mean, psychology is a fascinating subject and there is so much to learn, but it seems overwhelming at times. I have to remind myself that if I want to work with kids as a school psychologist, then I have to stick with it and persevere."

I stood there stunned, surprised by what he said.

He tilted his head to the side, giving me a slight frown, "What? You seem…I don't know…surprised."

"I am, actually. I've gotten so used to pushing myself to keep up with everyone else, that it didn't occur to me that you would need to do it too."

He looked at the floor then back at me, "Heh. You still work harder than most people, Jessie. That's what I like about you. To me, your strength is what shines the most. You've found a way to stay strong. That's what I want to help kids find: their own inner strength so that they can propel themselves forward in life."

I blinked. "Wow, you're already sounding like a psychologist. I think you'd be perfect role model for them, someone to look up to. It suits you," I said, giving him a warm smile.

"Thanks," he said softly.

"Anyways, I have to go. Thanks for asking me about fencing. Can you send me a text me next time?" I asked him as I made my way over to the locker room.

He nodded. "Sure."

He gave me a sad smile and waved at me. There was still a sense of coldness between us that made it feel like a vast lake of ice separated us. Our conversation was more cordial than anything else. I missed how close we used to be, I missed the warm and intimate connection. Weirdly, it felt like we were strangers again, trying not to step on each other's toes. Most of all, I missed his touch, the feeling of his warm hands on my skin and his soft kisses on my lips.

Chapter 18

I looked out the window in the kitchen, watching the leaves flutter to the ground. The trees were glowing in the sunlight, the leaves highlighted in bright shades of amber and red. Parker and Serena were sitting by my feet, curiously watching me, their heads swiveling back and forth as I moved around getting their supper ready. I scooped out the food onto their dishes and placed it on the floor in front of them. They eagerly gobbled it up. I was itching to go outside for a walk through the woods and take some pictures of the colorful landscape. One of my assignments was to capture fall scenery for my photography class, and I was determined to do it today before all of the leaves fell.

I went upstairs, grabbed my camera, and thumped back down the stairs. I opened the closet, pulled out a purple jacket and shrugged it on. A quick search through the bottom of the closet yielded a pair of vibrant pink running shoes. I smiled as soon as I saw them. Perfect, I thought. I sat down and tugged them on and laced them up. Parker and Serena scampered over to me, pressing their noses to my shoes, eagerly sniffing them.

"Did you want to come outside with me?" I asked them.

Parker gave me a loud yowl. Serena went over to the

door and spun around in circles. I chuckled. "I guess you do! Okay, let's go."

I opened the door and they ran out.

There was a slight chill in the air, a hint of an icy breeze. It smelled like winter was coming soon. I pulled out a pair of fingerless knitted gloves from my pocket and put them on. We marched on the well-worn path, which led us past the field of sunflowers. I stopped momentarily to snap a few shots of the golden flowers, their petals shining brightly in the sun. A chickadee fluttered over to one of the larger heads of the sunflowers and began plucking out the seeds. The cats watched in fascination, their eyes growing wide. Serena's broken tail wagged side to side and Parker wriggled his rump and short tail. I moved closer to the chickadee, trying to get a picture of it. I managed to press the shutter twice before it flew away.

"Aw, sorry, guys," I remarked. "I think I scared it."

I knelt down and took some shots of the cats. The outside light made their eyes shine brightly and their fur was more striking. They seemed happy to be out here with me. We continued our walk toward the valley, a heavily wooded area where the deer often roamed. The valley was filled with tall maple, birch, and oak trees. The leaves on the ground grew thicker and deeper, covering the tops of my shoes. Serena ran ahead of me, pouncing on the leaves. I didn't see Parker. I turned around and saw that he was moving more slowly than usual. My heart momentarily froze. I knew that he was getting old and having trouble getting around. I felt a pang of sadness for him.

I hung the camera around my neck. "Hang on, Parker, I'll carry you."

I went back up the hill and picked him up. He snuggled under my chin against me. I could feel him purring as he leaned into my neck. We followed Serena down to the bottom of the valley. I looked up and realized just how tall the trees were. I felt incredibly small in comparison. The wind shook the leaves, sending a ripple amongst them, causing them to shake and shimmer. There was a large tree off to my right, the thick roots forming a natural nook in the pile of leaves. I sat down, cradling Parker in my arms. We watched the trees sway above us. Occasionally, the breeze would scatter the leaves around us, sending them rolling across my feet. Serena scampered after them, leaping up in the air to snatch them. I pulled Parker closer to me, hugging him. I didn't want to lose him, not now. He was purring loudly against my chest.

Serena came over to where we were sitting, crawled into my lap, and glanced at me, giving me a squeaky meow. I reached out and stroked her soft, warm fur. She leaned into me.

"I miss you guys," I said, sniffling, feeling my eyes water. A tear rolled down my cheek.

Serena reached up and touched my face with her paw, as if trying to wipe away the tears.

"Thanks, Serena," I said, my voice sounding raw.

A shiver ran through me as a breeze sent more leaves scattering around us. Suddenly, the leaves started to swirl around us in a circular motion as if we were in the middle of a mini leaf tornado. I held onto the cats, keeping them close to me. The leaves continued to spiral, rising upward, shining brightly in the sun like golden coins. They rose high up into the air, then the wind ebbed away, causing them to fall like little boats gliding back down to us. I laughed as I watched them fall, trying to catch one as it fluttered within my grasp. I grabbed my camera and quickly took some shots.

I remembered a similar scene with Parker from several years ago when we were in the valley and the leaves did strange things in the air. I squinted my eyes at him in suspicion. "Did you do this, Parker?"

Even though he was my spirit guide, strange things seemed to happen around him. I wondered if Serena pitched in to help too.

We stayed for a little while longer, watching the leaves rain down on us as the wind shook the trees. The air began to grow colder and the sun was starting to set, sending long shadows across the forest floor.

I got up, cradling Parker, and headed back up the hill with Serena leading the way. As we reached the top and walked past the sunflowers, the sky turned deep shades of pink, lavender, and baby blue as the sun sank into the horizon. Once we reached the porch, I placed Parker down on the steps. He gave me a mix of a purr and meow, his signature greeting. We all marched into the house, grateful for the warmth and delicious smells. The house was filled with the aroma of gingerbread cookies, Mom's most popular request from her clients. She decorated them lavishly with brightly colored icing and sparkling edible sugar and beads. I headed over to the kitchen and found several trays of leaf and pumpkin-shaped cookies.

Mom's red apron was covered in white flour, and her hair was curling around her face from the heat. I quickly snatched up an unfrosted broken cookie and started nibbling on the edges, savoring the rich flavor. Parker and Serena sat at my feet watching me with wide, hungry eyes.

"No, you can't have any cookies, this is people food," I said to them.

"Purrup?" Parker replied.

Serena wagged her tail, hoping for a piece to fall on the floor. I placed my camera on the table, sat down, and scrolled through the shots. There were several of them that I thought would work for school. I particularly liked the shot of the leaves falling down, with the sun shining through them.

"Did you get any shots?" Mom asked, glancing up from pulling a tray out of the oven.

"Yeah, I think so. I'll know more when I load the memory card onto the computer."

"You picked a great day to take pictures. The trees looked beautiful," she said, lifting the cookies off the tray with a spatula.

"Parker seemed to have trouble keep up with me during our walk."

She nodded. "I've noticed that he seems slower lately, and I'd wondered if he's having joint pain?"

"What? Like arthritis, you mean?" I asked her, after taking bite out of the cookie.

"Yes. He is getting old, Jessie," she said, giving me a somber look.

My chest tightened painfully, and I took a deep breath, trying to ease the tension. It seemed to constrict even more.

After supper, I went to my room and sat on the bench by the window. Serena lay between my legs, her chin resting on my knee, while Parker was curled up in my lap. I was doing some sketches of Parker, trying to capture his facial features. I loved the feeling of their warm bodies on my lap, the sensation of their purrs through my legs. I definitely missed this. Soon after, I crawled into bed. Serena and Parker followed me, climbing on top of my blanket to curl up side by side with each other.

I grabbed a paperback book from the side of the table and started reading it. My eyes grew heavy fairly quickly, and I kept dropping the book on my face, jerking myself awake. Eventually, I gave up, after re-reading the same page three times, and put it away.

I became aware of a shimmering white light on the left side of my bed. Wide shafts of moonlight beamed through the window and onto the floor, creating brightly lit panels. I blinked my bleary eyes, wondering what was going on. Sparkly motes floated in the beam of light. Serena's spirit guide stood next to me, her human form was breathtakingly beautiful. Her long, silver hair shimmered and flowed like liquid mercury. The sleeves of her long robe flowed gracefully, the material sparkling like tiny diamonds in the moonlight. Her smooth skin glistened as if she was covered in starlight. Whenever she moved, tiny glittering stars fell and disappeared before they hit the floor.

"What's going on, Serena?"

"It's time," she said. As she spoke, I could hear her in my head.

"Time? Time for what?" I asked her.

Then my eyes slid past her shoulder. Parker's spirit guide stood behind her. That's when I noticed she was holding his hand. His luminous skin twinkled like shifting golden sand. Both of them were breathtaking.

That's when it hit me. I shook my head, "No."

Parker inclined his head. "It's time for me to move on," he said, his deep baritone voice clear in my head.

"Please don't go," I said, my voice trembling.

"I will always be in your heart," he replied, giving me a smile.

"But I'm so scared."

"Fear can compel you to move forward or hold you back. It's up to you to choose which way to go. Remember, you have a bright light within you, a beautiful and kind soul with so much to offer. Don't let anyone dim it."

I nodded, gulping back tears, my throat feeling very tight.

Parker started flickering. He was beginning to fade.

"Embrace the unknown, accept what you see in a renewed light. Let that sense of hope fill you with strength," he said.

"Parker, wait just a little longer."

"You have shown me your powerful capacity to love freely and openly. You have embraced me with your compassion and kindness and, for that, I will always be grateful. There is a great strength within you, all you need to do is find it. As long as you stay strong and believe in yourself, you will succeed greatly in life."

His voice was growing quieter.

"Remember the stars, that's where you'll find me."

His image was fading even more now.

Serena turned and slowly walked over to the window, pulling Parker with her, her hand gently guiding him. She reached out, her fingers dissolving into sparkling motes along the moon beam.

His last words were, "Hope will always guide you."

He walked into the shaft of moon light, tiny golden orbs swirled around him. Serena's robe dissolved into thousands of tiny stars. Both of them followed the path of the moon beam, rising up into night sky, swirling and dancing like sparks of glowing silver and gold embers. The last image I saw was their hands still joined together.

I sat up with a start, my chest heaving with gasping sobs. Tears streaked down my face. I wiped them away with trembling fingers. It felt as if he had taken a part of my soul with him. I looked down at the bed and saw Serena and Parker laying together, her paws sitting on top of his. I held my breath, cautiously extended my arm, and touched his fur. He was breathing, albeit a bit slower and more laborious than usual. Serena opened her eyes, blinked at me, then reached out with her paw and placed it top of my hand, as if comforting me. I sniffled and wiped away the wet tears on my cheeks then lay back down again. I tried to go to sleep but my mind had other ideas. It kept replaying the last scene of them leaving.

Morning came too soon, I woke up to Parker standing beside my shoulder, watching me curiously. He leaned in and gave me gentle kiss on my face with his wet nose, cold against my skin. Then he stretched out his paw and tapped my cheek, as if telling me to wake up and feed him.

I felt immensely relieved to see him. "Morning Parker, thanks for the kisses."

He meowed in response. Even though I couldn't hear him at all, I knew that he was talking to me by the way his jaw moved. I found it ironic that I could lip-read my cat. I gave him and Serena a quick kiss on their soft, furry foreheads then flung the cover off the bed and got out. The cats followed me downstairs, leading the way to the kitchen, eager for breakfast.

Mom was already up making coffee. She turned around

and signed to me. '*Morning, Jessie, how did you sleep?*'

I felt absolutely exhausted after tossing and turning so much last night, worried sick about Parker. "Not good, really. I had this horrible feeling that something was wrong with Parker."

She frowned, glanced down at him then back at me. '*What do you mean?*'

"I guess you could call it a premonition. I had this strange vision of him leaving me." I had a feeling that my voice cracked while I spoke, but since I couldn't hear myself talk, I wasn't sure.

'*Oh, dear,*' Mom signed.

"Is that possible? I mean, get premonitions?"

She nodded. '*Yes, I've had people tell me stories about their premonitions.*'

"Like what?" I asked.

'*One of them was traveling in a car with a friend on a highway in the mountains. He said that he had a strong and sudden vision appear in his head of a rockslide. To him, it felt so real that it shook him up. He had such a bad feeling about it that he asked his friend to pull over at a scenic lookout to take a break. Sure enough, a little while later, it did happen on that road. He saved their lives by trusting his instincts.*'

"Oh, wow, does that mean it will come true for us?" I said, feeling anxious.

'*No, honey. Sometimes our minds play tricks on us while processing things we've experienced during the day. It doesn't always make sense.*'

I felt marginally better, but I was still haunted and deeply saddened by it.

'*Can you tell me what you saw?*' she asked, her fingers spelling out the words.

"I guess."

I told her about Serena and Parker appearing to me in their spirit forms and the message they left me before they disappeared into a shaft of moon light.

'That's beautiful Jessie. They're like angels, giving you comfort and hope.'

"Do you really think so?"

Mom nodded and gave me a warm smile. She crossed her arms on her chest, the sign for love. *'It was a lovely message, especially about the stars.'*

My throat tightened painfully and my eyes started to water. Mom walked over to me and gave me a hug. After a few minutes, she took a step back and signed, *'I think it was a sign for you to appreciate special moments like today.'*

I felt something touch my leg, I looked down and saw Parker pawing at me.

"Did you want a hug too?" I said then reached down and picked him up, cradling him in my arms. I buried my face in his warm fur. I could feel his purring vibrate against my cheek.

'I think they want breakfast,' Mom said, gesturing at Serena who was doing figure eights around her ankles.

I snickered, put Parker down beside her, and got their dishes ready. After I fed them and made my own breakfast, I sat down at the table with Mom.

'Did you pack yet? The train will be leaving later this afternoon,' she asked.

"Sort of." I was putting it off for as long as I could. I didn't want to go to back school yet.

Mom put down the coffee cup and gave me a worried look,. *'Are you okay with going back on the train?'*

"Yeah, I guess."

She narrowed her eyes at me, not entirely convinced by my response. *'Are you sure?'*

"It's fine, Mom. I can't stop taking the train because I'm scared. I have to get used to it."

'Well, at least you have a story to tell at school.'

I gave a wry chuckle. "That's true."

After breakfast, I went upstairs and finished my packing. I sat on the edge of the bed and texted Jackson, checking to make sure he was going to pick me up at the station. My iPod displayed a message that said: *Will do. Anything exciting happen?*

I snorted and replied: *You could say that.*

And? he wrote.

I texted back: *You'll have to wait until this afternoon. I need an incentive for you to pick me up.*

You're totally evil.

I laughed at that.

A few hours later, I stood at the door, gave the cats a hug and kiss, then headed over to the van.

Dad glanced at me and the suitcase. "Are you sure that you packed everything? Did you need any food?"

"I don't want to carry too much stuff on the train, it gets heavy and cumbersome."

"Think of it as part of your exercise routine, like weight lifting," he replied cheekily.

"Dad!" I chided, rolling my eyes at him. "Can we go now?"

He hefted my suitcase into the car with a loud grunt, then we piled in. He continued to grin at me as he turned on the ignition and drove down the lane.

The scenery changed from lush rolling hills and farmland to sprawling subdivisions and tall buildings as we approached the city. He pulled into the parking lot, and all of us climbed out, Dad got my suitcase and insisted on carrying it for me. We went into the lobby of the train station, and I glanced up at the monitor near the ceiling, checking the status of the train. It was on time.

An announcement blared overhead, echoing around us. I had no idea what was being said. To me, it sounded liked a strange, alien language. It didn't make a lick of sense.

I gave out a disgusted sigh. "Why can't they do closed captions on the monitors? I can't understand what they're saying. It's like they're speaking another language."

"I know, honey," Mom said. "It doesn't help that the marble floors and high ceiling bounce the sound around.

Besides, you're partially right, they were speaking French too."

"Oh."

"I do like the idea of having announcements listed on the screens, that's a great idea. You should tell them," she added.

"What? Like right now?" I asked in surprise.

"Sure, why not?" Mom said. "They don't know how hard it is for you to hear the announcements. I'm sure a lot of people, especially the elderly, would benefit from it. You can help take a step in the right direction by making them aware of this issue. Who knows, Jessie? You may be the first person to start a cumulative effect for more accessible services. You could end up helping a lot of people."

"I agree, Jessie," Dad said. "You need to become a voice for others who may be too afraid to come forward with these problems."

"Yeah, but why me?" I asked.

"You're younger than most people with a hearing loss, and you need as much help as you can get, so you can function in society like everyone else. You deserve to be treated equally and fairly. The only way to do that is to be a leader and get that ball rolling so that others can follow. You can make a difference by educating other people," Dad said, his eyes twinkling, a sign of pride.

I stood there, taking a moment to ponder that.

"You're a natural leader, Jessie, you can do this," Mom added, reaching out to touch my shoulder in encouragement.

I took a deep breath, hauled my suitcase over to the ticket booth, and stood in front of the window. A man, several years older than me, was busy typing on the keyboard, his eyes glued to the monitor. He was slim, with short black hair and a narrow face. He wore rimless glasses perched on his nose.

He gave me a cursory glance. "I'll be with you in a moment."

I stood there, drumming my fingers impatiently on the counter top.

After a long wait, he finally turned around to face me. "Sorry about that. How may I help you?"

"I don't know if you've dealt with this before but I wondered if you have live captioning on the monitors for announcements?"

He blinked his at me. "Oh. I don't know. Why do you want to know?"

"I'm hard of hearing," I replied, turning my head to the side to show him my hearing aids.

His face immediately lit up. "I love those colors and adore the fact that you're not afraid to show them off!"

"Thanks. I wanted to make them look cool, like a fashion accessory. It's also a great way to remind people that I can't hear them."

"That is a marvelous way to do it. Good for you."

"Heh. Back to my original point, is it possible have a live captioning on the monitors? I actually can't hear the announcements. My hearing aids only work within a two-meter range and I cheat by reading lips."

"Ah, gotcha. Well, I honestly can't answer that question. You're the first person to inquire about it," he replied, folding his hands on top of the counter.

"Personally, I would feel a lot less anxious if that feature was available, and I imagine it would help a lot of other people too," I said.

"I agree. Tell you what, I will forward your comment to the head office, but in the meantime, I would suggest that you also contact them directly. I'm sure they would appreciate hearing it from your point of view," he replied.

He took a moment to rifle through the drawers beneath the computer, pulled out a business card, circled the email address on it, and handed it to me.

"Okay, I'll do that. Thank you so much."

"You're welcome. I hope they consider incorporating that feature," he replied, giving me a broad smile.

I turned around and walked back to my parents. "He said that there aren't any captions for the monitors, but will forward the idea to the head office. He suggested that I contact them directly." I showed them the business card he gave me.

Mom grinned. "That's great, Jessie. I hope it does happen. At least it will be a less stressful experience for a lot of people like you."

We sat down on the plastic bench by the large glass windows overlooking the tracks. At least this way, I could watch for the train. I was nervous and really wanted to get this trip over and done with. I jiggled my leg nervously as I peered out the window then looked back at the clock. "Do you really think I can change things, make them more accessible?" I asked Dad, who was reading a magazine beside me.

He nodded. "Yes. I truly believe that. All it takes is one person to make that little nudge to create a forward momentum. It may take a while but someone has to start the process."

"Jessie, you need to remember that most people don't realize how hard it is for you to have a hearing loss," Mom chimed in. "You make it look easy, even though you're working really hard to keep up. You have to show them how they can help you."

"I know. But it scares me to do that. What if they hate me or tell me that it's a stupid idea?"

"Then you need to find another way to explain it to them or find someone else who has a more open mind," Dad said. "There will always be someone out there who will challenge you, which means you'll need to be more creative with your approach."

"Oh, like showing them my hearing aids?"

Dad jerked his thumb toward the ticket agent at the booth. "Exactly. I saw how he smiled at you when you showed them to him. You're helping them realize that not everyone with a hearing loss is an old person. By you being honest about it, people like him will see it as sign of courage, and they'll admire you for that."

I shrugged my shoulders. "It's just the way I am, I chose not to hide it."

"That's what makes you more unique. You embrace it as part of your personality," he said.

Mom tapped my leg and pointed out the window. "I think that's your train, you should go."

I quickly grabbed my suitcase, and we all marched outside amongst the crowd. The train was just coming around the bend about a mile away, the headlight a tiny, bright pinprick. Within a few minutes, it roared up to the station, sending a blast of wind into our faces. It rumbled to a stop and the passengers climbed down the stairs. I turned around, gave Mom and Dad a hug, and said goodbye. I joined the line up at one of the cars. My heart was hammering in my chest, and my palms were all sweaty. When it was my turn to go up the steps, my feet froze for a moment. I gripped the metal handrail tightly then pulled myself up the stairs. I turned to my right, walked down the narrow hallway over to the luggage compartment, and tucked the suitcase on the lower rack. I went in search of my seat and sat down, waving at Mom and Dad, who saw me in the window. Once everyone was boarded, the train jerked forward then began picking up speed.

I picked up my iPod and texted Jackson, letting him know I was on the train. I tried not to think about the accident and, instead, focused on watching a movie. Every once awhile, I checked the map, watching the blue dot move quickly toward my destination.

After an hour, the train slowed down and came to a stop. It felt strange to have two homes now. I grabbed my suitcase and headed down the steps with shaky legs, grateful that nothing had happened. My eyes roamed over the crowd in search of Jackson. I found him at the far back, waving at me.

"Hey! You made it," he said enthusiastically, bouncing

up and down on his feet. He gestured at my suitcase. "Want me to take that for you?".

"Oh, sure. If you want to."

He eagerly grabbed the handle and marched alongside me, "How was the ride?"

"Better this time around."

He frowned at me. "Huh? What do you mean 'better'? Did something happen last time?"

"Yeah, there was an accident on the way. The train slammed into a car on the tracks."

He came to a complete stop, eyes bulging at me. "That was your train? I saw that on the news! I had no idea. Why didn't you say anything?"

"Sorry, Jackson, I guess I just wanted everything to be as normal as possible. It was a lot for me to go through, especially on my own."

He shook his head then continued walking across the parking lot. "Oh my, I can't believe you went through that. Yet you still took the train back home. That takes gumption."

I smiled. "I know, but I couldn't let that hold me back. I don't want fear to control my life."

We approached his car and he unlocked the door. "Good for you, darling!" he said as he lifted the suitcase into the trunk. "Oh my, this is heavy."

I snickered. "Just be glad it's not filled with soup cans." I climbed in the front seat and put on my seat belt. "How about you? Did you anything exciting this weekend?"

"Oh, you know, the usual, had a party, chugged lots of beer, and went to a local gay bar," he replied.

My jaw hung open, "You did not!"

"Ha! Gotcha. Of course not," he said, giving me a cheeky grin. "I did some homework, some new sketches, and went around taking some photographs for reference."

"Oh yeah, I forgot about that. I mean, I did take some pictures but not a lot."

We continued our conversation as he drove back to the

house, which still sounded weird to me. Once we got in, I happily dumped the suitcase in my room and headed downstairs for a snack.

I opened the microwave door to heat up some leftovers and discovered to my horror that Jackson had exploded more food in it.

Sweet cheese and crackers, what the heck happened here? I wondered. "Jackson!"

"What?" he bellowed from the hallway.

I gestured at the microwave, it was covered in a layer of icky, brown sludge. "Dare I ask what this used to be?"

"I don't know, burritos or a taco?" he replied, shrugging his shoulders.

I gave out a loud sigh. "Ew."

I didn't relish having my food flavored with the scent of the mystery meat and rummaged through the cupboards for a paper towel. I found one, ripped off a sheet, dampened it under running water, and began the process of cleaning out the microwave.

I glared at Jackson who gave me a mischievous smile. "Welcome home."

Chapter 19

Breakthrough

I was in the computer lab, doing some extra work during my spare time late in the afternoon at school when Jackson sauntered in and came to a stop beside me. He stood with his hands in his pockets, watching me. I got the impression that he was up to something.

"What are you up to now?" I asked him.

He gave me a sheepish grin. "Um…can I borrow you?"

I raised my eyebrows. "Me? Why?"

"I…uh…need a model," he replied.

I stared at him, waiting for the other shoe to drop.

"It's for my photography class," he added.

I balked. "I'm not exactly 'model' material," I said, miming quotes in the air with my fingers.

"Anyone can be a model, my dear," he said.

My eyes roamed around the room. I tilted my chin at one of the guys in the front row. "What about him?"

"Ugh." He shuddered. "Too Justin Bieber."

I snickered.

"Come on, Jessie, I know you can do this," he said, pleading with me.

"It just feels too weird for me."

He rolled his eyes. "Please?" He did a mock quiver with his lower lips, looking like a sad puppy.

I sighed. I knew it was cheap ploy but damn it, he was good at it.

"I'll pay for your cappuccinos and lattes," he added for emphasis.

He totally got me there. "Throw in organic dark chocolate, and you got a deal. But I will not pose in the nude."

He snorted. "You don't need to worry about that."

"When do you need me in the studio?" I asked.

"Now would be good," he said.

"Like right now?" I said.

"Yeah, that's kind of why I'm here."

Super, I thought dryly. "Okay, give me a second to save my work here."

A few minutes later, we headed out of the computer lab and walked down the long corridor over to the other wing. We went up several flights of stairs and turned to our left toward a door with the words, "Photography Studio." Jackson slid his ID tag in the key door lock, watching the light turn green, opened it, and went in. We entered into an alcove. The professor's desk was situated off to the right, and on our left were shelves filled with various photography equipment. I walked past the desk and leaned against the metal railing overlooking the spacious studio. There were several sets of backdrops along the wall to my right, and numerous lights, ladders, and stools sat in the middle. There were a couple of people in there, both of whom I recognized as second-year students. Their names were Erica and Rob. They were a couple, which was a rarity in our program, due to the heavy workload. They looked up and saw us. I waved at them and they happily waved back.

I watched them while they worked. Erica was sitting on a stool while Rob grabbed a light stand and changed the angle of the beam, highlighting more of her hair and face. I thought she was beautiful with her long auburn hair, brown eyes, and lean figure. She was naturally slim and tall, a perfect combination for a model. Rob was also good looking with his black hair in a messy style and chiseled features, as well as broad shoulders. The two of them were a natural fit as a couple and very good-natured people. They were always nice to me and gave me good advice from time to time.

Jackson and I went down the stairs and turned to the right where he had already set up a stool in the middle of a ring of lights.

I became more apprehensive as I sat down. "Are you sure you want me as a model? I'm not exactly dressed for it."

I was wearing an old, well-worn gray knitted sweater over a plum thermal top and black jeans. My pink sneakers were scuffed and dirty. I didn't feel very glamourous.

Jackson looked down at his black leather jacket. He shrugged it off and gave it to me. "Here, try this on."

I pulled off my sweater and put on his jacket. It was still warm from his body heat and felt really nice."

"Wow," I said, "This is a great jacket."

"I know, and it looks really good on you," he said, grinning broadly. "I had a feeling it would."

I watched him move the lights around and add a colored filter to one of them that changed the overall mood. It cast a peachy orange glow around us, like a sunset.

"I feel like I'm at a beach and incredibly overdressed for it," I remarked.

He snorted. "Don't worry, you look fabulous, dear. The golden glow really sets off your blonde hair, and there is a bit of a warm halo around you." He picked up a camera and tripod and set it up in front of me. I just remembered that my hearing aids were visible and pulled my hair down, trying to hide them. Jackson peered around the camera. "You don't need to do that, darling, let's show that bling to the world."

"Are you sure?"

"It's a part of you, Jessie, rock that look. Embrace it."

"Oh, okay. I thought I was already embracing it."

"Then prove it, be fearless, honey," he replied.

I took a deep breath and gave him a tentative smile, feeling so nervous that my palms were sweating. He pressed the shutter and the lights around me flashed. I blinked, feeling somewhat dazed.

"Good, Jessie. Okay, give me a bigger smile," he said, looking up at me, miming a ridiculously happy face.

"Okay, I'll try. It just feels weird to do this. I can't explain it, but I feel kind of naked."

He stood up, put his hands on his hips, and struck a pose, pretending to be a model.

His silly pose made me laugh out loud. "You look like Zoolander!"

He promptly took several more shots as I continued to laugh. Then he quickly ran over and stood next to me. "Quick! Let's strike a silly pose together."

He arched his back, pursed his lips the way a Victoria Secret model would usually do for a photo shoot. He was a natural at this and having fun with it. I joined him, trying to feel more glamourous. The flash went off a few seconds later.

Then Erica and Rob came over, carrying a portable music box, and plunked it down near the camera.

Erica stood beside me. "That looks like fun! Can I join you?"

"Sure! Maybe you can help me and show me how to pose?" I said.

"You're doing just fine, Jessie," she replied.

"Do you really think so?"

She nodded then told Rob to turn on the music. Loud dance music filled the room. I could feel the bass thump against my body.

"Feel the beat, let the music wash over you," Erica said, bobbing her head and shoulders to the rhythm.

Following her prompting, I began snapping my fingers.

"That's it!" she said.

The two of us became more energetic, striking more confident poses. Jackson ran back to the camera and took more shots of us. We looked over our shoulders at him in various positions. Rob gave us a thumbs up, bobbing his head to the tune and doing a little dance of his own. When I saw him, I laughed and spun around, feeling happier than I had in a long time. I felt a warm glow spread through my body, a feeling of joy.

"That's it, Jessie! You got it," said Jackson, who was quickly snapping more shots. He moved around us, shooting from different positions.

Then he gave the camera to Rob and joined us. Both of us got into the catwalk mode, doing fun poses together.

The energy in the room was lively with the loud music thumping away and growing warm under the lights. In fact, I felt rather hot. I could feel the heat radiating off the large lamps and that's when I noticed an acrid smell. Something was burning. I spun around, my eye searching for the source of the smell.

"What's wrong, Jessie?" Jackson said, noticing a change in my behavior.

"This may sound weird but does it smell like something is burning?"

He frowned for momentarily, took several deep breaths like a dog sniffing in the air. At that point, everyone stopped moving to the music and their faces grew more serious. Then Jackson's eyes grew wide as he spotted the smoking filter in front of the lamp. The plastic sheet was melting!

"Gah!" He ran over to a bench beneath the stairs, grabbed a pair of rubber tipped tongs, quickly pulled off the smoldering filter, and carried it briskly over to the metal sink. He turned on the tap and frantically ran water over it.

The room stank like burnt plastic. I covered my nose and mouth with my hand, trying not to laugh. He held up the badly distorted filter and heaved a heavy sigh.

I snickered. This was typical Jackson.

He glared at me.

"What? Only you could turn this into a memorable event," I said.

Erica and Rob guffawed. "She's right!"

Jackson's grumpy frown and sad pout gradually grew into a lopsided smile. "Why does this always happen to me?"

"I guess you're too hot to handle," I replied, chortling.

He rolled his eyes. "Well, I guess this shoot is over."

"It's just as well. It's almost time for supper, anyways," I said. I faced Erica and Rob. "Thank you, guys, for your help."

"No problem, I had fun!" she said.

"So did I."

We said goodbye to them as they left and Jackson showed me the shots on the camera.

"I look goofy in some of those, you can delete those ones," I said to him.

"What? No way. I like the way you look, see?" He paused on one image and I nearly gasped. It didn't look like me with the leather jacket, amber highlights backlit on my hair, and a golden glow across my face. It looked like it belonged in a magazine.

"Wow, Jackson, these are great. You're a good photographer," I remarked.

"I had help too," he said, giving me a nudge with his elbow and a wink.

"I wouldn't mind giving my parents one of those images for Christmas. I think they would like it."

"Oh sure, no problem. Thank you so much for helping me, Jessie," he said.

I gave him a smile. "I'm glad it worked out. I mean, aside from burning the filter. You showed me what it means to feel beautiful."

He tilted his head to the side. "How do you mean?"

"Well, I've never really felt pretty. I've always felt awkward about that. For me to love myself, even just for a little while, is hard to do. Today, you showed me how to do that. There was a sense of joy in me that I hadn't felt in a long time," I said.

"Oh, darling, now you're going to make me cry," he said then pulled me into a hug.

Chapter 20

INSPIRATION

As the weeks went by, our assignments and workload became heavier and more challenging. The closer we got to the holidays, the more worried I became. I had already done several all-nighters and, last night, proved to be no exception. I had staggered to my bed at three in the morning, only to be rudely woken up by my shaking pillow. I bleary glanced at my alarm clock. It was already seven-thirty. I groaned and rolled out of bed. My eyes felt like they were full of sand. I glanced down and realized that I still wearing my sweatpants and hoodie. *Funny, I could've sworn I put on my pajamas,* I mused.

I did remember waking up in sheer panic, thinking that I had forgotten to finish the assignment. It took me a frantic moment to recall that it was already completed. I felt like I was losing my mind. There were so many assignments to keep track of lately. My body felt sluggish, as slow as molasses, while I fumbled through the closet for a fresh change of clothes.

By the time I took a shower and got dressed, Jackson was already standing by my bedroom door, nibbling on a muffin. He tapped his watch impatiently. I was just putting on my hearing aids, waiting a few seconds for the sound to come on.

"I'm going as fast as I can Jackson," I said irritably.

I quickly bundled up my artwork, slid it into the portfolio case, slung it over my shoulder, and grabbed the tool box. When I walked past him, I snagged a piece of his muffin and tossed it into my mouth.

"Hey!"

"Serves you right for nagging me," I mumbled.

When we got into the car and headed to school, he said, "You know that you left the tap running last night?"

That bit of news surprised me. "What? Where?"

"The bathroom sink," he replied.

I slapped my forehead with the palm of my hand. "Gosh, I'm sorry. I didn't have my hearing aids and couldn't hear it."

He gave me a sheepish grin. "You know what's funny about that?"

"Aside from running out of hot water? No," I replied tersely.

"I was dreaming about a waterfall. I didn't realize that I was actually hearing the sound of running water, and it affected what I dreamt about," he said.

"Really? That's fascinating but I'm still mortified about that. It could've overflowed, and we could've gotten into a lot of trouble if there was any water damage. It would've been my fault," I said.

I felt horrible about that, not being able to hear something like that.

"It's turned out okay. At least, I'm learning how different your life is from mine."

"Okay, but that doesn't mean it should affect your life too."

"Don't worry about it, Jessie. It doesn't bother me," he replied.

"That's not what my brother used to say to me."

"What do you mean?" he asked.

"He didn't like what happened when I suddenly lost my hearing from meningitis. It changed the dynamics of the family. Even though he was the oldest, most of the attention was focused on me because of my issues. He blamed me for that."

"Oh, I didn't realize that. How are things between you now?" he asked, turning to face me while waiting for the lights to change.

"It's different since we don't see each other very often. He lives up north and is busy teaching at university. Our lives are more separate now," I said.

"Do you think it helped going to different schools?" he asked.

"Yeah, it gave us the space that we needed. I didn't mean to make things worse for my family. That's just the way it turned out."

"Interesting. Well, at least you're not boring, I'll grant you that."

"Says the guy who has a reputation for burning everything," I said.

He chuckled. "We're like a pair of misfits."

"Yeah, no kidding."

By the time we reached the parking lot, there were virtually no spots left. We had to circle around the lot twice until someone pulled out.

"There!" I said, pointing in that direction. "Quick! Before someone takes it."

Another car turned around the corner and headed toward it. Jackson pressed on the accelerator and just barely made it in the nick of time.

I was laughing as I got out of the car, grabbing my gear.

"I can't begin to tell you how crazy it is to find a parking spot here. It's ridiculous," I said.

He snorted. "At least it gives us an exciting start in the morning. It really gets the blood pumping, eh?"

Our boots squeaked loudly on the slick floors as we raced to class. We barely made it in time. Professor Knudsen gave us an exasperated glare as we rushed over to our seats. I blushed while I scrambled to find the FM system, marched up to him, and handed it over.

He quickly snapped it up, giving me a curt, "Thank you."

I could feel everyone's eyes on me. I kept my head down as I headed back to my chair. Once I turned on the receiver, his deep voice rumbled in my hearing aids. I turned down the volume a notch and continued pulling out my supplies.

Professor Knudsen was a slightly heavyset man with thinning hair. "As I was saying…" He paused, giving me and Jackson a long stare over his glasses. "…a professionally designed website features a clean look, easy navigation that loads quickly."

He paced across the floor as he spoke, which often drove me crazy. I had a hard time following his lips when he did that. Fortunately, the microphone picked up a lot of what he said. "Heavy animation and gifs may be fun to look at, however, they can bog down the site, creating slower loading times. No one wants to hang around a website for more than twenty seconds while waiting for it to buffer. Keep that in mind as you design your online portfolio. Think about what skills you are most proficient in and really showcase that talent. Remember that your website is what will sell you and your work. By the time you graduate, potential employers should be knocking on your virtual door wanting to hire you."

He paused, pivoted, changed direction. I resisted the urge to raise my hand and interrupt him. "Think about the clients you want to attract. If you want a career in the gaming industry, you'll need to focus on their requirements for suitable candidates. Do some research, in terms of where you want to go, and find out how to attract your target audience."

I waited for a few moments while he paused then raised my hand.

He looked at me. "Yes?"

"Isn't it too soon to be thinking about that? I honestly

don't know which area I want to focus on yet."

I noticed several people in the room nodding their heads, an obvious indication that we were thinking the same thing.

He wagged his head. "Yes and no. This is simply a starting point for you to create a basic portfolio. It should help you narrow down your choices in terms of career you want."

I raised my hand again. "So we can update the website as we change our focus?"

"Of course! Over the next few years, your skills will grow and become more specialized. The quicker you showcase your talent, the faster you'll catch the eyes of people who want to hire you."

That kind of scared me. I was already becoming more intimidated with the assignments. I wasn't failing any classes, but I wasn't super talented. Yet. I was so focused on learning the basics of illustration that it never occurred to me to consider where I wanted to work. My stomach quivered nervously as I thought about it.

The next class was in the computer lab, which was always fun. Today, we were learning about Photoshop and neat editing features. The professor for this class was a goofy kind of guy, very laid back and really open minded. He was about the same age as Dad. His short dark hair was starting to go gray on the sides, and he had a very cool-looking goatee. He looked like he worked out and was more fit than the other teachers we had. Today, he wore tight jeans and an orange long-sleeved shirt with the sleeves rolled up to his elbows. I had seen his portfolio online. His work had been featured in many galleries and appeared in shows around the world, as well in some magazines. Apparently, he was famous. He had also worked in the advertising and marketing industry, which gave him a wry sense of humor. Jackson and I got a kick out of teasing him. It all started with Jackson's obsession with the singer, Enrique Iglesias, and finding ways of incorporating him into his assignments as a joke. We did it to see the expression on the professor's face whenever we handed in the assignments. His reactions were priceless.

The last time we did this, he ran his hand over his face in exasperation. "Oh my word, you two will be the death of me."

Today, he stood at the front of the class. "Last week you learned how to shoot in RAW format. Today you will be learning how to use actions and double exposures."

Cool, I thought.

He turned on the large white screen behind him, which mirrored what was on his computer. The room was dimmed so we could see what he was doing, which made it more difficult for me to see his face. I had to rely on the FM system more heavily in this class and watched how he worked more closely. The screen showed him turning on the layers panel and actions panel in Photoshop. He showed us how to turn them into smart objects and edit the image, manipulating the colors to enhance the photograph.

"The beauty of using smart objects is that we can edit the image without losing the quality of the subject, it's essentially non-destructive editing. Quite often when you try to scale an image, it can become pixelly. That's where the smart object comes into play. It preserves the overall quality. Also, while you work on it, you can see the changes you make right away."

I blinked, trying to process this information, watching him work with the layers.

"Now, you will be working with two images. One will become a mask, and the other one will used as the background," he said.

He showed us two images on the screen and went through the stages to convert them. He had chosen a photo of a woman with curly hair and a city landscape. Within a few clicks, he made the city appear within her silhouette. It was one of the coolest tricks I'd seen so far, and I was eager to try it.

"You can change the opacity to allow more of the landscape become more visible," he said, demonstrating the technique. "Does this make sense to everyone?" He took a moment to wait for any questions, then said, "Great! Choose any model and background you want and start working on those layers. I'll come around and check on your progress."

I knew exactly what I wanted to do and did some searching for images to practice with. Once I found what I was looking for, I went to work. Jackson and I exchanged sly glances. He swiveled the monitor toward me. I snorted. It was a shot of Enrique. I gave him a thumbs up and mouthed to him, "I'm doing the same thing."

He mouthed back to me, "Awesome!"

I was smiling gleefully when Professor Kevin came to a stop beside me. He groaned and slapped his forehead when he saw what I was working on. "You're killing me, Jessie, killing me."

That made me smile even more. It was totally worth it.

I had selected a close up of Enrique singing on stage and incorporated a misty concert scene with vibrant spotlights and the crowd in his silhouette. It was a very cool effect.

"Should I make the background behind him more obvious?" I asked him.

He knelt down on the floor beside me so that he was eye level with me. "It depends on how dramatic you want it to be. If I was using this on a banner or billboard, I would allow the concert scene to be more visible in the background. Although, if you want more of a poster feel to it, you can make the background a lighter color to really make him stand out."

"Okay, thanks."

He nodded then looked past my monitor and saw Jackson's screen. He rolled his eyes dramatically, shaking his head as he headed over to him, wagging his finger at Jackson.

I was so absorbed with experimenting with the effects that I didn't realize that half an hour had gone by.

Professor Kevin stood up at the front of the class. "It looks like most of you are getting the hang of this technique, which is great. The more you practice working with these types of layers, the easier it will become." He paused momentarily to scan the room for any questions. "Since it's getting close to the holidays, I want you to come up with a design for a large paper shopping bag, using what you've learned today. I've written down the requirements for you to follow."

He picked up a stack of sheets and handed them out. When he gave me my copy, I quickly perused the rules. It listed the usual parameters such as the size of the bag, work area, background color, the company it would be designed for, and the overall theme. My eyes stopped partway through, and I started laughing quietly.

Jackson looked over his shoulder at me. "What's so funny?"

I gestured at the list. "Look at item number five."

He squinted his eyes at me suspiciously, scanned the list. A broad smile crept across his face.

Professor Kevin was watching us. He grinned impishly, waving his pencil at us. "That means you two."

It read: *You can feature animals, nature, sports, city scenes, and people, with the exception of Enrique Iglesias.*

Like I said, he had a great sense of humor and made the classes more fun.

"In advertising, we often work with teams to collaborate our ideas and maintain a consistent theme, especially for a particular brand. You can work with a partner to discuss potential themes, subject, colors, and fonts you want to use for the slogan. Bear in mind that I'm looking for witty slogans. Keep it short and sweet. If you need inspiration, go to the mall and look at the bags that are being used now. Think about which ones stand out and capture your attention. Consider the reasons why it works."

That was a great excuse to go to the mall. After I picked up the FM transmitter from Professor Kevin, I joined Jackson and headed to our lockers. He seemed to be in deep thought.

I nudged him with my elbow. "What'cha thinking about?"

"I was trying to come up with a design for the bag, and I can't think of anything."

"Did you want to partner up with me and see what we can come up with?" I asked him.

He snickered. "Do you think our professor could handle the two of us working together?"

I laughed out loud. "No, but it would be so much fun to try."

After we put our equipment in the lockers, we went over to the cafeteria. We purchased our food, carried our trays over to the lounge by the large bay of windows, and sat down. The light streamed in, casting beams with dust motes floating in the air across the chairs and tables. There was a light layer of snow outside, and the clouds looked gray and ominous, a sign that more snow would be on its way.

"It's a bit strange that we haven't seen much snow this year," I remarked before taking a bite out of my grilled cheese sandwich.

"At least it makes it easier to drive home. I really don't like driving in bad weather," he said, giving me an exaggerated shudder.

I hadn't thought of that. "Oh, hey, before I forget, did you want to visit my parents on your way home for Christmas? You would be going past our town anyway, right?"

"Yeah, you're right. Um, sure. If that's okay with them," he replied, munching on a carrot stick.

"Mom already suggested the idea so she's fine with it. At least it will you give you a break from the driving," I said.

"That's true. You live on a farm right?" he asked.

"No, we live in a rural community, although there are farms in the area."

"Oh, I see. Do you grow anything, though?"

I nodded. "Yeah, one of the farmers uses our field to

grow his crops and harvest them. He grows sunflowers and corn, depending on the season. The flowers are beautiful in the fall. It's like being surrounded by sunshine. I really should do some sketches of them next time."

"Would they be finished blooming by now?" he asked.

"Yes, it has already been harvested. We often have deer visit us. They use a path that goes past our house and into the woods out back," I said.

"It sounds peaceful," he said as he unwrapped his hamburger.

"Yeah, it's nice. It can be a bit isolated, though. It's not like here where it's different, being surrounded by so many people. For me, city life is kind of weird. It feels like there this constant sense of energy all the time."

"I like it, it's nice having the freedom to walk out the door and talk to people on the street or go shopping on a whim," he replied.

"You know what's funny? I keep getting the feeling that someone's watching me through the windows. I'm always closing the drapes around the house."

He barked out a laugh. "Okay, that explains why they're always closed. You know what? I really don't care about whether people can see me. In fact, I'll even dance in front of the windows."

I nearly snorted my smoothie through my nose, spilling the juice all over the table. "Jackson!"

"Sometimes you have to let go of your fear and be yourself. Who cares about what anyone else thinks?" he replied in a confident tone.

"That's a great attitude, Jackson, that's what I like about you. You don't take any crap from anyone," I said.

"I learned that lesson the hard way of after years of being picked on because I was gay. It wasn't until I made the decision to take control of my life that others changed the way they treated me. I had to become more confident about myself and it worked."

"I can see it. You're so brave," I said as I mopped up the juice with a paper napkin.

"So are you, Jessie. You're an inspiration to me. You don't let your hearing loss hold you back from anything. You go ahead full steam and tackle your challenges fearlessly," he replied earnestly.

"Oh, I'm definitely scared. I just don't show it. I think it's from years of sparring and not letting my opponents know that I'm scared."

He nodded. "Yep, that would do it" He looked at his watch. "We have class in fifteen minutes, we'd better get going."

We handed in our assignments after lunch for the other professors and spent the afternoon sketching nude models and watercolor painting, my weakest subject. I could never get the hang of it. My pictures had a tendency to go too muddy. By the time we got home, I was dead tired and ready to fall asleep. After supper, I went upstairs to work on my sketches. I found it to be a meditative experience and easily lost track of time. Several hours later, I went to the kitchen to make a cup of tea and found Jackson sitting at the dining room table, idly doodling in his sketchbook. His eyes held a faraway look. The table was covered with crumbled up balls of paper.

"Hey, Jackson, what are you working on?"

"Nothing, apparently," he groaned then plunked his forehead on the table.

I grabbed a chair and sat down beside him. "You're stuck?"

He mumbled something that I couldn't hear.

I sighed. "Jackson, you know that I can't lip read you in that position. What did you say?"

He jerked his head up. "Oh, sorry, I forgot." He let out a big sigh. "I'm trying to come up with an idea for the shopping bag but my mind is totally blank."

"Why didn't you ask for my help?"

"I thought you were busy," he replied.

"Well, I'm free now. You know, between the two of us, we should be able to do this," I said. I grabbed a sheet of paper and pencil. "Obviously Enrique is out, so…" I said, the pencil hovering over the paper.

We sat there for several long minutes. I started humming to myself.

A look of recognition flashed across Jackson's face. "Is that Jingle Bells?"

"I was trying to get in a festive mood."

"Is it working?" he asked.

"Nope." I drummed my fingers on the table. "Okay, let's make a list of things that we consider to be festive." I wrote down some ideas. "Christmas trees, ornaments, ribbons, poinsettias, Santa obviously, snow, stocking."

"Fireplaces, mittens, wreaths, candy canes," Jackson added.

I jotted them down. "We should add Hanukkah, dreidel, and candles," I said, writing as I spoke.

A slow smile crept across his face. "Fireplace, fire…" he said, letting his words trail away, his mind seemingly on a particular track.

"Does that mean you have an idea?"

"Yeah, I think so. Why don't we have large flames or a fireplace on the bag with the words 'This bag is hot.' What do you think?"

"Yeah, I like it. That could work, but how do we do use double exposure?"

He face fell as he struggled to come up with the answer. "Great. Now we're back to square one."

He grabbed the list, pouting as he scanned it. While he thought about it, he began playing with a pencil, tapping the end of the eraser on the table. After several minutes of incessant drumming, the rhythm was driving me crazy and I had to snatch it out of his hand.

"Okay…how about a large red bow across the bag with the slogan 'Unwrap me' and make the silhouette look like it's filled with gifts?"

"Ooh! That's a possibility. It would have to be a big ribbon to show that kind of scene though," I said.

"Yeah, that's true," he replied somberly.

"I love the 'Unwrap me' slogan, though." I began thinking about sports, which led to skiing, and I had an idea. "What if we featured several large Christmas trees on the bag and had skiers on a mountain within it?"

"Yeah, that might work. What should we say?" he asked.

Now it was my turn to be stumped.

Jackson heaved a heavy sigh. "Oh, dear, it looks like this is going nowhere."

I snapped my head up. "That's it!"

He blinked in surprised. "What?"

"A large deer with antlers with the words 'Oh, deer, did you forget someone on your list?' It's like a play on words."

He nodded, a slow smile blossoming. "I like it but how do we do a double exposure with it?" he asked.

"Red poinsettias?" I mused. "A snowy forest or a colorful shot of presents?"

"Any of those would work. We should experiment with that and see how it looks," he said.

"Okay, let's do that. I'm too tired to do any more thinking. My brain is totally fried tonight," I said.

"Me too. This is a great start, Jessie, we work well together."

"That's because you're so much fun to work with," I said, giving him a big smile.

I went back upstairs and got ready for bed. I grabbed my iPod and texted Mom, asking her how things were back home.

A message popped up on the screen: *Looking more like Christmas here.*

I replied: *Lots of cookie orders?*

Definitely a lot more than last year, she texted. *I've been baking and decorating cookies non-stop!*

Good, it means you're popular, I texted back.

I hope I'm not sick of cookies by Christmas.

Funny, I replied. *How are the cats doing?*

Serena is sitting by the fire, I think Parker is asleep on your bed.

I thought that was unusual. The two of them usually slept together. *Strange, why isn't Parker with Serena?*

I think it's too hard for him to go down the stairs, honey, she replied. *He hasn't been himself lately.*

A cold chill ran over me and I became worried.

I'd wondered if he missed me. My fingers tapped out: *Is it because I'm not there?*

I don't think so. I think he's just getting old. I've made an appointment at the vet for a checkup.

My heart skipped a beat. *I hope he's okay,* I replied.

Me too, honey.

I let her know that Jackson was going to stay at our house on his way home, and she said that was fine. The beauty of going with Jackson was that I could take more of my stuff home and show my parents the artwork I'd been doing.

I slept fitfully throughout the night and bolted upright early in the morning, drenched in a cold sweat and filled with a horrible sense of dread. It was like a foreboding, a bad feeling that I couldn't shake.

When I went downstairs for breakfast, Jackson looked at me. "You look terrible."

"Thanks, that's what every girl wants to hear," I replied tersely.

"Bad night?"

I nodded and stretched, feeling very stiff. "I'm just worried about my cat, Parker."

"Oh, dear. I hope he's okay."

"So do I," I replied, opening the fridge and grabbing some yogurt.

"Did the noise wake you this morning?" he asked, taking a sip of orange juice.

I gave him a perplexed stare. "Noise? What noise?"

"I did some vacuuming around the house."

I blinked. "Uh, no. I can't anything without my hearing aids on. You could literally vacuum around me and I wouldn't even notice." I narrowed my eyes at him. "Since when do you clean the house?"

"It was beginning to drive me crazy."

"What was? The mess?"

"Yep," he said.

That surprised me. "Says the person who has a tendency to burn things."

"That's my other talent," he replied cheekily.

"Uh-huh."

"Besides, I found a sticky note in the kitchen from Shirley asking us to clean the house," he said.

"What note?" I asked him.

"Oh, she left one on the fridge," he replied.

"Really? When did she do that?"

"No idea. I just noticed it today. It's probably been there for like a week or so," he said.

I began laughing. "Seriously? I can't even remember the last time I saw her."

"Oh well, at least it's clean now," he said.

I sighed. "True."

We headed over to school afterward, with me feeling more tired than usual.

I was standing in line at the cafeteria, scrolling through the messages on my iPod when I saw that there was a message from Mom. I thought that was a bit odd since we often chatted in the morning before I went to school or after supper.

I nearly dropped the tray when I read it. *I just got back from the vet. They said Parker was suffering from acute renal failure. I'm so sorry, we had to put him down today. He was in too much pain.*

My blood suddenly ran cold and my hands shook. A tear slid down my cheek.

I was looking forward to seeing Parker when I got home. Now I'd never see him again. Then I'd remembered the vision of Serena leading Parker into the moonlight toward the night sky and his words: *'Remember the stars, that's where you'll find me.'*

That's when it dawned on me that he knew it was his time to move on. He tried to tell me in his own way.

My legs suddenly felt wobbly, and I grabbed a nearby chair to sit down in. I was barely aware of the crowd of people milling around the cafeteria, their figures a blur. It felt like my world had come to an abrupt halt. I blinked away the tears, my eyes welling up quickly again. My chest felt so heavy. I couldn't believe it. He was gone.

Jackson appeared in my line of vision and sat down in front of me. He reached out with his hand, his skin warm against my cold fingers. "Jessie? Are you okay?"

I had to blink several times to focus on him. "What? Oh. I got a text from Mom," I said, holding up my iPod.

"You're as white as a sheet. Are you sure you're okay?"

I gulped loudly, my throat felt unbearably tight. "Parker died today." I spoke the last word in a whisper. I was afraid that I was going to start crying in a public place.

Jackson's face crumbled in sorrow. "Oh, dear, I'm so sorry."

His eyes flicked over to the counter then back at me, "Did you want anything to drink? Coffee or tea?"

"Sure," I said absentmindedly, my mind already a thousand miles away. I wished that I could go home today and hold Serena in my arms.

A few minutes later, Jackson placed a cup of tea in my hands.

"Thanks," I said, quietly.

Jackson sat with me, idly watching the people walk past us. He leaned forward with his elbow on the table and placed his hand under his chin. "You have another cat right?"

"Yes, Serena, she was best friends with Parker." My voice nearly cracked when I said his name.

"What's she like?" he asked, playing with a napkin, folding over the edges and refolding it.

"Um…she's unique. We found her on our front porch a couple of years ago during a snowstorm. She was in horrible shape, really thin and starving. The vet said that if we hadn't brought her in, she would've died. Somehow, I think that she knew we would rescue her."

"So it was fate that she fell in your lap?" he asked.

"Yes, we think it was meant to happen. Parker was the one who found her. He kept insisting that we look outside. Her tail was broken and there was something wrong with her hip, as if she had been in an accident. She doesn't swish her tail like most cats do, she wags it like a dog." I smiled thinking about her.

"Ha! She certainly does sound unique," he said, his eyes crinkling at the corner as he smiled.

"How about you? Do you have any pets?" I asked, taking a tentative sip of the tea.

He nodded. "Yes, a great Pyrenees, his name is Gilmour."

"Is that a dog?" I asked him.

"Think of a Newfie but with white fur instead."

"How cute." Then I paused, realizing where I'd heard that name before. "Did you name your dog after Doug Gilmour, the hockey player?"

"Heh, yeah. He's fast and scrappy like him. How did you know that? Not very many people know who he is since he's retired."

"I used to play hockey and grew up watching hockey games on TV with my cousins."

"Funny, I didn't peg you as a hockey player," he remarked.

"Because I'm a girl?" I replied.

"No. You just don't strike me as the 'type.'" He mimed air quotes with his fingers. "You know the cliché, a jock. What I'm trying to say is that you're too elegant for the sport."

I narrowed my eyes at him. "Elegant? What's that supposed to mean? Too fragile, afraid I'll break a nail?"

He snorted. "Heh, no. Martial arts and fencing suit you more. They're more creative and intelligent sports."

"Well, I never considered myself as a bookish type of person, you know, like an uber nerd," I replied.

"You're smarter than you think, Jessie. You tend to hide it for some reason," he said.

"Force of habit, I guess. I think it's because I find it hard to keep up with conversations."

"Is that why you don't talk as much in group situations? Is it too hard to hear everybody?" he asked.

I was impressed. He was very astute in his observation about that. I took another sip of the tea. "Yes. I get tired really quickly."

"I've noticed that you sort of...zone out...sometimes. You get really quiet whenever we're around a lot of people."

"You're right. I'm surprised that you picked up on that. Most people don't realize that I physically can't follow their conversations. To me, it's a like a game of verbal ping-pong, it's quite a workout for my brain. I'm often exhausted after doing a lot of lip-reading by the end of the day." I paused and took more sips of the tea, still feeling the ache in my chest. "You know, you're more observant than most people I've met. That's probably why you're such a good artist, you tend to pick up the more subtle details."

"Oh, stop it, you're making me blush," he said. "I'm not that good."

"Well, you are definitely more talented than me, that's for sure," I replied.

"Shush, that's not true." He glanced at his watch. "We need to get going, otherwise we'll be late for class."

I nodded numbly, my thoughts going back to Parker. I felt as if I was shrouded in a heavy blanket full of sorrow. I knew that I had to keep moving forward and focus on school. I joined Jackson at the lockers, picked up my supplies, then headed to afternoon classes. Time seemed to move more slowly than usual. The professors' voices sounded so far away. By the time we got back home, I promptly crashed onto my bed and fell asleep. When I woke up, it was dark outside. I checked the time. It was after seven in the evening. I had slept for several hours. Strange, I still felt really groggy. There was a message on my iPod, I picked it up and noticed it was from Ethan.

I sat up and read it. He had heard about Parker and wanted to know how I was doing. We hadn't talked to each other for several weeks, and it seemed odd to see his message. I wasn't sure what to do. My fingers shook as I typed in my reply.

He texted back within minutes: *You doing okay?*

No, not really, I replied:

Sorry to hear about Parker. You must miss him.

Fresh tears welled up in my eyes, turning the iPod into a watery blur. I tried hard not to cry, blinking back the tears. *Yes. I wish I could've seen him one last time and given him a hug.*

Wish I could be there for you.

I was surprised he said that since we hadn't been together as a couple for several months, not since my head injury. I didn't want to give him the wrong impression, and I had to think long and hard about what I wanted to say. I was about to respond when he texted me again.

When are you coming home?

My fingers typed over the tiny keyboard: *In a couple of weeks. We get a long break here.*

Okay. Want to do some fencing?

Sure, can I bring Jackson? I replied.

There was a distinctly long pause and I wondered if I offended him.

Of course, he typed back. *Has he fenced before?*

No, but I think he would get along with Tristen, the two of them should meet.

You know that Tristen is gay, right? he replied.

I had to laugh at that. *Perfect.*

Aha. I get it now. Is he one of your classmates?

Yes, and my roommate.

Now I'm intrigued, he texted.

He's pretty cool. I think you'll like him.

I'm impressed...that he'd put up with you in the same house, Ethan said.

Is that a joke? I didn't think you were that funny.

I do have a sense of humor, he typed back.

I smiled. I had been a long time since we talked like this and I missed it. At the same time, it also felt strange, as if there was an incredible distance between us. There was a sense of coldness instead of the usual warm connection, and I felt a pang of sadness.

We bantered a little bit longer, then I spoke to Mom for a few minutes, which made it even harder for me since I was missing her even more today. After we finished talking, I didn't feel very hungry and decided to work on my assignments. I was sitting at the drafting table, working on a pen and ink drawing, getting more frustrated with it. No matter how hard I tried, I couldn't capture the scene that was in my head. I crumbled up the paper and tossed it over my shoulder. I stared at a new sheet of paper. For some reason, it wasn't working. I felt sapped of my creativity. I began sniffling and tears threatened to well up which made me more angry with myself.

"What the heck happened here?" Jackson exclaimed when he came in, picking up the wadded balls of paper.

I flinched so hard that I nearly fell off my stool. I spun around and ended up knocking the cup of inky water onto the white carpet. Both of us gasped in horror. I had been using the cup to clean my brushes from my previous homework and had forgotten to empty it. Now it lay on the pristine white carpet as a pooling, muddy blob.

"Oh, dear, I'll grab some paper towels and cleaning supplies from the kitchen," he said, rushing out the door.

I frantically grabbed an old towel that was sitting on the

table and began mopping up the liquid. When I lifted the towel from the carpet, I'd discovered that I was making it worse. Some of the stains on the towel were still wet from the paint! It made the carpet even darker with additional blotches. I began sobbing, out of control. Jackson came running back in and immediately pressed a thick layer of paper towels on top.

"Don't worry, honey, it's not the end of the world," he said.

"It feels like it. It has been such a sucky day! Why does this stuff keep happening to me?" I wailed in between sobs.

"Okay. I've got an arsenal of cleaning tools here, I'm sure we can get this clean in a jiffy," he said, grabbing a scrubbing brush and spray bottle of heavy duty cleaner.

We spend several minutes, scrubbing and spritzing the carpet. The ugly blob grew fainter but it was still a stark contrast against the white carpet.

"Oh, dear," Jackson said, leaning back on his heels.

"What kind of insane person uses a white carpet?" I said.

"I think most people do, honey," he replied.

I snorted. "Not at our house. It's mostly wooden floors. Living in the countryside doesn't give us the luxury of white carpeting. It would be impossible to keep it clean."

"Well…" he said, his gaze roaming around the room. "It looks like you won't be getting your security deposit back."

I gave him an incredulous stare then began laughing. He chimed in, grabbed a waste basket, and placed it on top of the gray stain. "That'll work."

I laughed even harder.

"I think you need a break, darling. And some food. It's been a long day for you. We should watch a movie tonight. How does pizza and a marathon of *The Flash* on Netflix sound?"

"Perfect."

Chapter 21

HOME

I was giddy with excitement as I awkwardly carried my heavy suitcase down the stairs.

Jackson was already by the door. His portfolio leaned against the wall beside him.

I raised my eyebrows at him. "That's it? What about your suitcase?" I asked.

"It's already in the car, I was waiting for you. Are you going to bring your portfolio too?"

I nodded. "It's the last thing I'm getting."

"Okay," he said, grabbing my suitcase when I plunked it down in front of him. "Holy cow, Jessie! Did you pack your entire wardrobe in here?"

I glared at him and headed back up the stairs. The portfolio was leaning against the bed. I went over and slung the strap over my shoulder. I took another look around the room, making sure I got everything, then skipped down the stairs.

"Is that it?" Jackson asked, holding a set of keys in his hand.

"Yeah, I think so," I replied.

"Great. Let's go."

I put the portfolio in the back seat and slid into the front, while Jackson locked the front door of the house and ran over to the driver's side.

"Whew!" he said as he started the ignition and turned on the heat.

While it was cold, there wasn't much snow. It was mostly a thin layer of white frosting on the lawns and homes, turning them into sparkling gingerbread houses.

"At least the sun's out and it's a nice day for driving," I remarked.

He nodded. "Let's hope there's not much traffic today," he said, backing the car out of the driveway.

We drove through the subdivision then headed south on the highway. There were a lot of cars, but it didn't seem too congested.

"It's not too bad, eh?" I said.

"Yeah, so far, so good."

"Are you looking forward to going home?" I asked.

"Oh, yeah, it will be nice to see everyone again," he said.

"Will Wesley be there too?"

"He'll be coming a few days before Christmas," he replied. "How about you? Are you looking forward to seeing your family?"

"Yeah, it'll feel different, though, without Parker," I replied, looking out the window.

We were approaching smaller cities, zipping past the industrial areas.

"What about your boyfriend? Do you think you'll get back together?"

I shrugged my shoulders. "I don't know. I was hoping time would give a more definitive answer, but instead I'm left with more questions about us."

"May I ask what drove you apart?" he inquired.

"He hit me so hard that I passed out," I said bluntly.

He jerked the steering wheel to the side in reaction to what I said. Fortunately, there were no cars in either lane at the moment, the traffic was thinning out. He stared at me in shock, "What?"

Belatedly, I realized I had phrased it incorrectly. "Oh! I meant that he hit me during a sparring match in karate. One of his kicks just happened to connect with the side of my head."

"I see." He placed one hand on his chest, appearing relieved. "For a moment there, I thought he was abusive."

"No. He's a karate instructor, like me. We were both sparring pretty hard and got caught up in the heat of things. A rush of adrenaline, I guess."

"That must've been a hard hit to knock you out like that," he said.

"Well, you see. I took another hit a few years ago that made me lose my memory. I still can't remember what happened that day. Only bits and pieces of it."

He frowned. "Did he do that too?"

"No, it happened at a tournament," I said. "I do remember how terrified he was, though. He stayed by my side the whole time."

"Oh, dear, you've been through a lot. Did he push you away?"

"No, I did. After the last hit, my doctor told me that I can never compete in contact sports again, which meant no more sparring. It completely changed my life, and I blamed him for that."

"I get it. You were angry at him," he sympathized.

"Yes. In fact, I was furious."

"This may sound like a ridiculous question, but could've this happened if someone else had hit you?" he asked.

I thought about it. "Yeah, I guess so." I shrugged my shoulders. "I can remember thinking that it felt like we were getting out of control really quickly. We were so pumped up, throwing lots of punches and kicks and everything was happening really fast."

"So, it wasn't necessarily him that made you push him away, was it?" he asked, giving me a quick glance.

That startled me. His honesty was making me see thing from a different perspective. I hadn't realized that I was holding in so much anger from everything that I had gone through lately. That day just happened to be the trigger when I finally snapped. I had fallen to pieces so quickly, and Ethan was the target of my frustration. "I guess not. I had been through so much and finally came face to face with the anger and frustration that day. It was as if my world had fallen apart. Being told by my doctor that I couldn't spar anymore was the last straw. I had worked so hard to get to that point, only to have it so rudely taken away from me by an errant hit. It felt like I had lost a part of myself that day."

"That makes sense," he said, nodding. "We often hurt the ones we love the most."

"It certainly feels like it," I said.

"I'm curious, has your relationship been better or worse since you took a break?"

"I've discovered just how much of an impact he had on my life. In some ways, being away from him made me more independent. In other ways, I feel more lost."

"What do you mean by being lost?" he asked.

"Um…more isolated. Remember when we were at the bar and there was a comedy show and I couldn't follow it?"

He nodded. "Yeah."

"That's what I mean. I felt left out and alone."

"So, what would've Ethan done?" he asked.

"We would've gone to a movie that had captioning instead," I replied.

"Oh, so he tried to find other ways of making you feel more inclusive?" he inquired.

"Yes. His grandmother, Rose, has a hearing loss too, and he has seen how hard it is for her."

"Oh my god, that totally makes sense. It's like fate wanted you guys to be together," he added.

"Do you really think so?" I asked.

"Yes, I do. And you know what? I think that if you forgive him, you'll also forgive yourself."

"I think forgiving myself will be the hardest part," I said.

"Why is that?" he asked.

"I suppose it's from years of being told by others that I don't fit in or belong. Growing up with the message that I'm not worthy to be in the same class, or on the same team as everyone else, hit me really hard. Ironically, the harder I tried to fit in, the worse it got."

"I'm so sorry that you had to go through that, Jessie," he said.

"So am I. Those experiences changed me. I still have those insecure moments where I feel like I don't fit in. It's a potent reminder of what I went through as a kid. It's like I'm crippled by this horrible sense of anxiety, and I can't escape from it."

"I know what you mean. Obviously, I didn't have a disability like you, but being openly gay was quite an eye opening experience for me. I learned the truth about people around me very quickly. It took me a long time to overcome my own fears and accept myself for who I am. I also had to come to terms with the fact that there will always be someone who will not embrace it the same way I do. It's my life and I'm in charge of it," he replied.

"That's what I admire about you, your confidence. You're so sure of yourself and you know what you want," I said, feeling as if a huge burden was beginning to lift off my shoulders.

"That's from having to stand up for myself," he said, giving me a smile and a quick glance. "I lost some very dear friends when I came out, and that was a harsh reality I had to accept. But it also saved me a lot of pain and grief had I continued being dishonest with everyone. What I found odd, though, was how quickly their perceptions changed when I spoke the truth. I was still the same person, but they saw me in a different light and didn't want to be my friend anymore. That hurt me deeply. However, I needed to be true to myself and I had to feel good about that."

"Do you find it hard to trust some people?" I asked him.

"I'm slower to trust people. Although I want to give

them a chance to get to know the real me," he said.

"I know the feeling. It's very hard for me to trust people," I replied.

"I've noticed that. It's not necessarily a bad thing. It can be a bit off putting, though," he said.

I frowned. "How do you mean?"

"You often come across as being a strong person, you have a dominant personality," he replied.

"Really? I didn't know that. It's probably from having to deal with the bullying and the teachers all the time, you know, showing them how to use the FM system."

"Do you think it encouraged you to mature more quickly than your classmates?" he asked.

"I guess. It still bothers me to have to go up to the front of the class and approach them. I don't like having an audience watching me all the time."

"Let me guess, it's like the feeling where there's a roll of toilet paper stuck on your foot and everyone can see it except you?"

"Ha! Yes, that's exactly how it feels like."

We both spend a few minutes chuckling about that.

"You're stubborn," he said. "I'll grant you that. Don't worry, it's a good thing. It seems to give you a strong sense of determination."

I thought about that for a moment. "Yes, that's true. But there's something else too. You see, I grew up with the feeling of constantly being rejected, and that made me afraid of it. I have a tendency to keep my heart close to me." I was struggling to explain to him how I felt, "It's as if I have a shield around me, you know, like a wall to protect me."

"That makes sense, it takes longer to get to know you," he said.

I felt bad about that. I didn't realize it was that obvious. "I'm sorry about that, Jackson. I didn't mean to push anyone away from me, that wasn't my intention."

"Don't worry, darling, I'm wasn't offended. It's a part of you. I suspect it's an old habit of yours. I think that learning to love yourself can go a long ways toward forgiving Ethan. You deserve to have some happiness in your life, Jessie. Don't let your past overshadow your future," he replied.

I was constantly amazed at how observant he was. "Thanks, Jackson, that means a lot to me."

"You're welcome, my dear," he said.

I looked out the window and noticed that it was becoming more overcast. There was a large swath of clouds looming on the horizon. It looked like we were heading into a snow storm. Jackson turned on the radio, filling the car with holiday music. By the time we reached the city limits, snow began to fall. I gave him directions, telling him where to go. Finally, we turned onto the long driveway with trees on either side. Their large branches created a snowy archway above us as we drove through. I saw Dad standing on the porch, putting up the lights on the eavestrough. He turned around and gave us a wave when we came to a stop.

When I stepped out of the car, Dad came down the steps and pulled me into a hug. "Welcome home, Jessie."

Jackson stood beside us, carrying our portfolios, one on each shoulder.

"This young man must be Jackson." Dad's voice boomed as he reached out and gave him a hearty handshake. "Come on in, you can put those in the hallway."

As soon as we opened the door, I was greeted by the scent of Mom's baking. The house smelled like a bakery, making my mouth water. Mom came through the kitchen, wearing a red apron covered in flour. She was holding a dish towel, wiping her hands on it. Her auburn hair was done up in a clip at the back, the long curls falling around her face. Her cheeks were red from the heat of the oven.

"Oh my! It smells so good in here," Jackson exclaimed.

"That would be Mom's cooking. She has her own catering business," I said.

Mom came forward and pumped Jackson's hand. "The holidays are definitely a busy season for me."

"I must admit that I'm looking forward to have a nice

home-cooked meal for a change," he said.

I snorted. "I think we both are, Jackson. It would be nice not to have something explode or burn for a change."

Mom gave us a quizzical glance.

"Jackson and the microwave are not a good mix," I explained.

Jackson mimed an explosion with his hands. "Let's just say I'm not a good cook."

Mom bit her lip trying not to laugh.

"Oh! We forgot the suitcases," I said.

"I'll get them," he said, turning around and going back outside.

Mom came over and gave me a hug. "So, how was the drive?"

"It was fine, sunny most of the way until we close to here. When did it start snowing?"

"About an hour ago," she replied.

"It's starting to look like Christmas around here. It's just not the same living in the city," I remarked. I felt more relaxed than I had been for a while.

"We haven't put the tree up yet. Your father and I have been too busy, and we thought you might like to help with the decorations."

I nodded. "Yeah, I would like that."

"The guest room is ready. Can you show Jackson where it is? I've got some food in the oven I need to attend to," she said and went back into the kitchen.

"Sure."

I went outside to check on him, he was already coming up the porch steps with my suitcase.

"Thanks, Jackson," I said, grabbing the handle and bringing it in. "Did you already bring in your suitcase?"

"Yep, we're good," he replied.

"Great, I'll show you to your room. It's down this hallway," I said, leading the way to a small bedroom.

The walls were painted a soft shade of purple that reminded me of lilacs. There was a hand-made quilt on top of the bed in the same shade, with butter cup yellow pin-wheels. A cute mini sofa was tucked in the corner next to the window. Beside it was a small table for a book or cup of tea. The soft, fresh colors of the room and simple country decor reminded me of spring.

"This is a lovely room, Jessie," he said as he walked in.

"I hope the bed is comfortable for you," I said then gestured toward a set of doors on the wall next to the bed. "There should be room in that closet for you to hang your clothes."

"Perfect. It's so nice of you and your parents to let me stay here, Jessie."

"It's nice to have company here. We rarely get any visitors since we live in the country," I replied. "I'm going to put my stuff upstairs in my room and start unpacking. You should show Mom and Dad some of your art. They would love to see it."

"Sure, if you think they're interested," he said.

"Of course, they are, don't be shy about it," I said then turned around, grabbed my suitcase, and lugged it up the stairs, the edge of the suitcase hitting each step as I went up. *Guess Jackson was right that it's a tad heavy,* I thought. The suitcase landed with a heavy thud once I reached the top.

Serena's head popped up from where she was sleeping on my bed, blinking her sleepy eyes at me. My heart sank when I saw the empty space where Parker used to sleep beside her. I promptly went over and sat on the bed beside her. She got up, sat in my lap, and began to purr loudly. I tried really hard not to cry. "I'm so sorry, Serena, that you're all by yourself now."

I pulled her into my arms, snuggling my face into her fur. I didn't realize how much I'd missed her until now. It made me miss Parker even more. A quiet sob escaped from my throat. She reached up with her paw and gently touched my face. I leaned in and she rubbed her cheek against mine. A few minutes later, I got up and began unpacking. Serena jumped down and pounced into the pile of clothes in the suitcase, happily burrowing through it like a mole, her tail wagging. I giggled at her playfulness. I felt a buzz in my pocket and pulled out my iPod, there was a message from Ethan.

Are you home yet?

We just arrived a few minutes ago, I replied.

Great! Want to go fencing tonight?

Sure. Can Jackson come too? I asked him.

Of course, he replied. *We have lots of extra equipment. I'll bring some of my gym clothes for him to wear.*

Thanks. It should be interesting to see if he likes it.

Do you want me to pick you guys up? He asked.

Yes, that would be great.

I'll pick you up after supper at six thirty.

I typed in: *Okay.*

I went downstairs, looking for Jackson to tell him the news. He was in the library, using Dad's desk to display his artwork. Both Mom and Dad were admiring his sketches.

"Isn't he talented?" I said when I stood beside them.

"He certainly is, both of you picked the right school," Mom said.

"You should show them your work, Jessie," Jackson said, urging me to get my portfolio. He made some room on the desk while I pulled out some of my sketches. I handed them to Mom.

"Oh my, Jessie, these are beautiful," she replied as she went through them. Some of them were nude models and still life drawings of various objects, like fruit and vegetables. "We should frame some of these."

"Sure, if you think so," I said.

Everyone nodded their heads.

"Before I forget, Ethan will be picking us up after supper for fencing tonight," I said.

Jackson gave me a thumbs up.

"I didn't know you fenced," Dad said to Jackson.

"Not yet," he replied, giving us a big grin.

Dad gave him a rueful look, chuckling. "Uh-huh."

"It can't be that hard," Jackson said, looking at us. "Can it?"

I snickered. "We'll see. On the plus side, even if you don't like it, you'll definitely like some of the guys."

Mom rolled her eyes. "Oh dear."

"What?" Jackson said, noticing our expressions.

"You do realize that it will be quite a workout right?" Dad asked him.

Jackson nodded. "Yeah, of course. It's not a big deal," he said, shrugging his shoulders.

"Anyway, supper will be ready soon," Mom said, heading out to the kitchen.

Jackson took that cue to pick up his portfolio and head back to the guest room. I was about to leave when Dad asked me to stay behind. "Are you sure that Jackson is aware of how much work goes into fencing?"

"To some degree," I replied. "He can handle it. He's stronger than you think."

"Good to know. So you two are getting along okay?" he asked me, crossing his arms over his chest.

"Yeah, he's been so helpful and understanding. I mean, because of his own experiences," I replied.

"Ah, because he's gay?"

I nodded. "He knows what it's like to be on the receiving end of negative attitudes. I know it's not the same thing as having a hearing loss like mine, but at least he understands what's it like to deal with 'being ostracized,'" I said, miming finger quotes. "He's more open minded than most people I've met."

"That is certainly understandable. I'm glad that you found a friend at school," He paused for a minute. "How are things with you and Ethan?"

I shrugged my shoulders. "I'm not sure yet. I mean he's polite to me at karate, but it's not the same as it was before when we were together."

"There's nothing wrong with that, Jessie. Sometimes, you just need time to heal," he replied.

"I know. I'm still trying to get used to these changes in my life."

"Because of school?" he asked.

"That and what happened to me," I replied, gesturing at my head.

"You've been through more trauma than most people and you've done remarkably well."

"I know," I said.

I saw Mom standing by the door. "Supper's on the table," I said.

After supper, I headed upstairs, grabbed my gym bag and placed it on the bed. I was rummaging through my closet for something to wear when Jackson came in and casually leaned against the door. I nearly did a double take. For a moment he looked like Ricky Martin with his strong jaw, chiseled features, and hair swept across his forehead. He wore a black shirt, leather jacket over top, and slim black jeans with a silver belt. He had on several black leather bracelets with silver beads on his wrist. There was this air of casual sexiness about him.

"How can you look so good just standing there? It's like everything fits you perfectly," I said to him.

"What?" he said, looking down at his body then back at me.

I sighed and rolled my eyes. "You're making me look bad in comparison."

"Sorry. I can't help it. It's just the way I am."

"Ridiculously good looking?" I said.

He snickered, strode into the room, and sat down on the bench by the window. "Funny. Okay, what's really bothering you?"

"I don't have anything to wear. It's like nothing feels right anymore," I said, tossing a sweatshirt on the bed.

"Ah, gotcha. Nervous about seeing Ethan tonight?" he asked.

My hands stilled while rummaging through the close. I turned around. "I guess. That's so weird. I shouldn't be this nervous."

He gave me a smug smile which made him look more handsome. *Damn it, stop doing that,* I thought.

"Maybe it's because you're ready to forgive him?" he asked.

I crossed my arms and tilted my head to the side, "I am? What makes you say that?"

"You seem different, more open and relaxed."

"Oh. I didn't realize that. I'm only taking it one step at a time. I'm still being cautious about it," I replied.

He gave me a thumb up. "It's a good start and that's what counts."

I went back to the closet and rifled through the clothes. "Ugh! How come I don't like anything?" I said, my frustration mounting.

"Here, try this on." Jackson stood up, walked over to me, took off his jacket, and held it out. I turned around and shrugged it on. It was still warm from his body heat. It was little big since he was taller and more muscular than me.

"How does it feel?" he asked.

"It's nice. I feel better about it."

"That's because it suits you, darling. You've changed, you're growing into a new person who's becoming more sophisticated."

"But what about you?"

"Don't worry about me. Let's make tonight memorable for Ethan," he replied.

"Do you really think so?"

He nodded and gave me a big smile. "Let's blow Ethan's socks off!"

I laughed. "I'm not sure I can do that, but I'll try."

"That's the spirit, darling!" He gave me a gentle shove toward the door. "Go on, *viva la vida!*"

I managed to grab my gym bag before we headed down the stairs. I waited anxiously at the bottom of the stairs while Jackson went to his room and came out wearing another leather jacket, this one in a dark shade of indigo blue.

"Wow, you look great in that, Jackson," I said.

He put his hands in his pockets and rocked on his feet. "I know."

I shook my head and snickered. I pulled on my boots and grabbed a scarf and gloves to wear. Ethan showed up several minutes later. I opened the door to find him standing on the porch with his hair and shoulders covered in snow. Suddenly, I felt very shy. My heart skipped a beat for a moment.

"Hi, Ethan, come on in."

His eyes lit up and he gave me a generous smile. "You look lovely, Jessie."

I felt my face grow hot. I'd hoped he didn't notice that I was blushing. "Oh, thanks."

Jackson was standing next to Ethan and mouthed at me, "Told you!" giving me a thumbs up.

"I think I like this new side of you. It's different," Ethan said.

"I didn't think I changed that much," I replied.

"You seem more sure of yourself. I noticed that at the dojo last time," he said.

"Oh, I didn't realize that," I said. I gestured at Jackson, "Ethan, this is Jackson."

"Hey, it's great to meet you," Ethan said, turning around and giving him a handshake. "Are you ready for some serious fun tonight?"

Jackson snorted. "I think that's the first time I've heard someone use the words 'serious' and 'fun' together in the same sentence about a sport."

Ethan gave out a bark of laughter, giving Jackson a hearty slap on the shoulder. "I think Tristen will get a kick out of you."

"I'm liking this club already," Jackson replied with a broad grin.

I gave Ethan my gym bag, and we followed him out to

the car. We piled in, Jackson climbed into the back while I slid into the front seat beside Ethan. Once we reached the main road, Ethan asked Jackson if he had been to our city before.

"No, not to my recollection. I'm sure my parents have been here on several occasions, but I don't remember it. I was probably too young."

The two of them got along quite well, chatting animatedly about where they'd traveled, the different cities and countries they'd visited. It didn't surprise me that Jackson had been to many locations around the world. Somehow they had gotten onto the topic of summer activities, namely jet skis, by the time we reached the gym. When we got out of the car, strolled down the long hallways, and emerged into a spacious gym, there was already a group of people here. They were chatting with each other and gave us a brief look.

"Locker rooms are this way," Ethan said to Jackson, gesturing to his left.

We headed off to the respective rooms. I shucked off my clothes and pulled on my black yoga pants, pink T-shirt, white socks, and pink running shoes. By the time I walked out the door, Jackson and Ethan were already with the group of guys. Some were on the floor, doing stretches, while others rummaged through their bags, pulling out various equipment. I joined them just as Ethan finished introducing Jackson who was shaking hands with everyone. I noticed that he was standing next to Tristen, wearing a smug grin. I recognized most of the guys here from last time, including Neal, Chris, and Stephane.

I waved at them. "Hi!"

Patrice, the coach, came over to us. He wore black track pants, black running shoes, and a red warm up jacket. "It's good to see you, Jessie, welcome back," he said.

Ethan introduced Jackson to Patrice. "It's always nice to see new faces here," Patrice said, giving Jackson a handshake. "Don't worry if you can't keep up, just do the best you can, okay?"

Stephane snorted, elbowing Chris in the ribs. "I don't think anyone can keep up with us."

Patrice gave them a knowing glance. "Oh, shush. Don't forget that you had to start somewhere yourselves. You didn't become experienced fencers overnight. Let's not get too cocky tonight."

They started snickering then couldn't contain themselves. "Cocky? Us? Pfft, yeah, right."

"*Mon dieu*," Patrice said wearily, rubbing a hand over his face. He looked at Ethan. "Since you have guests today, would you like to do the honor of leading the warm ups?"

"Sure coach," Ethan said then began an easy lope around the room. "Follow me, guys."

After a few minutes, he picked up the pace, adding more moves, running from side to side, and doing leg stretches. I was able to follow him fairly well since I was familiar with his voice and teaching style. While we followed Ethan around the room, I noticed that Patrice set up several stations on the floor, including a rope ladder, hula hoops, and wooden boxes.

I was feeling quite warm and sweaty by the time we took a short break. I grabbed my water bottle, took a long sip, and passed it over to Jackson who eagerly gulped it down.

"So? What do you think so far?"

Jackson gave me a thumbs up.

"That was the easy part," I told him.

He paused mid-gulp and gave me a suspicious look.

In return, I gave him a sly grin. Suddenly, the room was filled with loud music. I turned around and noticed that Brandon was at the stereo system at the back wall, fiddling with the volume, making it blare from the overhead speakers. I sighed, knowing that it was going to make things much more difficult for me. We lined up at one end of the rope ladder and proceeded to go through each station, doing various stepping drills, jumping over the boxes, and leaping from one hoop to another. I could feel my legs burning by the time we went around the fourth time. Patrice had us line up near the wall facing him and went into the en garde stance. I shifted my right foot forward and turned my left foot out to the side, lowering my stance. Ethan was between Jackson and me. He turned to help him adjust his feet.

Patrice stood facing us in the middle. "When I clap my hands, I want everyone to do a lunge. When I clap them twice, do a step lunge."

Since he was so far away from and the music was so loud, I could barely hear him. I squinted at him, trying to read his lips. We slowly shuffled forward, taking tiny steps, waiting for his command. Suddenly, he clapped his hands. Everyone burst forward, stepping into a deep lunge, our legs spread far apart, as if our back leg was stuck on the floor. We recovered our position and continued moving forward, following his claps. I managed to get the hang of it quickly, keeping a watchful eye on Ethan and mimicking his moves.

Patrice added more sequences to the footwork, moving forward then backward. "I'm going to turn around and yell out the required steps, so you guys can't cheat."

I froze. There was no way I was going to be able to hear him or read his lips. With the music blaring overhead, it was turning into a virtual nightmare for me. This created an impossible drill for me to follow. I was about to raise my hand when he promptly spun around and began yelling out the commands. Everyone began to move forward and do lunges. I tried to copy Ethan who was busy helping Jackson. I felt absolutely helpless, not being able to participate. When Patrice turned around, I quickly raised my hand.

"Can you do this drill facing us? I can't follow you since I can't hear you or see your face."

He shook my head. "No, I'm sorry. I cannot change this drill for you."

My heart sank. "Can you at least turn down the music? I'm having trouble hearing you."

He gestured at the guys. "It's up to them since it's their music."

I turned and looked at them. They all shook their heads

at me. They were glaring at me with such intensity that I could feel the heat of their anger coming at me in waves.

Before I could say another word, Patrice turned around and continued the drill. A hot flame of anger shot through me. I started to walk away from the group when Ethan reached out and grabbed my arm.

"Wait, Jessie. I have an idea," he said.

I watched him curiously. He strode out in front of me, stood near Patrice, and proceeded to repeat what the coach said in sign language. My jaw nearly dropped. That was a big surprise to me. I had no idea that he had become so proficient in it. He had taken some sign language classes before, but just the basics. This was a huge leap in his skills.

My heart surged with renewed hope, and I could feel my chest glow with warmth. I followed Ethan's instructions, feeling more at ease. Even after Patrice turned around, Ethan continued to sign the rest of the drills.

"All right everyone, go suit up," Patrice said to the group.

Ethan walked back to us.

"Wow! When did you become so good at signing?" I asked him.

He blushed momentarily. "I've been taking an advanced sign language course at school. I needed another credit and this made perfect sense. I really wanted to learn more about it."

I wanted to cry. "That means a lot to me, Ethan. Thank you."

He shrugged his shoulders and smiled. "I was going to surprise you later, but it looked like you needed to use it now."

"I did need it," I said then clapped my hand over my chest, feeling so overwhelmed.

Just then Chris, a tall lanky guy wearing red track pants and a white T-shirt, came over to me wearing a very angry expression on his face. He jabbed his finger in my face and yelled, "This is not your club. You had no right to tell our coach to turn around for the drills. No right at all!"

Ethan turned around and glared at him. "She had every right to tell him that she couldn't hear!"

Chris's face turned an ugly shade of red. "She doesn't belong here and you know it!"

"She deserves to learn fencing like everyone else, Chris!"

"And what's with the turning off the music? That's our tradition," he said, his voice rising in pitch as he got angrier.

Ethan stood face to face with him, creating an imposing presence. He stared at Chris unflinchingly. "Maybe it's time we made some changes to be more accessible. Have you thought about that?"

Christ took a step toward me, clearly intending to get in my face. "People like you shouldn't play sports."

I flinched at that remark, the angry barbs hitting me like shards of ice.

He shoved at Ethan who, in turn, grabbed his wrist and gave it a twist. Chris immediately bent over, straining against his locked arm.

"You're a jerk, Chris, you know that? You give fencing a bad name. It's people like you who shouldn't be here," Ethan said in a firm voice. He was gritting his teeth and he stared at Chris with cold, hard eyes. "Jessie deserves an apology."

Patrice saw what was going on and started heading over to us.

"Ethan," I said urgently. "Look."

His eyes followed my gaze, and he promptly released Chris who stood up and pulled his shirt down, still seething with rage. Chris shoved his hand in my face, gave me the finger, and stormed away.

Patrice stared at us, perplexed. "What was that about?"

"You, sir," Ethan replied.

"Because I wouldn't accommodate Jessie?" he asked.

"Yes," I said. "Chris told me that I shouldn't have said anything to you. But you know what? I was right to speak up and voice my concerns."

Patrice let out a heavy sigh. "Look, I'm sorry, Jessie, but I can't change tactics at the last minute like that. It's too disruptive to this group."

"That's fine and we respect that. But you singled her out by doing that," Ethan said. "Try to see it from her point of view. She couldn't hear you at all. She tried to fix that, and it took a lot of courage for her to even ask you that."

Patrice thought about that for a moment. "I appreciate that, but you have to remember that I wasn't trained to deal with athletes who have a disability. It's not in the coaching manuals. I wasn't taught how to coach fencers with a hearing loss," he said, gesturing at me. "I don't have any experience in this regard. This is a new field for me and it terrifies me."

I looked at him in surprise when he said that. "You're afraid of me?"

"Not you as a person. I'm afraid of screwing it up as a coach. It's hard work teaching it to guys like Chris," he said.

"I know. I'm an instructor too," I said.

For a moment, he seemed stunned. "Wait, you teach?"

I nodded. "Yes. I have a black belt, I teach karate."

"I didn't know that," he said. "Anyway, please accept my apologies. I didn't mean to cause any undue hardship for you."

"Thank you," I said.

Even though he was trying to ease the tension, I still felt shaken up. We went over to the cage locker filled with various equipment.

I rifled through the white jackets and pulled out one for myself and another one for Jackson. I grabbed some gloves, chest protectors, wires, and masks and added them to the growing pile.

"I think that's the first time I've heard a coach say

they're scared of someone with a disability," Jackson remarked.

I helped Jackson put on his jacket and slipped the wires through the sleeve. "I wish it wasn't like that, though," I replied. "It bothers me."

He frowned. "How do you mean?"

"I guess it hurts my feelings because it's my fault," I said.

Ethan abruptly stopped putting on his equipment, laid his hands on my shoulders, and looked me in the eyes. "It's never your fault, Jessie. It's their problem, not yours. You amaze me every day with your determination and ability to rise above your hearing loss."

I blinked. "I do?"

"Yes, of course you do," he said.

Jackson chuckled. "Although she can be a little scary sometimes. After seeing her in action, she can be my bodyguard anytime."

Ethan blinked "What are talking about?"

"Oops. You didn't tell him?" Jackson said, looking at me.

"Uh, no. I didn't think it was important," I replied.

A look of concern washed over Ethan's face. "Tell me what?"

Jackson grimaced. "We were attacked by a drunk guy at a bar, and she did a pretty good job at kicking his butt."

Ethan's eyes grew wide when Jackson said that. "Why didn't you tell me about that?"

"Since we weren't together, I didn't think that you wanted to know what was going on in my life," I said.

He gave me a despondent look. "Jessie, I will always care about you."

"Even after I pushed you away?" I said.

"Yes. Letting you go was the hardest thing I had to do, and it tore me apart when I couldn't be there for you. I wanted to stand by your side and help you get through this.

There were so many times when I wanted to talk to you or just hold you in my arms."

My chest contracted painfully. "I don't know what to say."

"I wish that you hadn't shut me out like that. I mean, I get it. You needed time to process everything. But I felt so helpless when I couldn't be there for you."

I felt bad for him. "I'm sorry."

He started to reach out and grab my hand when Patrice clapped his hands loudly. "Let's go, folks, we need more fencers on the pistes."

Ethan dropped his hand and went back to putting on his equipment. I helped Jackson shrug into the lamé, a metallic vest over his jacket, and clipped the wires on the back of the hem. He slid on the glove I gave him while I attached the short wire to the back of his collar for the mask. I handed him the foil which he took and made some swishing motions with it.

He grinned at me. "Ooh, I like this, it's very sexy in a manly way, you know?"

I snickered.

"Now I know why Johnny Depp liked sword fights so much. There's something empowering about it," he remarked. He moved back and forth with it, stabbing at an imaginary opponent.

While he did that, I grabbed my white shield and slid the hard plastic over my chest. I felt supremely self-conscious and deeply embarrassed as I strapped it on.

Jackson turned to face me and glanced at my chest. "Oh my, they really need to rethink the whole design of the protective equipment. You resemble a storm trooper from *Star Wars*."

I gave him an exasperated glare. "Is that a bad thing?"

"Didn't they always miss?"

I snorted. "Yeah. I know what you mean about this stupid shield. I wish it was more like Katniss's style."

"Oh, yeah! Like the black one she wore in *Mockingjay*."

"Uh-huh. That's way cooler than this."

Ethan rolled his eyes at us. "At least it works. Even some of the guys wear them."

"Really? I had no idea," Jackson said.

"That's because those guys are secure enough in their masculinity and smart enough to protect themselves," Ethan replied.

Jackson looked puzzled. "Protection from what?"

Ethan gave Jackson a wicked grin. "You'll see." He clasped his hand on Jackson's shoulder. "Ready to fence?"

He gave him a shove toward the long metal piste on the floor. I helped Jackson attach the short coiled wire to his mask and hooked the metal plugs into the wires on the hem of his lamé. Ethan showed Jackson how to do a salute with his foil then began the match. I watched the two of them dart back and forth, trying to score a point. Ethan was taking it easy with Jackson, letting him learn how to do parries and ripostes. He deftly blocked Jackson's strikes with casual ease, following them up with quick stabs to the heart.

After a while, Ethan held up his hand. "Halt!" He took off his mask, approached Jackson, and gave him a hearty handshake. "Okay, Jessie, it's your turn!" Ethan said, waving me over.

I gleefully took Jackson's place, unclipping his wires and attaching them to my equipment. Jackson walked past me, rubbing his chest. "Ow. Now I know why you wear those tacky shields."

I gave him a cheeky grin in return.

Once I got my mask on, I saluted Ethan and stood on the en garde line. I reigned in my focus like I did for sparring, coiling in my energy, ready to explode. As soon as the match started, I moved quickly toward him, watching his reactions, teasing him with my foil. I lunged at him, trying to strike his chest. He quickly leapt out of the way, parried my attempt, and followed it up with a hit over my heart. The buzzer went off, indicating he got the point. We went back to our starting positions and went again. There was tension in the air as we moved back and forth, our foils clashing loudly. Ethan moved quickly and easily, from years of practice. His long legs slid across the floor in a few short strides, I had to scramble backward to avoid his reach. His hand moved with such fluid grace that his foil seemed to slide around mine like a snake. His moves were elegant and wicked fast, like lightning. I was dripping with sweat by the time he halted the match, my chest was heaving from the exertion. I took off my mask, saluted, and shook his hand.

"That was fun, thanks, Ethan."

"Fencing suits you, especially your aggression," he replied.

"How do you mean?" I asked.

"You're a tenacious fighter, Jessie. I could tell that you were tapping into your inner strength. There's so much power in you," he said.

I shrugged my shoulders. "It's nice to be able to vent my frustrations like this."

"It's kind of therapeutic, isn't it?" he said.

"What? Stabbing people? Totally," I said.

He let out a bark of laughter.

As I unhooked the wires and left the piste, I saw Jackson and Tristen fencing together beside us. Jackson was doing well and quickly learning on the fly. He embraced the speed of this game very well, moving out of Tristen's range quickly.

I was approached by Brandon, a slim teen with long, reddish brown hair that hung in rumpled waves just past his shoulders. He looked like he belonged on a beach, surfing the waves. He had this laid back attitude. "Hey Jessie, want to fence with me?" he asked.

I nodded. "Sure."

Once we got hooked up to the wires, we saluted. He raised his hand, alerting me to wait. As soon as he lowered it, we began the match. He tested my reflexes, hitting my foil with a sharp flick. He took a quick leap toward me, and I managed to parry it, frantically scrambling backward, trying to get out his reach. I gulped loudly. He was being smart and patient with me, watching my reactions. I surged forward and tried to hit his chest. He brought up his foil with a loud ping and hit me squarely in the chest. I rocked back from the force of his hit and was grateful for the chest protector. The buzzer went off. He got the point. Obviously.

He said something, but I couldn't hear him over the loud beeps from the electronic scoring machines, squeaking shoes, and clashing of blades. Brandon pulled off his mask, his wet, curly hair was plastered to his forehead. Concern was etched on his face. "Are you okay?"

'Yeah, I'm glad I have this on," I said, tapping my chest.

He winced. "Sorry, I forgot how strong I can be."

"Don't worry about it. I'm used to sparring against guys like Ethan."

He looked at me then him. "Sparring? As in fighting?"

"Yes. We both teach karate."

Ethan would've looked like an imposing figure next to me, since I was smaller than him. He was more fit and muscular, and I could understand why Brandon had a hard time visualizing the two of us sparring.

"Doesn't it scare you to compete against guys like us?" he asked.

I got the impression that his question had a double meaning to it. I chose my words carefully. "No. I'm used to it, and it helps me become a stronger fighter."

"Cool," he said then put his mask back on.

We started the bout again. He strode quickly toward me, his long legs covering the distance easily. He taunted me with his foil, flicking it. He was waiting for me to make a mistake. I circled around his foil. He rapidly circumvented it and slid the blade along mine to hit me in the chest. He got another point. We went back to our respective positions and started again. Midway through, he suddenly leapt through the air with his foil held out like an arrow and stabbed me in the chest. He was so fast that I didn't even have time to react.

The light on the scoreboard lit up along with a loud beep.

He took off his mask and gave me a salute. I repeated the same moves. He came over to me and shook my hand.

"That was so cool!" I said. "What do you call that?"

"A fleche. It took me a long time to get the hang of it."

"It's so fast!" I exclaimed.

He gave me a warm smile. "It's one of my favorite moves."

I continued to rotate with the other fencers, excited by the fast paced energy and speed. It was so different from sparring. By the time we were finished, I was completely whipped. Exhaustion washed over me and my legs felt heavy from the exertion. My T-shirt was completely soaked when I peeled off my jacket and chest protector. Jackson joined me a minute later, stripping off his equipment.

"Whew! That was quite a workout," he said.

"So, what did you think of fencing?" I asked him.

He gave me a thumbs up. "It's a fabulous workout for my tushy. I wonder how many calories we burned today."

I rolled my eyes at him, not surprised by his response. "And what did you think of Tristen?" I inquired.

"He's delightful and my cup of tea," he replied, grinning broadly.

We put the jackets back on the hangers in the locker along with the rest of our equipment. I grabbed my gym bag, headed over to the locker room, and took off my wet clothes. I quickly pulled on a pair of jeans, sweater, and leather jacket. I gave the water bottle a squeeze, gulping down the cool liquid. I was so hot and grateful for the drink. Then I headed back out to the gym to join Jackson and Ethan who were already changed.

"You okay, Jessie? Your face is quite flushed," Ethan said, reaching out to touch my cheeks. I'd missed the feeling of his hands and his soft touch against my skin.

"Yeah, I'm just really hot."

"You always look hot, darling," Jackson remarked.

I snickered. "Thanks, Jackson."

Ethan let out an exasperated sigh. "I can see why you two get along so well." He dropped his hand. His touch left a lingering sensation on my face. He hefted the heavy fencing bag over his shoulder. "Ready to go?"

I nodded, giving my water bottle another squeeze, feeling very thirsty and somewhat uncomfortable. Something wasn't right and my neck was starting to tense up.

"Is there any place where I can refill this?" I asked Ethan, shaking the empty water bottle.

"Yeah, there's a water fountain down the hall. We can stop there."

"Great."

We waved at the guys as we left, and Ethan led us down the long corridor, turning several times until we came to a stop at the wall where a silver fountain jutted out. I put down my gym bag, unscrewed the lid off the bottle, and pressed on the metal lever. Water gushed up, and I placed the bottle under it, letting it fill to the top. I put the lid back on and bent down to slurp up some water from the fountain. When I stood back up, the room spun around momentarily. Fear raced through me, and I shot my hand out against the wall to brace myself.

The water bottle fell out of my grasp and landed on the floor.

Ethan dropped his bag and stood beside me, placing his hand on my back. "Jessie! What's wrong?"

"I just felt dizzy all of a sudden," I said, closing my eyes for a moment.

My neck and shoulders felt awfully tight, and I could feel the tension rising upward to my head, which was a bad sign. That meant a headache was on its way. I gulped audibly, trying not to throw up.

I could feel Ethan standing beside me, the heat of his body radiating out to me.

"Is it coming from your neck?" he asked, placing his hand on the back of my neck.

I nodded.

"Crap. That means you're overheating," he said. He turned to Jackson. "Can you grab the white towel from my bag and soak it in water?"

"Oh, sure." Jackson quickly rummaged through the bag in search of it.

I leaned against Ethan while he massaged the muscles on my neck.

"Here you go," Jackson said, giving him the wet towel.

Ethan placed it against my neck, a sudden cool sensation. "How does that feel?" he asked.

"Better. Just give me a moment until the pain goes away."

Ethan looked at me with deep concern in his eyes.

"Do you want me to put your bags in the car for you?" Jackson asked Ethan.

"Yeah, that would be great," he said, fishing the keys out of his pocket and handing them to Jackson. "Thanks."

"I'll wait in the car for you guys. Take the time you need, okay?"

I watched Jackson walk down the hallway and turn around the corner, leaving us in silence.

Ethan reached up and brushed the bangs away from my forehead, his fingers gently stroking my skin. "You still feel feverish, Jessie. Do you want to go outside for a minute to cool down?"

"Sure," I said softly, feeling very tired.

He slid his hand down my arm and linked his fingers with mine, an automatic and familiar gesture. Once we reached the doors, a blast of cold air greeted us. It felt good against my cheeks. I looked up at the night sky, watching the snowflakes fall lazily, swirling around us.

"Are your headaches getting worse since your head injury?" he asked, his eyebrows furrowed.

I thought about it and realized he was right. There was a pattern: whenever I worked too hard, my headaches would return.

"Yeah, you're right. It's worse when I get overheated," I replied.

"I'm sorry about that," he said.

"You don't have to worry about me, you know?"

"Jessie, I will always worry about you," he said. "I don't like to see you in pain, and you don't have to go through this alone. Let me help you."

He pulled my hand to his chest, placing his overtop of mine. I could feel the warmth of it against my skin. I looked up into his eyes. Snowflakes fell onto his hair and face. Some landed onto his eyelashes. There was a hush in the air and, for a moment, it was just the two of us standing together.

"I love you, Jessie," he said, his eyes welling up. He began to lose his composure. His lips quivered as he visibly struggled to hold back the tears. "I can't lose you," he said, his voice beginning to crack.

He sucked in a deep breath as tears rolled down his cheeks. I reached up and wiped them away with my hand. He placed his hands gently on my neck and pulled me to him. His lips touched mine, as soft as a feather, leaving a warm and tingling sensation. I wanted more. I leaned into him, savoring his kisses and eagerly returning them.

The ice that seemed to cover my heart, cracked open. It shattered and broke free. The pain that was there suddenly disappeared. Now it was filled with an incredible warmth like sunlight. We continued to exchange passionate kisses. My fingers held on to his silky hair, pulling him closer to me.

"I've missed you," I said when we broke apart.

He laughed as relief washed over his face. "So did I."

He reached up to cup my cheek, inadvertently causing my hearing aid to squeal loudly. It was my turn to laugh.

He looked at me in confusion. "What?"

"Remember when that happened the very first time we met?" I asked him.

He thought about it, then recognition dawned on his face.

"Do you mean in the gym at your school when Dad and I taught self-defense?"

I nodded. "Yes! I don't know why, but this is fate. It's happening all over again."

Ethan brushed my bangs aside, stroking my skin with his fingers, a soft caress. "What is?"

"I'm falling back in love with you," I said.

His eyes lit up and he laughed. "So am I."

He pulled me in, giving me more kisses, his soft lips sending delicious shockwaves throughout my body in waves of passion. A few minutes later, we leaned our foreheads together, an intimate connection. We felt reunited, once again.

"I think Jackson has waited long enough for us," Ethan said.

I nodded. I'd forgotten about him. "We should get going."

"So, are you feeling better?" he asked.

"Yes, I think so," I said as we began walking back to his car. "Thanks, Ethan."

"For what?" he asked.

"For waiting for me," I replied.

He gripped my hand, lacing his fingers with mine, and giving them a squeeze. "Always."

When we got back in the car, Jackson gave me a knowing look, wearing a smug grin. I knew he was secretly hoping that we would get back together.

I leaned my forehead against the window, the cool glass a relief against my warm skin.

"You okay, Jessie?" Jackson asked.

"Yeah, I get bad headaches sometimes," I replied.

"Oh dear," he said.

"I think she pushes herself too hard, gets overheated easily," Ethan added.

"Ironically, it seems like it's not enough, you know?"

"What do you mean?" Jackson asked.

"I find that I have to work harder than most people to

keep up. In sports, it takes a lot more energy and effort to hear what's going on. I feel like I have to prove myself and work even harder as a result."

"I don't think you should worry about that. You're already stronger than most people I know," Jackson replied.

"I agree with Jackson," Ethan said.

That gave me pause. Was I really overdoing it? I wondered.

When we got home and stepped out of the car, the air was fresh and crisp. The snow had stopped falling. It covered everything in a heavy blanket of softness. Ethan walked with us to the front porch, carrying my bag for me. We stopped in front of the door, and he placed my bag on the floor beside me. Jackson went ahead and stepped inside. Just as I was about to follow him, Ethan reached out and grabbed my hand, pulling me toward him.

"Jessie, wait," he said.

I waited, watching his facial expressions as he looked at me.

"There's something I want to tell you," he said.

"What's that?" I asked.

"I just wanted to say that you've really grown as a person. Even though your life is headed in a new direction, you've become a new woman that I admire even more. Don't fight it, embrace it."

He reached up with his hands, gently cupping the sides of my neck, his thumbs stroking my jaw. He leaned in and gave me slow, feather-like kisses. I melted into him. For a moment, I felt like I was floating, the euphoric sensation pulsing through me. I felt dizzy with love, glowing from the inside out.

When he took a step back, there was a rush of cold air between us, and it made me want to go back into his arms and hold on tight. I didn't want to let go.

"I've missed you," I said.

"So did I, Jessie. So did I," he replied. He gave me another kiss. "Goodnight."

"Goodnight, Ethan."

He turned and walked back to his car, got in, and drove down the lane. I waved at him then bent down, picked up my bag, and headed back inside. Jackson was munching on a cookie when I came in. He gave me a smug grin.

"What?" I asked him.

"Told you forgiveness goes a long ways," he said.

I shrugged off his jacket. "I think this helped, too."

He shook his head. "You were already beautiful, Jessie. It was just a matter of seeing you in a different light."

"Aw, thanks, Jackson. For everything," I said then gave him a hug.

"You're welcome, darling. You deserve it."

Chapter 22

reflections

The next morning after breakfast, I was sitting on the bench, with Serena curled up on my lap, and going through my messages on the iPod, when there was a knock on my bedroom door. I looked up to find Jackson holding a large envelope with a bright red bow stuck on it. He came in and handed it to me.

"What's this?" I asked.

"Think of it as a thank you gift," he replied.

"For what?" I asked.

"Being my friend."

"You really didn't have to do this Jackson," I said.

He shrugged his shoulders. "Go on, open it."

I opened the flap and pulled out several glossy eight-by-ten photos. They were shots of me and Jackson and close ups of me posing as a model. I sucked in a quiet gasp. They were stunning.

"Jackson, these are amazing," I gushed.

He glanced down at the floor. "Thanks."

As I perused them, I couldn't believe what I was seeing. He was a natural photographer and made me look like a model right out of a magazine. I didn't realize that I could look like that.

"I can't believe that's me," I said.

"It's all about perceptions, Jessie. We all see ourselves in a different light. This is what I see in you," he replied.

"You made me look beautiful," I said.

He sat down beside me. "That's because you are beautiful, Jessie. That's the real you."

"Is that what you and Ethan meant last night?"

He nodded and gestured at the pictures. "This is what he sees in you. You just need to be true to yourself."

I looked at the pictures, taking it all in. It was a very revealing moment. "Thank you so much, Jackson. You have no idea how much this means to me."

After he left, I decided to frame them and give them to Mom and Dad and Ethan for Christmas.

❧❦❧

When the time came, they were all sitting around the fireplace and sipping peppermint hot chocolate. Mom had holiday music playing, and I recognized one of the songs. It was Michael Bublé singing "Baby, Please Come Home."

It couldn't be a more perfect moment. I handed everyone their gifts and anxiously watched their reactions as they unwrapped them. Mom gasped and covered her mouth with her hand. Ethan's eyes lit up, and he gave me a broad grin.

"These are beautiful photos of you Jessie," Dad remarked. "Who took these?"

"Jackson."

"Oh my. He did a wonderful job. He captured your true spirit," Mom exclaimed.

I turned to look at Ethan who was gazing at the picture. '*You're beautiful,*' he signed to me then pulled me into his chest, hugging me close.

Serena jumped up onto the couch and sat down beside us. Ethan pulled out a small wrapped box. The shiny silver paper was adorned with tiny blue hearts and blue curly ribbons that cascaded down the sides. I quickly unwrapped it and opened the lid. There was a note inside, it read *Always.* Underneath it was necklace with a sparkling, heart-shaped pendant. I held up the silver chain. The light from the fire made the clear glass sparkle like a polished diamond. Serena reached up with her paw, touching it curiously.

I giggled. "This is beautiful, Ethan."

"It's to remind you that I will always love you," he said then placed it over my head and clasped it around my neck.

At the moment, it felt like all of the pieces of a puzzle fell into place. There was a sense of renewed hope within me. It couldn't be more perfect.

About the Author

Growing up surrounded by a seemingly never ending supply of books provided an ample playground for Jennifer Gibson's imagination. A voracious reader at a young age, she delved into the rich worlds created by talented writers like Madeleine L'Engle, *A Wrinkle in Time,* which planted the seed of her passion for unique adventures. Encouraged by her creative writing teachers, her love for books blossomed into a full grown talent when she became inspired to create an original series based on her life as hard of hearing teenager.

Gibson's novels have received numerous awards: Silver in the 2014 Literary Classics Book Awards, Finalist in the Stargazer Literary Prizes, Readers' Favorite 5 stars, and Official Selection in the 2015 New Apple Book Awards. She is a recipient of the Oticon Focus on People Award, and a HearStrong Champion, for her dedication to helping change the stigmas surrounding hearing loss through her books.

9 781626 946996